LEGACY OF THE WITCH
A MYSTERY
KIRSTEN WEISS

misterio press

COPYRIGHT

Copyright © 2024 by Kirsten Weiss

All rights reserved.

No part of this publication may be reproduced, distributed, or transmitted in any form or by any means, including photocopying, recording, or other electronic or mechanical methods, without the prior written permission of the publisher, except as permitted by U.S. copyright law. For permission requests, contact kweiss2001@kirstenweiss.com.

The story, all names, characters, and incidents portrayed in this production are fictitious. No identification with actual persons (living or deceased), places, buildings, and products is intended or should be inferred. AI has not been used in the conceptualization, generation, or drafting of this work.

NO AI TRAINING: Without in any way limiting the author's [and publisher's] exclusive rights under copyright, any use of this publication to "train" generative artificial intelligence (AI) technologies to generate text is expressly prohibited. The author reserves all rights to license uses of this work for generative AI training and development of machine learning language models.

Book Cover by Dar Albert

ISBN-13 ebook: 978-1-962292-01-6

ISBN-13 print: 978-1-962292-04-7

ISBN-13 color print: 978-1-962292-05-4

Worksheet illustrations licensed via DepositPhotos.com. Firepit, map, and love knot illustrations by Articult.

misterio press / ebook edition February, 2024

Visit the author website to sign up for updates on upcoming books and fun, free stuff: KirstenWeiss.com

CONTENTS

Get the UnTarot App!	VIII
About This Book	X
A Note to the Reader	XI
SUBJECT: JUST START	1
Chapter 1	2
Kings Rail Trail Map	12
Chapter 2	14
Chapter 3	22
Chapter 4	28
Chapter 5	35
Chapter 6	45
SUBJECT: WELCOME	53
Chapter 7	55
SUBJECT: CONGRATULATIONS	63
Chapter 8	67
Chapter 9	69
Chapter 10	77
Chapter 11	85
Chapter 12	93
SUBJECT: ALCHEMY	100
Chapter 13	105

Chapter 14	115
Chapter 15	122
SUBJECT: TRUTH	127
Chapter 16	131
Chapter 17	138
Chapter 18	146
Chapter 19	156
Chapter 20	164
SUBJECT: CONSCIOUSNESS	169
Chapter 21	173
Chapter 22	180
Chapter 23	187
Chapter 24	188
Chapter 25	194
SUBJECT: SPELLWORK	205
Chapter 26	208
Chapter 27	211
Chapter 28	222
SUBJECT: CHANGE	229
Chapter 29	234
SUBJECT: FAITH	241
Chapter 30	244
Chapter 31	251
Chapter 32	258
Epilogue	261
SUBJECT: BEAUTY	268
Grab the UnTarot App:!	271
Book Club Questions	273

About the Author	275
Other misterio press books	276
More Kirsten Weiss	278
Connect with Kirsten	281

GET THE UNTAROT APP!

EMBARK ON A JOURNEY that intertwines fiction and reality as you dive into the captivating world of Kirsten Weiss's Mystery School series. With the UnTarot app, you can wield the very cards the characters from the books receive, tapping into a wellspring of ancient wisdom and boundless magic.

Imagine harnessing the power of the UnTarot cards to unlock hidden insights and unravel the threads of fate. With the UnTarot app, you gain access to a treasure trove of captivating readings and interpretations. As you explore this mystical experience, you'll be drawn into a world where the boundaries between fiction and reality blur.

- **Authentic Connection:** Immerse yourself in the enchanting ambiance of the Mystery School series. The UnTarot app faithfully captures the essence of the books, allowing you to connect with the characters and their adventures on a whole new level.

- **Ancient Wisdom, Modern Convenience:** The UnTarot app marries centuries-old divination techniques with cutting-edge technology, creating an accessible experience for both seasoned practitioners and curious novices.

- **Free Exploration**: Yes, you read that right! The UnTarot app is entirely FREE, ensuring that everyone can join in the magical journey of self-discovery, insight, and revelation.

Ready to embark on a journey that defies the boundaries of time and space? The UnTarot app beckons you to step into the wondrous world of Kirsten Weiss's Mystery School series. Download the UnTarot app and let the magic unfold before your very eyes!

Download the UnTarot app for FREE today and embrace the enchantment that awaits!

About This Book

SEEKER: AS SOCIETIES GROW *increasingly fragmented, hopelessness, nihilism, and division are on the rise. But there is another way—a way of mystery and magic, of wholeness and transformation. Do you dare take the first step? Our path is not for the faint-hearted, but for seekers of ancient truths.*

All April wants is to start over after her husband's sudden death. She's conjuring a new path—finally getting her degree and planning her new business in bucolic Pennsylvania Dutch country. Joining an online mystery school seems like harmless fun.

But when a murdered man leaves her a cryptic message, she catches glimpses of another reality she's unwilling to acknowledge. A reality where bygone enchantments cast cryptic shadows, and the present brims with unanswered questions.

As April works to unearth the mystery, every step brings her closer to a truth she's been evading. And to a conspiracy of hexes that may end in her demise.

Legacy of the Witch is a spellbinding, interactive tale of a woman's midlife quest to understand the complexities of her own heart. A paranormal women's fiction murder mystery for anyone who's wondered if there might be more to their own life than meets the eye...

Book 1 in the new Mystery School Series featuring the **UnTarot**, a deck of cards for meaning making. Start reading now!

UnTarot deck app included!

A Note to the Reader

I'D LOVE TO INVITE you to post photos of your completed exercise sheets (feel free to color them in), quotes, and/or insights related to *Legacy of the Witch* and the UnTarot on social media using the hashtag #MysterySchool, #UnTarot, or #KirstenWeiss so I can see and then repost yours on my page! If you'd like weekly mystery school inspiration, I invite you to join the school's email newsletter at https://bit.ly/join-the-mystery

This book and the exercises in it can be read on your own, with a friend, or as part of a book club. You can also create your own Mystery School: a group of people who gather together to discuss the book, the UnTarot concepts, and the exercises. See the book club questions at the back of this book for some ideas of things to discuss.

SUBJECT: JUST START

SEEKER:

Just start.

Yes, reading more about the subject is great. Talking to people with experience, doing your research, taking the class—good, good, good.

But these things can also be excuses to procrastinate. And the best way to learn is to just do it. (We're not talking about throwing a bunch of money at something you know nothing about. We at the Mystery School understand the power of frugality, which is one reason why these emails are free).

So just start. Stumble. Screw up. It's okay.

But just start.

Action item:

You know what you've been thinking of doing. Baby steps are encouraged, but just start.

CHAPTER 1

OF ALL THE LIFE-RUINING mistakes I'd ever made, being late was not going to be one of them.

I double checked the campus map. My advisor's office *should* have been directly ahead of me. Instead, there was a wide swathe of grass dotted with crimson leaves and way-too-young students.

At least they seemed too young to *me*. They had to be too young, because the alternative was that at forty-seven, I was too old. Too old to start over. Too old to rid myself of my growing collection of ghosts. Too old to get a degree. Too old to use that degree as a springboard for my dream business and dream life and dream whatever the hell I was doing.

But I couldn't think that way. I had to have hope or I'd be stuck in the purgatory of widowhood.

I crumpled the campus map in my gloved hand. What *was* I doing? Everything was shifting—inside and out, above and below, and—

"You lost?" A man who could have been in his twenties grinned, attempting a covert up and down glance. At least I still warranted the occasional masculine appraisal.

"I'm trying to find the Heritage Building," I said. And I hated being late. My usual timeliness came from the Penn German in me, though I'd never lived in Pennsylvania before now.

He pulled a phone from the rear pocket of his ripped jeans, tapped the screen. The man nodded past a maple, its remaining leaves splashes of fire. "It's thataway."

I grimaced. "Thanks." *Duh*. I could have used my phone to find the building. But I'd grown up on paper, not screens. "You're a lifesaver." Stomach churning, I trotted across the damp lawn.

"Any time," he called after me, and I gave him a wave without looking back.

I'd only been on campus a few days in the last year—quick flights in and out. Most of my folk art program was online. Until now. Today would be my first in-person meeting with my thesis advisor.

Ghosts of disappointments trailing behind me, I jogged across the pavement to the three-story brick building dotted with cupolas and white-painted eaves. I pushed open a door and hurried inside the high-ceilinged foyer, its pointed arches adorned with elaborate wood carvings.

The campus wasn't as grand as the bigger colleges and far from Ivy League. But Babylon College was up and coming. More importantly, it had the degree I wanted in the area I wanted to be.

Though it hadn't come cheap, it didn't come with an Ivy League price tag either. Still, at the thought of the expense, guilt tangled with my anxiety, and suddenly, I found it hard to breathe. The life insurance had been there to get my life back on track after—

"It was supposed to be an investment," my husband whispered. "A safety net."

My throat tightened. I shook my head, trying to dislodge the echo of David's voice. The past was past, and this was present, and present wasn't the time for ghosts. If I didn't focus, I'd be late for my future.

Office 302. Third floor. I glanced at a cluster of students waiting outside an elevator. Jogging past them, I climbed the wide, wooden stairs.

I huffed down a hallway, my low heels click-clacking on the linoleum. How late *was* I? I skidded to a halt in front of room 302. A brass nameplate glittered on the door:

Dr. Ezekial Stoltzfus.

The air molecules in the hallway compressed, my ghosts squeezing closer. My father, skeptical. My mother, curious. My husband, sardonic. Not for the first time, I wished I could see rather than just sense them. If I could see them, I'd know they were real.

Forcing myself to breathe, I reached for the door.

It opened before I could touch the knob. An auburn-haired woman in a navy jacket looked back over her shoulder. "Nonetheless, if you think of anything—" She plowed into me, and we stumbled apart.

"Whoops," she said and laughed. "Sorry. You okay?" She was a little shorter than me—maybe five-seven. Her hair was darker than my true, pale red. And of course she was younger, somewhere in her late thirties. A professor? Another not-too-young student?

"No harm done." I straightened the front of my forest-green blazer.

A man with thick, dark hair streaked with gold loomed over her shoulder. "April?" he asked. He wore a navy suit with faint, gold pinstripes, his white shirt open at the collar.

I nodded, and he broke into a grin. He had a lovely, even smile, the outside corners of his brown sugar eyes crinkling, and my stupid heart jumped. "You're right on time," he said. "Come in."

The woman sidled past me.

I was definitely *not* right on time, but I wasn't going to argue the point. "Thanks for seeing me, Dr. Stoltzfus." I walked into the office.

"We're too old for titles. Call me Zeke."

My mouth pinched. I wasn't *that* old, and my advisor couldn't be over fifty. But *Zeke* was less of a mouthful than *Stoltzfus*.

He shut the door behind us and motioned toward a cluttered wooden desk. "Have a seat."

Bookshelves lined the walls. Spider plants lounged on a windowsill overlooking the lawn I'd just raced across. Behind the glass, students scurried, heads bent, across the thick grass.

I pulled back a rolling chair and sat, tugging off my gloves.

My advisor walked around his desk and dropped into the executive chair opposite. He gusted a breath and motioned toward the closed door. "Sorry about that. It was another of those witches."

I blinked. *Ah, what?* Had the college's folklore program expanded to witchcraft? "Witches?"

He pulled a tie from the pocket of his suit jacket and dropped it beside a stack of papers marked in angry red ink. "You'll come across a share of them in your research. *Braucherei* is hot in the witchcraft world these days. American witches are looking for western magic so they can't be accused of cultural appropriation."

My gaze clouded. "You mean… powwow?" It was old Pennsylvania Dutch faith healing. Silly stuff, superstition. I was surprised the practice still existed.

"There's some controversy over that name," he said. "Not that the Penn Dutch care. They're in their own world. But the pagan community and the academics do."

I glanced back toward the closed door. "And she was a witch?" I asked, twisting the gloves in my lap.

"Has her own online mystery school, if you can believe it," he said cheerfully. "But let's talk about your thesis proposal." His brown eyes grew serious, and his chin lowered. "Tell me the truth. Why are you *really* studying Pennsylvania Dutch folk art?"

I froze in my chair. *Dammit.* He knew. How did he learn about my plans? I'd only told a few friends, and they were far from Pennsylvania. I cleared my throat.

"Why?" I repeated stupidly.

"Yes," he said patiently and flashed that Hollywood smile again. "Why?"

I hesitated. I couldn't tell him the truth, that I wanted to start a business selling modernized versions of Penn Dutch décor. He'd think I wasn't serious about my masters.

Though I hadn't been a student long, I already knew the drill. *Real researchers were doing the research for its own sake, not for crass commercial purposes.* Women like me, women who wanted a degree to bolster their credentials after decades with no work history, were unserious.

I pasted on a smile in return. "My parents were Penn Dutch. They moved to California before I was born, but we spoke Penn Dutch in the home—"

"Right, I remember reading that you spoke it. That's a real advantage in this work. Aside from me, there aren't many people on campus who speak the language."

"It's been super useful," I said dryly, and he chuckled. Only 300,000 people spoke the language, a High German mashup. Penn Dutch was a dying tongue. At the thought, an ache pinched my chest. There wasn't much I could do about it, but I hated to see the old culture vanish.

I cleared my throat. "Anyway," I continued, "I love painting—"

"Most folk artists do."

I shifted in my chair, its wheels squeaking on the linoleum. *Artist.* The word sounded pretentious—at least when applied to me. "I think of myself more as a craftsperson. Anyway, I fell in love with the primitive style, with the folk art, but I wanted to make it my own."

"The mark of a true artist."

My face warmed. *Flattery will get you everywhere.* "But I realized if I was going to make it my own, I needed to first master the original forms. Which is why I'm getting this degree."

It wasn't a lie. I *did* want to know more, to be better. There was always so much to learn.

"Those are all good reasons," Zeke said. "Maybe that explains your proposal."

The office darkened, a cloud passing before the sun. In the window, the spider plant's green stripes seemed to fade.

I glanced down at the gloves in my lap. "What do you mean?" I'd thought my proposal explained itself. After all, it was a *proposal.*

"What you're proposing to research is old ground, I'm afraid. You're going to need to find something new."

Oh come on. I mustered a smile. "But... it's folk art. It's history. It's *all* old ground."

"Then find a new angle on it. Maybe look at how other local artists are re-interpreting the folk art."

My stomach plunged. I didn't want to study modern artists. I didn't want their work to influence mine. Worse, what if a technique or idea lodged in my subconscious, and later I came to believe it was mine?

Zeke cocked his head. "Actually, that witch may have done you a favor. Apparently, someone's been putting up odd hex signs in the woods." He chuckled. "It's causing a minor panic. It's probably just a prank, but who knows? Why don't you look into it? It's folk art. It's new. It's interesting."

I relaxed. *Hex signs.* I hadn't planned on selling them, since they mainly went on barns and my shop would focus on interior decor. Hex signs could work. "I'll look into it."

"Not that you have to do hex signs," my advisor said quickly. "It's just a suggestion."

"No, no," I said. "It's a good one. I'll check it out." Though I was a little annoyed I'd have to. I'd liked my old proposal.

"Unfortunately," Zeke said, "the only hex sign manufacturer, Zook, went out of business during COVID. But there's a local farmer who's painting hex signs in the modern style. You might want to chat with him..." He scrolled through his phone. "Here's his contact info. What's your cell number?"

I recited it to him. A moment later, a contact pinged into my texts.

"There you go." He rose. "I hear you got one of the king's cottages?"

"The what?"

His smile broadened. "Mr. King, our local philanthropist. I heard you got a scholarship to stay in one of his cottages. I hope you got one close to campus."

"Not exactly. I'm up in Mt. Gretel." It was about a thirty-minute drive—reasonable given the low rent.

"Oh." His voice lowered as he drew out the word. "They stuck you in the haunted forest."

Haunted? I shifted in my chair, and my gloves whispered to the linoleum floor. I bent to retrieve them. "The what—?"

He lifted a well-manicured hand. "No, it's not really haunted. It just seems that way off-season. Mt. Gretel's lovely, if a little lonely this time of year."

Far off or not, I was lucky I'd got the cottage. Mr. King had made them available to only a few grad students. And the woods were gorgeous in October, when the leaves were turning.

We said our goodbyes, and I made my way back to my Honda. *Hex signs.*

The colorful round signs actually had nothing to do with hexes or witchcraft. A guy who'd written tourist books in the 1920s had gotten confused, saying the signs were used to ward off curses and bad luck. Later, enterprising folk artists had realized that the supernatural sells and had run with the idea.

Scowling, I pulled onto the highway. *New ground.* Why did it always have to be *new ground* in academia? Why couldn't I just prove I knew my stuff and move on?

The highway narrowed, gold and crimson and tangerine branches blocking out the weak sunlight as I rose higher into the hills. My Honda crested a ridge, and the highway sloped downward.

My grip loosened on the wheel, and I rolled my head. A few droplets of rain splattered my windshield.

I stopped at a supermarket for supplies then continued on to Mt. Gretel. *Haunted.* I snorted. If the tourists were too dumb to come to Mt. Gretel in the fall, that was their problem. The resort village was gorgeous any time of year.

I drove past 19th century Gothic Revival and Queen Anne cottages. Thick fall foliage partially hid the homes' faded pastels. Slowing, I passed in front of an old yellow meeting house and turned onto a narrow road.

I spotted the squat driveway to my temporary home, Cornflower Cottage. Painted a soft blue, the cottage was built into the hillside, with parking at the mid-level. Beside the porch steps was the stack of fallen branches I'd cleaned up after yesterday's storm.

I'd have to figure out what to do with them. They were too wet for firewood.

I stepped into the cheerful entryway, my hobbit-door keychain swinging in the lock. Extracting it, I kicked off my shoes, and walked toward the open kitchen with my paper bags.

Something brushed against my ankle, and I yelped, lurching away at the touch. A black cat hopped onto the wooden dining table in front of the stone fireplace. Unblinking, she gazed at me, her eyes golden.

My pulse steadied, and I laughed unevenly. "Who do you belong to?" I set my bags on the nearby kitchen counter. The room was open plan, the high, gray granite counter dividing the kitchen from the front entry and dining area.

The cat yawned, displaying razor teeth. It was an appropriate response to an inane question.

"Well, you don't belong to me." I moved to pick her up. The cat deftly evaded my grasp, hopped from the table to the rag rug, and scampered out the open door.

I shrugged. The cat probably belonged to a neighbor. Though she hadn't worn a collar, she had looked too sleek to be a stray.

"Okay then." I closed the door behind her and unloaded the bags, filling the modern fridge.

Though Cornflower Cottage was historic, it had a modern kitchen and baths. I climbed the stairs, careful to duck before I hit my head on the low overhang. Some wag had taped a handwritten reminder on it that simply read:

OUCH.

The second to highest step groaned theatrically at my weight. I walked down the narrow hall to my cramped bedroom. Its floors bowed, angling downward toward the four walls.

I dropped onto the bed, and the mattress squeaked a protest. A *cat*. I flexed my foot. Maybe a cat was what I needed.

I hadn't had a pet since I'd married David. He'd said we moved around too much to be fair to an animal, and he'd been right. He was always right. It had been about as annoying as you'd expect.

I switched from professional clothes to jogging gear. I'd followed David on his jobs across Europe and Asia. Wherever we'd gone, there'd been two consistencies in our lives: *The Lord of the Rings*, and my jogging.

Alas, a shared love of Tolkien had not been a solid foundation for a marriage, and David had hated exercise. He'd claimed it wore the body out sooner. I hated running too, but I'd kept it up to be contrary. *Stop thinking about David.*

I locked the cottage when I left, though there seemed little point. My advisor, Zeke, had been right. The village was mostly deserted, the windows dark in the cottages I passed. *Haunted.* The oaks shivered in a sudden gust, their dying leaves fluttering to the pressed stone.

I consulted my trail map, then folded it into my jacket pocket. Jogging down the leafy road, I cut down another lined with pines and found my way to the King Railway Trail.

According to the tourist brochures, my patron, Mr. W. King, had been the driving force behind turning a disused railway track into a hiking trail. The track was now gone, replaced by a pavement and pressed stone trail that ran from Babylon to Mt. Gretel.

I liked the idea of the trail. I liked the hopefulness behind it, of taking something disused and turning it into something new and beautiful and loved.

At the trailhead, grasping branches arched above the sign. Curtains of spiderwebs hung from the bushes and rippled eerily. Insects—prey—hummed in the thick bracken. Resolutely, I pulled my thoughts from Tolkien's dark forest and its giant spiders, and I checked the map again.

Start Here➤

Jamming the map into the side pocket of my thick leggings, I started off. My running shoes drummed a heavy beat on the pressed stone dotted with damp, yellow leaves.

David, David, David. My heart heavied. He didn't like how I was spending his life insurance money. Though his opinion now shouldn't matter. David was gone. And though he'd never really approved of my interests, somehow, it still *did* matter.

Through the oaks, I could occasionally catch a glimpse of a distant cottage. A shudder of droplets plopped from sodden leaves to the ground. I glanced between the snare of branches at the mercury sky and hoped any serious rain would hold off.

I didn't pass anyone. The trail was as deserted as the village, and the muscles between my shoulders loosened. I put on more speed, driving out thoughts of the past, the future, my thesis, my imaginary business.

A creek chattered, invisible, in the woods. It could have been ten feet away or a hundred. It was impossible to tell from my vantage on the trail.

I rounded a bend. A low ring of stone, about ten feet in diameter, stood beside the trail. I slowed, curious. The circular structure was too big to be an old well.

Panting, I walked toward it. The stone ring had a pagan feel, reminiscent of ancient stone barrows. Something bright and yellow and slick peeked from the undergrowth inside the ring.

I propped my foot on the stone ledge, bent to stretch my hamstring, and gasped. My hands turned clammy.

A rain slicker. It was a rain slicker.

And there was someone inside the yellow coat. A silver-haired man.

For a moment I thought it was a bad joke, he wasn't real. Then, heart banging, I hopped over the stone ledge.

Heedless of the brambles tugging at my clothes, of the muck squelching beneath my shoes, I stumbled to the supine man. He lay staring with one broad hand pressed to his chest. Blood stained his neck and pooled in the hollows around him.

"Oh my God," I breathed, fumbling for the phone in my jacket pocket.

His head turned toward me, and I yelped.

I dropped to my knees beside him. "You're alive. It's okay. I'm calling for help now." What had happened to him? Had he tripped and fallen? But what had he been doing in the circle?

"Can you put pressure on the wound?" I asked. If he couldn't, I'd need to. I'd need a cloth, something to staunch the flow.

But first, help. Hands shaking, I called 9-1-1.

He lifted a hand and pointed toward the trees. "Look beneath," he whispered. "The brotherhood."

"It's okay," I said. "I'm calling now." I pressed the phone to my ear. "I'm calling..." My voice faded.

His blue eyes grew as cold and impersonal as the Atlantic, and he stared without seeing at the sky. A thick dullness fogged my chest. I was too late. He was dead.

KINGS RAIL TRAIL MAP

King's Rail Trail

Key:
- T — Trailhead & Parking
- ... — King's Rail Trail
- — Highway
- ● — Mile Marker

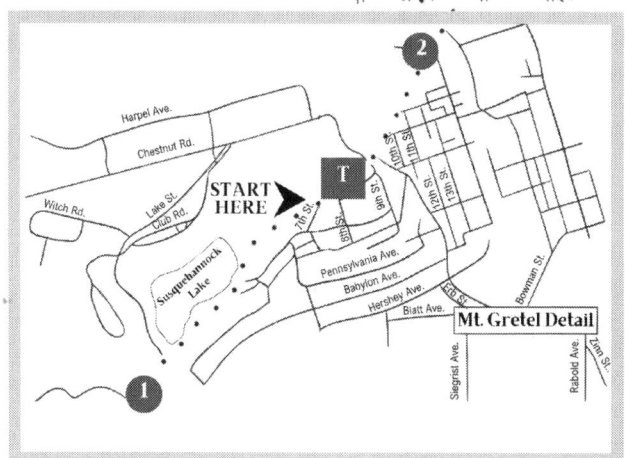

CHAPTER 2

I'D NEVER MET A man as wide as he was tall. But that was impossible of course, an illusion, since Sheriff Yoder was well over six-feet tall and couldn't possibly be six-feet wide. He rested one foot easily atop the mile three marker post, a post that was hip height for me.

I didn't bother to try to glance past the sheriff at the men and women swarming the damp stone ring. Even if I could see around him, I didn't want to see any more. My jaw compressed. I'd already seen enough of the sad, dead figure in the yellow rain slicker.

"You say you're a student?" Yoder's sunburnt brow lowered. Rain dripped from his broad-brimmed hat and plastered the thin caramel-colored hair to his head.

"Grad school." I wiped the water dribbling down my face. I didn't wear much mascara, but what I had was running, burning my eyes.

He grunted and scribbled something in his notebook. Apparently, audio recorders for interviews hadn't made it to this part of the state. "Where are you staying?" he asked.

"In Mt. Gretel, at Cornflower Cottage."

His pencil tip snapped on the page. The sheriff looked up, his piercing blue eyes meeting my gaze. "Cornflower?" he asked sharply.

"Yes." I shifted my weight. Was something wrong with my cottage? My advisor's remark about the haunted woods stuck in my brain. "I got lucky. There are a few houses provided to students at cost, and that was one of them."

"I know." His arm drifted to his side. He studied me. "Tell me again what he said to you."

"He said, look beneath the brotherhood."

The sheriff scratched behind his ear with the eraser end of the pencil. "That doesn't make much sense."

"He was dying, probably confused..." And why was I trying to explain on the dead man's behalf? It wasn't my tragedy. I had enough tragedy in my own life.

"Are you sure that's what he said?"

Was I? It had all happened so fast. "It's what I remember. He said, *look beneath the brotherhood*. I'm sorry. I didn't know what to do. Maybe I could have saved..." I glanced toward the stone circle, cold sorrow blossoming in my chest.

"You couldn't have saved him." A dark-haired man in a black raincoat strode toward us. He looked to be about my age, and his close-cropped beard and mustache gave him a Byronic air. "There was nothing you could do."

The newcomer's gaze flicked over me, then locked on mine, and my breath caught. *Those eyes*. They were blue-gray and tempestuous as the Baltic in winter. They were David's eyes.

"It was too late," the man said. "So he couldn't have spoken. With that neck wound, he would have bled out in under a minute."

"But... he *did* speak," I insisted.

The newcomer ran a hand over his beard and scowled. "You're mistaken. Unless you came across him within a minute of him being stabbed. And if you found him when you said you did, that doesn't seem likely."

Why not? I stiffened.

"You have time of death already?" the sheriff asked him.

"As close as I can get under these conditions." The man grimaced. "It's only my best guess, but I'd say he's been dead over an hour. I'll need to do an autopsy to be sure."

"You're the coroner?" I asked. The town was in trouble now. If this guy thought he'd been dead an hour, he didn't know what he was talking about. It had been thirty minutes since I'd called 9-1-1, and that had been seconds before the dead man had spoken.

His brief smile looked unnatural, and I guessed it didn't appear often. "Local doctor," he said. "Ms...?"

So he's a family practitioner with delusions of grandeur. "Miller," I said. "April Miller."

"I'm Josh, Josh Zook." He stuck out his hand, and automatically, I shook it. His grip was painfully strong, and I'm almost certain I didn't wince. Zook. Was he related to the hex company that had gone under?

"You must not have come across him when you say you did," the doctor continued.

The sheriff cleared his throat.

"I called 9-1-1 immediately after finding him," I said. "The time is in my phone."

"Did you see his killer?" the doctor said with a maddening condescension. "Because if what you say is true, he'd just been stabbed. The killer would have been close by at that time."

A chill followed the trail of water trickling down my neck. I swallowed. "No. The trail was deserted."

"Then either you're wrong about the time you found him," the doctor said, "or you're wrong about him speaking."

My shoulders tightened. How could I be wrong about either? I wasn't delusional, and I wasn't lying. "He definitely spoke to me," I said hotly. "I didn't imagine it. He even motioned toward the trees." I pointed toward the thicket of pines to the west.

"That's ridiculous," the doctor said, voice taut. "There was no way he would have had the strength—"

"What's going on?" A Hispanic man, tall and of solid build, ambled up to the group. In an elegant trench coat, he'd done a better job dressing for the rain than I had, but he'd forgone an umbrella. His dark hair lay damp against his head. He squinted, deep lines fanning at the corners of his brown eyes.

The sheriff made a low noise in his throat. "Mr. Mayor, it's under control."

"Is this a witness?" The mayor smiled at me. "I'm Santiago Morales, by the way."

"I'm not a constituent," I said.

The doctor snorted.

"Sorry," I said, my face heating. *Rude*. Where had *that* come from? "I'm April Miller."

"Now that the introductions are out of the way," the sheriff said caustically, "I'd prefer to interview Ms. Miller without interference."

"Apologies," the doctor said. "But she couldn't have heard Woodward say anything."

I blinked. *Woodward?* They *knew* the dead man? But I shouldn't be surprised. Babylon was a small town and Mt. Gretel smaller. Why wouldn't they know him?

"He spoke to you?" The mayor turned to me, his gaze serious.

"He couldn't have spoken to her," the doctor snapped. "He was dead by the time she found him."

"Your time of death is wrong," I said. "Because he *did* speak. Like I said, he even pointed into the trees, that way."

The doctor's dark brows lowered.

The mayor burst into laughter. "Not used to being told you're wrong, are you, Josh?" He clapped the doctor's shoulder, scattering droplets from the black fabric. "You couldn't have prevented this either," he said to the doctor in a low tone. Then, more loudly, "Okay, let's leave the sheriff to his work. And maybe your witness to a hot bath."

A uniformed policeman jogged to us. "We found tracks." Panting, he gestured toward the pines.

"That's where the dead man pointed," I said. Not that I always needed to be right. But dammit, I had been right. He *had* gestured to the woods.

"All right," the sheriff said to me. "You can go. I may have more questions later."

Shivering, I nodded. It would have been nice if someone had offered to drive me back to my rental. But no one did. A stake had been driven through chivalry's heart decades ago. I jogged in my wet clothes all the way to the cottage.

The cat was nowhere about. I hadn't been expecting her to stay, but her presence would have been nice about now.

It wasn't until I'd stripped my clothes off in the white-tiled bathroom that I noticed the bloodstains. Pink threads writhed in the puddle I'd left on the tile floor. Gut twisting, I followed their trail to the source.

My leggings. I must have knelt in the dead man's blood.

Closing my eyes, I swayed and grasped the door frame to steady myself. I hadn't fainted when I'd found the man—Woodward. I wasn't going to faint now. But it would be par for the course if I did, when I was alone, without any handsome—if annoying—strangers to catch me.

Sickened, I showered, changed, then mopped up the mess, tossing the clothing in the downstairs washing machine. To heck with Mother Gaia. I wasn't going to wait for a full load. I turned it on, and the machine rumbled to life.

Downstairs, I paced restlessly through the cottage, touching random objects. The fireplace mantel, with its display of leaves and pine cones I'd added. The bowl on the wooden kitchen counter filled with fruit.

I opened the refrigerator, contemplated the cheese inside, and closed the door. I didn't want to eat, probably couldn't keep anything down.

In the dining room, a handsome, live-edge table with a blue river of epoxy running down its center stood sturdily in front of the stone fireplace. I wandered into the living area. The owner had decorated this as well with modern wood furniture. Matching chairs that followed the natural curves of their wood, each unique and each shockingly comfortable.

The modern look could have been off in the old cottage. But its woodsy feel meshed well with the oaks on the other side of the picture windows.

Returning to the living area, I stopped beside an inset bookshelf, painted white, and trailed one finger along the spines. Someone had alphabetized the spines by subject, a Beastie Boys biography beside a book by Condoleeza Rice.

My finger stopped on a slim, green and yellow pamphlet beside what appeared to be trail maps. I pulled the pamphlet from the shelf.

WITCHCRAFT IN PENNSYLVANIA IS A THING!

By Elmer Fenstermacher Jr.

I laughed shortly at the title. It must have been written by someone much younger than me.

The stapled booklet was amateurish. A handmade price sticker for $1.99 decorated its paper cover. I was surprised anyone had paid that much. But I was more of a Tolkien than Beastie Boys fan, and maybe there would be something I could use about hex signs in the pamphlet.

Booklet in hand, I wandered to the leather sofa by the window and gazed out over the side porch. Rain splashed off the railing.

Despite the weather, an auburn-haired woman picked her way around the brown-painted cottage beside mine. She brandished a smoking bundle of sage. I wondered how she kept it lit in all this rain.

I started, unease prickling my chest. I'd seen that woman before. She'd been coming out of my advisor's office. *The witch.*

I glanced down at the pamphlet in my hand and laughed. Witchcraft really *was* still a thing in Pennsylvania.

Turning my back on my neighbor, I dropped onto the couch, the leather squeaking beneath me. I opened the booklet and read. The booklet didn't take long to finish, though the writer's somewhat pretentious style slowed me in places.

Someone had underlined portions of the text. Baffled, I reread those sections, trying to figure out what had made them so interesting. But it was the usual fare. Demons. Witches persecuted over land disputes or just because they were unpleasant. Pennsylvania farmers terrified over what walked in the woods.

And who could blame the early farmers for their paranoia? Isolated in dense woods. High childhood mortality. The occasional deadly Indian attack...

I glanced out the window and pressed my back deeper into the cushions. The day had darkened, the rain thickening, a steady drum on the roof, punctuated by the bang and clatter of the occasional falling acorn.

No, I couldn't blame the early settlers. Even now, when the woods were glorious in ruby and gold, there was something uncanny about those dark spaces between the trees. As if something was waiting...

I shook myself. Bad things happened in the woods because they were filled with predators and ankle-breaking branches. And breaking an ankle, alone, without aid at hand or cell service, could be a life-ender even now.

A chill stole across my skin. Grabbing the blue throw blanket, I pulled it across my lap and tucked it over my shoulders.

I skimmed the booklet again, studying the underlined bits:

For while good witches can be solitary practitioners, <u>both good and bad are known to work in groups to exert their will</u>...

The old Germans believed <u>evil was a force in the world</u>...

Like everything in this universe, <u>these signs have their inverse, dark symbols to cast curses, or hexes</u>. The most infamous is the pentacle. While this five-pointed star within a circle is a symbol of life, <u>turning it upside down creates</u> a symbol of evil. This is because <u>the Devil is an inversion of good, opposing Truth and perverting Love</u>...

But like so many accused witches, Susan just didn't get along with her neighbors. Her family had been <u>feuding with another family since 1876 over a parcel of land</u>...

I turned to the last page and sighed. The booklet had been a waste of time. The paragraph on hex signs had been brief and inaccurate. But the booklet had done its job, diverting me from the—

Man staring at the sky, one broad hand pressed to his chest. A bloody wound stained his silvery hair.

Leaping to my feet, I tossed the pamphlet to the couch. The throw blanket whispered to the wood floor. *Stop thinking about—*

He lifted a hand and pointed toward the trees. "Look beneath," *he whispered.* "The brotherhood."

My teeth chattered. I retrieved the throw blanket and swung it over my shoulders like a cape. Why was it so damned cold in here?

I moved toward a space heater disguised as a wood stove. The back of my neck prickled.

The murderer would have been close by. My footsteps slowed, as if I were walking through molasses. And then I stopped.

I wasn't alone.

Heart thumping, I turned. A column of gray mist hovered beside the coffee table in front of the couch. The mist darkened. Despite the chill, a clammy dampness sheened my skin.

My breath rasped. A mercury form seemed to be struggling to take shape. The mist lengthened, solidified.

I blinked rapidly. I was seeing things. It was an optical illusion. Maybe a gas leak. I was hallucinating.

The mist swept toward me. I stumbled backward and tripped over a child's rocking chair. The mist brushed my outflung hand, an icy, paralyzing touch that flowed upward from my fingertips to my chest, and I screamed.

CHAPTER 3

Wood crashed against wood, a door banging against a wall as my back hit the wood floor. Disoriented, I twisted, the miniature rocking chair tangling around one ankle. I kicked it free and scrabbled to my feet.

A strange man stood beside the cottage's kitchen counter. He was tall and broad shouldered and wore a damp, tight white t-shirt and jeans that left zero to the imagination. His wavy, brandy-colored hair was tousled, his five-o-clock shadow gleaming like fool's gold.

He scanned the living room. "I heard a scream."

"And so you broke into my house?" I snapped. In the kitchen closet, the washing machine thumped and whirred.

His mouth compressed. He backed toward the open door, his broad hands raised. "The door was unlocked, and it's not your house, it's a rental."

"Pedant," I retorted.

The man stopped short, his green eyes widening, then he burst into laughter. "Pedant? Did you actually just call me a pedant?"

I scowled. "It's a perfectly good word, and in this case, it's accurate."

He shook his head. "Okay. Let's start over. I'm Mitch."

"And you're still in my cottage."

He sobered. "Woodward King's cottage. He was my uncle."

"Was? He..." I felt the blood drain from my face. *Woodward. W. King.* I swallowed. The body I'd found. It had to be...

The man's jade gaze bore into mine. "He was found dead today along the rail trail this morning. I'm his executor. I just came to make sure you were okay out here, and then I heard a scream. Why *did* you scream?"

I couldn't tell him what had really happened, that for a moment, I thought I'd been sharing the cabin with a ghost I could actually *see*. "Did I?" I asked lightly. "I tripped over that chair." I motioned toward the rocking chair, sprawled on the floor. "I didn't realize I'd yelled."

His green eyes narrowed, focusing on my hand. I glanced down at the slim booklet I gripped there.

Mitch's upper lip curled. "The witch booklet? Keep reading that and you'll give yourself nightmares, if you haven't already."

Oh, for Pete's sake. I hadn't scared myself with a silly book...

I crinkled my forehead. But *was* that what had happened? Had I begun to doze and created a ghost in my mind? Because whatever I'd seen was gone now, the cottage returned to its damp warmth.

"Thank you for coming," I said crisply. "And I'm sorry for your loss."

His head jerked sideways, a quick negation. "Don't be." His voice hardened. "We weren't close."

But he was Woodward King's executor. And so help me, my next thought was to wonder if he'd allow me to keep staying in the cottage now that Woodward was dead. It was a selfish, awful thought, and I bit my bottom lip, ashamed.

"I heard you found him," he said examining the front door. He shut it and tested the lock, opened and closed it. Seemingly satisfied it wasn't broken, he left it open.

"Yes," I said in a low tone. "I didn't know it was him though. We hadn't met, I mean. The cottage..." I motioned toward the burnished wood furniture. "The rental was organized through the college. I didn't know it was him until you..." I trailed off.

Mitch's gaze was fixed on the dining table. "What—?" He stopped, swaying. "What?" he repeated more softly. A dazed expression on his chiseled face, he moved to the live edge table, ran his hand along its blue river. "It's mine," he said wonderingly.

I stiffened. His uncle hadn't been dead a day, and this man was already taking possession of the furniture? *What a creep.*

I don't know why I suddenly felt so defensive of my dead landlord. Maybe it was guilt over my earlier selfish thought. Maybe it was because he had been my patron, of a sort.

Or maybe it was because of the rail trail. Absently, I rubbed my chest. The kind of man who could do something so creative, so smart, seemed like the kind of man I'd have liked to have known.

"Never mind." He shook himself. "The cottage. Do you need anything? Are there any problems?"

I jammed my hands into my pockets. "The bedroom door sticks, and the faucet in the shower leaks. The oven door doesn't close properly either." If Woodward King's ungrateful nephew was going to take over his empire, he could damn well enjoy the responsibilities that went along with it.

But Mitch just nodded in an infuriating fashion. "I'll take care of that." He hesitated. "If you need anything, let me know." Without another word, he left. The door banged shut behind him.

I retreated to the leather couch and boneless, sank onto it. I'd found King's body three hours ago. How had Mitch found out about me so quickly?

My hand curled on the sofa's arm. It beggared belief that his first thought on learning of his uncle's murder was to check on his tenant. So why *had* he come?

I unrolled the pamphlet in my hands.

The story of the *Brauchers* was familiar. Vaguely, I remembered my father, his blue eyes twinkling, telling me about someone removing a wart from his hand with a potato. Had his uncle done it for him?

I wished I could ask him now, and I sank lower in the couch. But my parents were gone, and their ghosts unwilling to answer questions. Though they had plenty of unasked-for opinions. What would they think of…?

Rising, I returned the booklet to its place on the shelf. It didn't matter what they'd think. They were gone, like David. I was a functioning adult, and I was on my own.

The next morning was still dripping. After breakfast, I took my coffee from the kitchen and made my way down to the walkout basement. I'd turned it into a studio, and my muscles relaxed at the cheerful chaos of easels filled with half-finished paintings of salt box villages and Pennsylvania barns.

Art. A lump hardened my throat.

My paintings weren't art. They were pretty, and they were original works, but I was a craftswoman, not an artist. And that was okay.

I rummaged through my tackle box of acrylics and thought about a second breakfast. A hearty appetite was the *only* thing that made my early morning jog worthwhile.

The doorbell rang. It took me a moment to recognize the sound for what it was, since it was the first time I'd heard anyone ring it. Frowning, I trotted up the basement stairs and opened the door.

My advisor, Zeke, stood hunched on the doorstep. Rain dripped down his classically handsome face and glistened in his burnished hair. "Hi." He wore a short, charcoal raincoat over his matching suit. "Is that your cat?" Zeke pointed at the black cat, curled on the porch rocking chair..

"No. It must be a neighbor's." I rubbed my forehead. What was Zeke doing here? "Come inside and get out of the rain." Baffled, I stepped away from the door.

"Thanks." He hurried past me and shook off his coat, spattering droplets on the wooden floor. "Sorry to drop in on you like this. I just thought it would be best to tell you in person."

My stomach clenched. *What now?* "Tell me what?"

"I've got some bad news. The man who owned this cottage, Woodward King, he's dead."

"Oh," I said. "Yeah. I know."

Zeke blinked. "You know?"

"I was the one who found his body yesterday."

He blanched. "What? My God. Are you okay?"

"Yes, I'm fine. I mean, it was awful, but... I'm fine."

His smile was faint. "Of course you are. I should have known you would be. You're a mature adult."

And I *really* wished he'd stop reminding me of my maturity. Yes, I was glad my twenty-something impulses were far in the rearview mirror. But forty-seven wasn't exactly ancient.

He rubbed the back of his damp head, ruffling his dark hair. Wet, the gold streaks looked bronzed. "The thing is, now that he's gone, I'm not sure what your status is with the cottage."

"You mean you don't know if I'll be able to stay here," I said. "It's fine. I'll figure something out." But I wasn't sure what that something might be. The cheap rent on the cottage had been a godsend.

"I'm still hoping you won't have to find a new place. But I didn't want you to be blindsided." His brow wrinkled. "You found Woodward? What happened?"

I leaned against the high kitchen counter. "I don't know. I found him—his body." But *had* he been dead when I'd found him? After that thing I'd seen in the living room yesterday, I was starting to doubt my senses. "So I called the police."

"My God." He scrubbed a hand over his face. "What a thing. How did he die? Do you know?"

I swallowed. *All that blood.* "I couldn't say."

"I'm sorry you had to see that. It's not the best start to your research quarter."

"No."

"Have you given any more thought to your thesis?" he asked brightly.

"I haven't had a chance, what with—"

"Of course," he said, "of course. Take all the time you need. And let me know if you need anything."

"Thanks," I said, drawing out the word. He could have told me this on the phone. Had he really driven all the way to Mt. Gretel because he thought the news had to be delivered in person?

"Okay," he said. "I'll let you get back to your morning."

I watched him get into his black BMW, and I closed the front door before he drove away. *Take all the time I want?* We both knew that was BS. I'd paid my fees for the quarter, and if I wanted to take more time, I'd be paying for that too.

I shot the door bolt harder than necessary and shook my head. *Focus.* I couldn't think about what might happen with my housing or anything else. I needed to focus on what I could control. Like contacting that farmer who painted those modern hex signs.

I walked to the kitchen counter. My phone wasn't beside the bowl of fruit. Neither was it on the dining table, between the couch cushions, or in my purse.

Hurrying upstairs, I finally found it beneath the end table beside my bed. I scanned through my texts, found the artist's contact info, and called.

After three rings, a man answered. "Yeah?"

I shifted on the edge of my unmade bed. "Hi, this is April Miller. My advisor at Babylon College, Zeke Stoltzfus, suggested I contact you about—"

"I'm busy." The line went dead.

Dammit. I felt like a telemarketer, making unwelcome cold calls. On the other hand, he didn't need to be such a jerk about it. I blew out my breath.

Okay. I'd just focus on something *else* I could control and finish one of those paintings.

I descended the stairs. Which was exciting me today? The barns or the salt box village?

I reached the living area. Wood creaked on the front porch, and I stilled. Behind the door's curtained window, a bulky shadow shifted, and my mouth went dry.

CHAPTER 4

THEY SAY NOT TO make decisions when you're angry, and this is probably good advice. The problem is, when you're angry, it's hard to follow advice, so I resorted to Tolkien: What would a wizard do?

He'd attack, staff blazing.

Jaw tight, I yanked open the porch door. A man stood on the other side, one hand raised to knock. He was olive skinned, with graying hair and even features, his eyebrows straight slashes above espresso eyes.

And he was beautiful—a term I don't often apply to men—but he *was* beautiful. He could have been a Hellenic statue or a middle-aged model. His eyes were soulful, his body sleek and muscular beneath a charcoal sweater and jeans. I caught myself staring and tore my gaze from his carved cheekbones.

The man stepped backward. "Oh. Hi. I was just—"

"Coming to ask about the body I found yesterday?" Mitch and Zeke had been interested enough in the corpse. Why not this guy? I scanned the porch. The cat had vanished.

"Uh…" He scratched his temple. His shawl-collar fisherman's sweater glistened with beads of water. "Yeah."

Seriously? We stared at each other. His mouth quirked.

"I'm your neighbor." He motioned toward the big, shingled cottage to the left of mine. It was the largest on the block, two storied with green trim, gables, and wraparound porches. "Ham Powers."

"April Miller. But I'm guessing you already knew that."

He rubbed the back of his neck. "Yeah," he said slowly and winced. "Sorry. When I heard about the trail murder, I just thought… We outsiders should stick together."

"You're not from around here either?" I asked.

"Nope. I'm a corporate guy from California."

"I'm from California too." *Long ago.* With David's work hauling us from one country to the next, I wasn't sure where I belonged anymore. Was that why I'd clung to my Penn Dutch heritage? A need for connection?

Ham brightened. "Really? Where?"

"The Bay Area."

"San Diego." He tapped his chest. "I'm a site acquisition director for Emotion Technology."

"ET is expanding here?" I asked, disbelieving. This was farm country. Why would one of the world's biggest tech conglomerates want to open offices here.

He laughed. "Not exactly. I'm doing some work for our foundation, the Global Development Fund. We're looking at buying farmland."

I leaned against the door frame. "Is farming a good investment?"

"It can be, if we can make it more productive. Ed thinks we can, and that will bring in more jobs."

"Ed... Sharpe?" Ham knew the ET founder personally? Sharpe was one of the richest men in the world.

Ham nodded. "He's a great guy, despite what the conspiracy theorists say."

I rubbed my cheek. Conspiracy theorists? I hadn't heard any conspiracies. But I didn't spend a lot of time online, either.

"What brought you to Mt. Gretel?" he continued.

"Research. I'm getting a masters in folk art at Babylon College."

"Cool. Anyway, I just wanted to let you know that if you need anything, I'm right next door."

"Thanks. Same."

Ham turned as if to leave, then he hesitated. "So you really did find that body on the trail?"

"It was a little off the trail, but yes." I swallowed, remembering.

"I'm sorry," he said soberly. "That must have been terrible. I heard he was stabbed in the neck."

I studied a potted fern on the porch railing and tried to force the image of the man in the circle from my mind. "It seemed that way."

"At least you didn't run into whoever did it. I hope Sheriff Yoder brings in some outside help. This seems a little out of his depth."

"You know the sheriff?"

Ham's smile was brief. "I've been shaking hands and making friends with all the local officials, from the governor to the mayor. It's part of the job. They're good people."

"And Woodward King?"

His mouth firmed. "Yes. He was one of the big players in the area. What happened to him is shocking."

"Yes," I said dully.

"Yeah. Well. Like I said, if you need anything, I'm right next door."

"Oh, hey." I straightened off the doorframe. "Do you have a cat?"

"A cat?" His brows lifted. "Uh, no. Why?"

I shook my head. "There's been a black cat hanging around. I thought she might be yours."

"Nope. Hey, if the weather clears, I'll have a bonfire tonight. Stop by if you want." He jogged down the steps and across the uneven slope to his shingled cottage. Opening a green door in its side, he strode into his house.

Thoughtful, I tilted my head and closed the front door. I'd never been this popular when David and I had lived overseas, or when we'd finally returned to California.

I looked down at the phone, still in my hand. The contact Zeke had given me for the farmer included an address. If he was painting modern hex signs, maybe he'd at least have some out on display. They were made to be displayed on barn exteriors, after all.

I grabbed my keys. Jamming my phone into my slouchy brown purse, I locked up and left.

The sun broke through the clouds as I crested a hill, green and gold patches of farm country spreading beneath me. I drove past ivy-covered grain silos and red barns, and my shoulders unknotted. A few of the barns had quilt designs painted on their sides. Others sported raised metal stars for good luck.

The red paint on the barn's sides was faded above the stones forming the structure's base. My car crunched to a halt in the long drive as I stared, astonished. As I'd hoped, circular hex signs decorated its exterior. But what signs.

Broken geometrics, cracked circles and swirls in deep, vibrant colors. Ryan Shaffer had deconstructed the traditional patterns and created a gorgeous chaos of color. Stunned, I stepped from my car and pulled my jacket tighter.

This was art, real art. Not the decorator stuff I was painting. Not that there was anything wrong with decorator. Creating a beautiful home was important. But this...

Neck craned, I let myself through the cow gate and wandered across the soft earth to the other side of the barn. There had to be more hex signs. A few black and white cows turned their heads to study me.

And there *were* more. The signs on this side had darker tones, recalling starry nights and far-off galaxies. I remembered to pull out my camera and started taking pictures.

A cow lowed, and I glanced over my shoulder. Half a dozen cows ambled toward me, and I remembered that I was a trespasser here. Ashamed, I retreated across the damp, uneven grass toward the metal gate.

The cows trotted toward me. I hugged my purse closer and swallowed.

Come on. They were only cows. It's not like they were going to hurt me. I broke into a jog.

The cows sped up, closing on me. My foot skidded in a puddle, and I hit the ground with a squelch.

My heart leapt into my throat. I was going to be trampled. By *cows*. Hastily, I rolled onto my side and planted a foot on the ground. It slid from beneath me, and I slapped wetly onto one elbow.

"Hey!" Muck covered boots and a pair of mud-spattered jeans appeared in front of my nose. A firm hand grasped my upper arm and hauled me upright. "What are you doing here?"

The man's brown-gray hair was short and tight against his head, accentuating his long nose. He wore a yellow rain slicker, though the rain had stopped. His gray eyes crackled with annoyance.

"I'm sorry," I bleated. "I got carried away by your hex art. I'm trespassing, I know. It's unforgivable." And I was very glad I wasn't in a state where trespassers could be legally shot on sight.

His expression relaxed. The grip on my arm did not. "You're the woman who called earlier."

And he must be the artist, Ryan. "Yes. I'd hoped you'd have hex signs on your barn, and when I saw them... I had to see the others."

He released my arm. "Playing to my ego?" His gray eyes held a suspicious glint.

"Is it working?"

He snorted.

Taking that for encouragement, I continued. "My advisor, Zeke Stoltzfus, suggested I talk to you. I'm working on my masters in folk art. My research project is Pennsylvania Dutch, specifically, how folk art is changing with the times. Yours is..." I motioned wordlessly toward the barn.

He grimaced. "And I was rude on the phone." His gaze raked me from my tennis shoes to the top of my head, and I realized what a muddy disaster I was. I tugged at my jacket collar.

He reached into the pocket of his barn jacket and pulled out a white handkerchief. "You've got, uh..." He handed me the handkerchief and motioned toward my neck.

Hastily, I swiped at the cool wetness there then tackled my hands. When I was finished the handkerchief was a wreck. "Ah, thanks." I made to hand it back to him, but he shook his head and stepped away. Awkwardly, I crumpled the sopping handkerchief and stuffed it into my jacket pocket.

"You're here now," he said. "The least I can do is show you my studio."

"Oh, you don't have to. Not after I just showed up like this."

Ryan's full lips quirked. "Now the lady's protesting too much. Come on." He turned and opened the cattle gate, waiting until I'd come through to close it.

I followed him to a small white outbuilding. He opened the door. "Are you an artist?" he asked.

"Oh, no." Distractedly, I rubbed my forearms, transferring more mud to my hands. *Great.* I retrieved the handkerchief in my pocket, studied the muddy cloth, and jammed it back inside.

Locating a clean spot on my jeans, I wiped my hands there. "I think of myself more as a craftswoman."

His square jaw jutted forward. "Why?"

"I paint American primitive style, but it's really more decorator. I suppose that's why I was drawn to folk art. So much of it is practical—"

"Art can be plenty practical. People are just too damned lazy to make beautiful things anymore." Ryan walked into the white building.

I hesitated, then followed him. Inside the door, I stopped short. Circles of color blazed from the walls.

I wobbled, momentarily dizzied. I'd walked into a celestial jewel box, an alternate reality of shocking color and otherworldly geometrics. "It's gorgeous," I whispered.

He folded his arms beside a stack of enormous, rectangular canvases, leaning against one wall. "They're for sale."

I wandered deeper into the studio and stopped in front of a sunburst hex sign. "It's perfect. Somehow you've managed to keep the... spirit of the hex signs, but you're using geometric abstraction."

He grunted. I walked past more, some in black and white, most three-colored.

"See anything you like?" Ryan asked, pugnacious.

I stopped in front of circles of blacks and purples, grays and yellows. "The problem is, I like everything."

"That one's a thousand."

I shifted my weight, my jeans squelching uncomfortably. For original art, a thousand bucks was well worth it. A steal, in fact. I sighed. But I didn't have a thousand to spare.

"Like I said, I'm a grad student," I said. "I'm saving to start my own business selling modern, folk-art inspired home decor."

"Designed by you?"

I nodded. But maybe, some day, I could bring in artists like Ryan.

"Selling modern hex signs?" he asked.

"Not after seeing what you've done. Anything I could design would pale in comparison."

His thick brows lowered. "So why are you interested in my signs?"

"My proposed thesis is apparently covering old ground." I put the last two words in air quotes. "I need something new. And to be honest, I feel better studying something that I'm not planning on painting later myself. And I know that's stupid—"

"It's not stupid. It make sense. If you really want to juice your creativity, it's useful to study art that's outside what you're making. It can inspire you in surprising ways. There's a hex sign self-driving tour. Self-guided. You can get the map from any visitor center and online."

"I'll do that," I said. "Thanks. Zeke mentioned someone was putting modern hex signs up in the woods—"

"That's not me," he said sharply.

"You know of them?"

For a moment, he didn't move. Then he nodded. "I've seen a few. But if I were you, I'd stay out of the woods. You might get shot by a hunter. Or worse."

Scalp prickling, I slipped my hands into my pockets. I didn't want to think about what was worse. I knew what was worse.

I'd imagined that if I could see my ghosts, they'd look like they had in life, not like that thing I'd seen in the cottage. That was worse.

CHAPTER 5

"Why does this smoke smell so good?" I sipped wine, a red provided by Ham, from my plastic tumbler.

It was cozy on the darkened hillside, a fire crackling in the pit, the occasional star glinting between the clouds and treetops. Lights glowed from the windows of his shingled cottage.

"It smells good because the smoke's not blowing in your direction." Ham laughed. Maybe it was the wine, but my impression that he looked like a Greek sculpture, a fit, middle-aged Dionysus, grew stronger.

"I'm cursed," he continued. "The smoke always blows toward me, so I decided to splurge on wood that actually smells good."

"Pear?" The woman staying in the cabin on the other side of me, Karin, lounged in an Adirondack chair. She looked prim and proper in neat jeans and navy jacket, her auburn hair loose about her shoulders.

Did the woman really believe she was a witch? I adjusted the soft scarf around my neck and swallowed.

Ham's graying brows rocketed upward. "Good nose." He coughed and walked to the opposite side of the stone firepit.

"The smoke really *does* seem to follow you," I said.

Karin's gaze lost focus. She frowned and her head turned toward me. "Your hair color is marvelous. Did you know the eastern Europeans once thought red hair indicated you were more susceptible to becoming a vampire after death?"

"Ah, no," I said. WTF *kind of fireside conversation was that?* Or maybe it was the perfect sort of conversation for a night in the October woods. The oaks seemed to lean toward us, as if listening.

"Karin's a Californian too." Ham motioned toward her with his tumbler. A column of dense smoke drifted in his direction. "I've been learning all sorts of things from her."

"Where are you from?" I asked.

"A little town in the Sierras called Doyle," she told me, but her gaze returned to Ham.

"How's your research coming?" Ham asked me.

"Good." *Good* was a grotesque overstatement. But no one really wants to hear a near-stranger's problems. I shifted in the Adirondack chair. "I met with a modern hex sign artist today."

"Ryan Shaffer?" Karin asked.

Surprised, I nodded.

"His work is interesting." She rubbed one thumb along the rim of her tumbler. "What did you think of it?"

"It's like he deconstructed and modernized the traditional hex sign," I said slowly. "But it's beautiful."

Ham laughed. "*But?*"

My face warmed. "It's just... So often when artists deconstruct things, the effect is disjointed, ugly." I shook my head. "Postmodern art isn't to my taste. But what Ryan did... It's beautiful."

"The same is true with writing," Karin said. "I can't stand most post-modernist novels. The characters are awful and nihilistic, and the narratives are so disjointed as to be unreadable. But you're right. Ryan's work is... different. Have you tried automatic painting?"

I shook my head. "I'm painting in the primitive style. It doesn't lend itself to..." *To what?* I wasn't entirely sure what automatic painting was, but I assumed it was like automatic writing, where one just let the hand wander, probably guided by the spirits. "Why do you ask?"

"No reason." Karin's mouth twisted. "Something Ryan said, I guess, that he was surrounded by ghosts."

I started. The ghost comment had to be a metaphor, because I hadn't sensed any at his farm. Or Ryan's ghosts had been avoiding mine. If so, I couldn't blame them. "What do you know about the hex signs in the woods?" I asked her.

"What hex signs?" she asked.

"I just heard someone was posting odd hex signs." Embarrassment ribboned through my chest. I was certain Zeke had said she'd told him about the strange hexes. But maybe I'd misinterpreted. "Sorry, I thought you knew."

She cocked her head. "Why?"

"Something my advisor said. I must have misunderstood. What brought you to Mt. Gretel off season?"

She swung one leg over the other and jiggled the toe of her caramel-colored boot. "Book research. I write paranormal romance. I'm interested in Pennsylvania Dutch knot magic."

"Knot magic?" Ham asked.

"It's part of their *Braucherei* tradition," she said.

"That's a sort of faith healing" Ham sipped his wine. "Isn't it?"

"I think it's more than that," Karin said. "But I'm just at the beginnings of my research. For example, why are they called Pennsylvania Dutch when they're German?"

"*Deutsch*," I said. "The German word for German, *Deutsch*, was bastardized to *Dutch*."

"Oh?" She cocked her head.

I studied my wine goblet. "My parents were Penn Dutch."

"I don't suppose they know any *Brauchers*?" she asked.

"My parents are dead," I said shortly then grimaced, regretting my tone.

"I'm sorry," Karin said.

"I take it you're not one of these... *Brauchers*?" Ham asked me.

"Hardly. I don't believe in magic." It wasn't a lie. Ghosts weren't magic. They just were. And I couldn't even *see* them. I wasn't entirely sure I even sensed them. I just... believed.

"And you?" she asked Ham. "How's your land acquisition going?"

"Slow." Expression rueful, he rubbed the back of his neck. "We need a parcel big enough to build on—"

"Build on?" Karin asked sharply. "I thought you were buying farmland to farm?"

"We are," he said. "But if we're going to increase production and efficiencies, we'll need our own facilities as well."

She sat forward in her Adirondack chair. "What sort of facilities?"

"Storage." Ham waved smoke from his face. "Shipping, that sort of thing."

"What did Woodward King think of that?" she asked.

I bit the inside of my lip. Her interest seemed... intent. Excessive.

He stiffened. "King?"

"I heard he owned farmland in the areas you were looking to buy," she said. "That he was leasing the land to Mennonite farmers."

I cocked my head and studied her. Maybe her curiosity meant nothing. It would be natural for a murder to be of interest to a writer—even a paranormal romance writer. But...

"Yes." Ham shifted his weight. "He was quite the land baron."

"Woodward King," I said. "The man who—"

"Was murdered," Karin finished for me.

Ham's laugh was strained. "You can't be suggesting I killed the man to get his land? Who knows how his heir will want to dispose of it? And even if his heir was inclined to sell to the GDF, no job is worth going to prison for murder."

My mouth puckered. Ham had leapt to defense awfully fast. Karin's comment hadn't sounded like an accusation to me.

"He?" Karin asked. "You know who King's heir is?"

Ham coughed and edged from the smoke. "No. I'm assuming it's his nephew, but he could have given everything to the local animal shelter for all I know." The wind shifted, the smoke groping toward him.

"Of course." Karin relaxed back in her Adirondack chair.

Puzzled, I studied the two. Why did a woman researching knot magic—whatever that was—know so much about local farmland sales?

And Karin's interest wasn't the only thing that seemed off. There'd been an odd tension between Ham and her since the moment I'd arrived at his fire pit.

"Did you know Mr. King?" I asked her.

Karin lowered her head. "No. He sounded like an interesting man though." She stood. "And I have a call scheduled with my family in ten minutes. Enjoy your evening."

She strode, surefooted, across the hillside and vanished around the corner of my blue cottage.

"At least the neighbors aren't boring." Ham raised his tumbler to me. "I've got a writer *and* a folk artist."

And possibly, a witch.

***

BANG BANG BANG.

My head jolted off the pillow. I groaned.

The heavy knock came again.

Cursing, I threw off the white duvet and swung my feet out of bed. I'd been up later than I'd planned last night, drinking with Ham at the fire pit.

I was dehydrated. My head throbbed. And I'd never been in love with mornings.

I stumbled to the closet, pulled on my fluffy blue robe, and made my way down the stairs at a careful angle. The steps weren't wide enough for an adult-sized foot.

I glanced to the kitchen. The clock on the stove read 8:05. Who the hell was knocking before nine o'clock?

I yanked open the door just as Mitch had raised his fist to knock again. He scowled at my fluffy robe. "Did I wake you?" he asked, his tone disbelieving.

"It's just after eight!"

"This is farm country." And he looked the part, in jeans, work boots, and a flannel shirt. His brandy-colored beard had a rough, piratical look.

"I've got no chickens to feed," I said. "I don't need to wake up at the butt-crack of dawn."

"That was over an hour ago." His lip curled.

"What do you want?"

"You said you had a leaky faucet."

I folded my arms. "Among other things."

"Well, I'm here to fix 'em." His gaze raked me, from my bare feet to the top of my rumpled hair. And suddenly I felt like I was in an adult movie, the old cliché of the plumber showing up at the doorstep.

Drawing myself up, I pulled my robe tighter. "Wait here. I need to get dressed." I shut the door on him before he could protest.

I took more time putting on my jeans and t-shirt than a jeans and t-shirt warranted. But what was he thinking just showing up? We didn't have an appointment. I tied my hair into a neat ponytail, put on some makeup, and returned downstairs.

I opened the door. Mitch scowled through his neatly trimmed beard and mustache. "Ready?"

"Yes," I said serenely and held the door wider. "You may come in."

He stomped into the house and up the stairs. Had I made the bed? No, I had not. Was I going to make the bed just because he'd be able to see it from the bathroom? No, I would not.

I'd made the bed every day I'd been married to David, for... reasons. Ignoring that chore now was a happy perq of my new single life.

Making myself a cup of coffee, I retreated downstairs to my makeshift studio and got to work. I couldn't imagine being married again. Having to compromise on basic issues like when to wake up and when to eat and what to eat and who was going to make the bed...

No. I'd compromised enough for one lifetime.

I hadn't been working thirty minutes before a bang from upstairs made my hand jerk, crimson paint splattering the canvas.

I exhaled slowly. There was another loud thud.

I put down my brush and stormed upstairs to my bedroom. A pair of denim-clad legs dangled from a hole in the ceiling above my bed. Fluffs of beige insulation drifted down to the sheets.

"What the hell?" I shouted. The bathroom was next door. He had no reason to be in my room.

The legs swung free, and Mitch dropped to the floor in a crouch. He straightened beside my bed. "You must be freezing at night."

"That's what blankets are for. What were you doing up there?"

"Checking the insulation. It hasn't been replaced since 1978. Squirrels have been up there and gnawed a hole in the fascia. I'm going to need to remove and replace the insulation, then fix whatever hole the animals are using to get inside."

"Now?" I asked, disbelieving. I'd swear he'd gone into the attic just to mess up the unmade bed even more. I couldn't just brush that stuff off the sheets. Now I'd have to do laundry.

"No, I'll need to get some supplies first."

Good. Fine. Go.

"But the frame around the bathroom window is rotting," he said. "I can replace that today. It'll only take a couple hours."

I massaged the bridge of my nose. "Hold on. I can't just..." Belated suspicion clutched at my throat. He was *inside my bedroom*. "How do I even know you are who you say you are?"

"Do you often have random guys showing up to do home repairs for you?"

If only. "You say you're Woodward King's nephew, but how do I know that's true?"

He pulled a wallet from the back pocket of his jeans and extracted a Pennsylvania driver's license. "This is me."

I glanced at it. "Congratulations. You're Mitch Black. But that doesn't prove you're Woodward King's nephew."

"Call the sheriff."

I shuffled back a step and touched my bare throat. Calling the cops seemed a little extreme.

"Or, I can call him." He pulled a phone from his other rear pocket, tapped the screen, and showed me the display. SHERIFF JOE YODER. He pressed the dial button and handed me the phone.

"Sheriff's Department," a woman said. "How can I direct your call?"

"I'm trying to reach the sheriff," I said uncertainly. "Sheriff Joe Yoder."

"And who may I say is calling?"

"April Miller."

"One moment please." She put me on hold. After a short period, a man answered. "Joe here. What can I do for you?"

"Mm, I'm here with a man named Mitch Black. He claims to be Mr. King's nephew and executor—"

He sighed. "Is he making a pest of himself?"

Yes. "No, I wouldn't say that. He's making some repairs at the cottage. I just wanted to verify he is who he says he is."

"Let me talk to him."

I handed Mitch the phone.

"Yeah?" Mitch said.

There was a long pause. Mitch's angular jaw tightened. He barked a laugh. "Not since '86... Okay." He passed the phone back to me.

"Mitch is who he says he is," the sheriff said. "And if I know—knew King, the lease will say that the landlord has the right to enter the property at will."

I rubbed my forehead and shot a glance at Mitch. He could just walk in whenever he wanted? True, today he'd knocked first, but... "Thanks," I said.

The sheriff hung up.

"Satisfied?" Mitch asked.

Not by a long shot. I returned his phone. "I've got research to... research."

"Don't let me stop you."

I grabbed my purse off the rocking chair. Shrugging into my turquoise jacket, I stormed down the stairs, remembering just in time to duck. I never should have mentioned that drippy faucet.

I also didn't actually have any idea what research I should be doing right now. In my Honda, I scrolled through my phone for inspiration.

Hex signs... The hex self-driving tour that Ryan had mentioned... I found a tour map on my phone and plugged it into the GPS.

The hex tour seemed to start in Mt. Gretel, though I hadn't noticed any barns or hex signs so far. But since I wanted to get away, I drove to the other end of the trail, in rolling farmland. I cruised past old barns and stopped to snap photos of their colorful hex signs, unsure what I was really doing.

But it was a sunny morning, and research was research, and you never knew when inspiration would strike. The hex signs were the traditional distelfinks and unicorns and stylized flowers. The patterns hadn't changed since...

Hm... Had any of the patterns changed in the last century? Or had all the innovations, like Ryan Shaffer's, been recent?

I smiled. At last, I had *something* to dig into. I drove through tunnels of trees in their autumnal glory. Leaves like drops of fire drifted onto the country roads and spun up behind my wheels.

And I started to get excited about interpreting Pennsylvania's patchwork quilt of amber fields and fall foliage, of Amish buggies and miniature horses... Why *were* there so many miniature horses?

Finally, I found myself driving up the steep slope toward Mt. Gretel. The forest darkened here, the trees growing taller, the sunlight dimmer, yellow leaves spiraling lazily across the road.

"Take a slight right at the next intersection," the GPS lady purred from my phone, angled in the cupholder.

I slowed to turn.

"Turn left," she said.

I stopped the car and frowned. I'd swear she'd told me to turn right earlier.

"Turn right," she said.

Okay. Right. I edged my Honda forward.

"Turn left."

"Oh, come on, lady." I glanced up at the green street sign.

WITCH ROAD.

A shiver convulsed the back of my neck. But it was only a coincidence that my GPS had chosen this spot to have a mental breakdown. It had to be.

I hesitated, swallowed, and turned onto Witch Road. A bald hilltop rose on my left, the tall grass edging the shoulder brown and bent.

A dark object appeared in the middle of the street, and I braked. My hands slipped down the wheel. A black cat sat on the double yellow line. The animal stared at my car, creeping forward.

Was that...? I pressed back in my seat. That *couldn't* be the cat that had walked into my cottage.

I stopped. I could have gone around her, but something about that cat, about her unblinking, golden-eyed stare, raised the hairs on the back of my neck.

Suddenly, I couldn't have driven forward if I'd wanted to. And I really didn't want to.

I couldn't say how long our staring contest lasted. But the cat finally stretched and rose. She ambled to the hillside and vanished in the tall grass.

Slowly, I exhaled. It was only a cat. On Witch Road. I laughed, and the sound was high and false.

Clearing my throat, I continued on to the next hex signs on the tour, at a barn on Witch Road. The structure was gray, small, and ramshackle, and dwarfed by fading trees. I pulled up beside a silver SUV and stepped from my Honda.

An auburn-haired woman rounded the bumper of the SUV, and I sucked in a breath.

It was the witch.

CHAPTER 6

THE BLACK CAT EMERGED from a purpling hedge of blackberry bushes and twined around Karin's low-heeled boots. Smiling, my neighbor bent to pet the animal. The fabric of her navy blazer rustled.

"Is that your cat?" I asked, still embarrassed by my earlier rank superstition.

So Karin—a supposed witch—was on Witch Road too. There were all sorts of logical, tourist-related reasons for the coincidence, starting with the hex sign tour.

Slipping my hands into my jacket pockets, I glanced at the hex signs on the weathered barn. Their geometric patterns had faded to weak outlines.

"No," she said. "Though I don't think cats really belong to anyone. If anything, it's the reverse."

"What are you doing out here?" I asked.

"Hex sign tour," the writer said. The cat rolled onto its back and writhed ecstatically against her brown boot. "Since it starts here in Mt. Gretel, it seemed like fate."

Ha. Logic. I'd been right. "Hex signs aren't really designed to repel curses or provide good luck," I said. "They're not magic."

"Aren't they?" Karin asked, straightening.

"They're just *for nice.*" It was an old saying. The Penn Dutch were used to correcting tourists about the signs. The signs were for nice, to brighten up a barn, not for magic.

I motioned toward the barn, and the remains of three hex signs marching across its top. "The whole hex business was a mistake by a travel writer in the 1920s."

"And yet, many of the signs include sacred geometry and celestial symbols."

Facts were facts. The signs weren't magic. "It's *geometry*." Artists relied on geometry all the time.

"Hm." She nodded. "I see what you're saying. I just wonder... if people believe they're magic, why couldn't they be magic?"

"Is magic only a matter of belief?" I tipped my head to one side, my fists tightening in my pockets. "Wouldn't that make it... psychology?"

"Exactly." Karin snapped her fingers. "There's a story from Britain—I can't remember exactly where. Some sociologists were studying human behavior and ghost stories. They took their test group to a certain tourist site and told them it was haunted. They gave the group a very specific story about the ghost and what it looked like. Several members of the group claimed they felt the spirit's presence."

"So, they tricked their brains. People freak themselves out all the time." But I shifted my weight, uneasy.

Was that what my brain had been doing when I'd seen that... thing at the cottage? I'd probably still been unnerved after finding Woodward King's body. And my GPS going crazy just now had been a technical blip. And the black cat in the road...

I looked down. The cat had vanished.

"Yes," Karin continued, "but here's the interesting part. After the study was over, this previously *unhaunted* location grew a reputation for being haunted. Visitors reported seeing and experiencing the ghost that the researcher had planted into the minds of their test subjects."

"The story must have gotten out somehow." I folded my arms over my lightweight jacket. "That's all."

"Maybe. But the broader point is you can't cast spells unless you know how to control your mind. You can't focus your intention until you truly know what your intention *is*. Call it what you want, but unless you can focus your will—*all* your will, conscious and subconscious, spells either won't work at all or won't work as intended. The foundation work, the psychology, matters."

This was ridiculous. *Witch Road. Ghost stories. Magical theory.* She was trying to freak me out. And as my mother always said, the best defense, etc., etc. I raised my chin. "I hear you have a mystery school."

"I do," she said, unruffled, and brushed back her auburn hair. "Well, it's not only mine. There are others involved in the management too. How did you hear about it?"

"Zeke mentioned it."

A pucker appeared between her eyebrows. "Zeke Stoltzfus, at the college? I wonder how he knew? I didn't tell him."

"He *is* a professional researcher," I reminded her. But how *had* my advisor known? Assuming she was telling the truth about not telling him. Or maybe she wasn't intentionally lying but had forgotten mentioning it. "Is your mystery school very profitable?"

"Oh, we don't charge. That's not what the school's about."

Sure it wasn't. "Then what *is* it about?"

"Transformation."

Great. She was a guru. "Transformation," I said in a flat voice.

"Transformation can happen at any time, if we let it. But it's usually sparked by life changes. When we get married or have children. When the kids move on or a relationship ends. Or there never were any kids, and we're left wondering what could have been."

My throat tightened. Children had never been a could-have-been. Not for me. I couldn't have children. Period.

David and I had talked about adoption, but with his traveling... We'd figured we'd do it when we returned to the US for good. And then I'd realized having children with David would be a mistake, and I hadn't pressed the issue. Neither had he.

A crow, hidden in the oaks, screeched a call.

"Transformations can be rough," Karin continued. "Especially for people with magical inclinations. Which you say you don't have. But how's your research going?"

Had she emphasized the word, *say*? "It's not."

"Oh. I'm sorry to hear that. I thought..." She motioned toward the faded gray barn.

"I'm not sure what I'm doing." My words jounced over each other. "I need to come up with a unique angle. I hope the continuing evolution of the hex sign is it. And if I'm writing about evolution, I need to start with what the signs evolved from. But..."

My initial enthusiasm faded. Surely someone had done this research already? "I don't know."

"What's your end goal?" she asked. "I mean, what happens after the thesis and degree?"

"Starting a home decor business based on modernized Penn Dutch folk art." I spoke without thinking, but it was unlikely she'd blab to my advisor.

She leaned against her SUV. "Do you need a masters in folk art for that?"

"I do if I want to be taken seriously."

"In my opinion, being taken seriously is overrated." Karin smiled. "But I write paranormal romance and have two kids, so I'm used to not commanding much respect." She straightened off her car. "I'll let you get back to it."

I waved half-heartedly as she drove off, then I turned to the barn. *Children. What could have been.*

I blinked away unexpected tears. I couldn't go back in time. I'd been making the best decisions I could with the knowledge and information I'd had. Regret was pointless.

I exhaled slowly, and the tightness in my throat and chest eased. A black tail snaked from a blackberry bush and vanished.

I returned to my cottage and checked my mailbox before remembering no one knew my address. Also, no one wrote letters anymore. And I certainly wasn't interested in the week's junk mail.

But inside there were no coupons or flyers for pizza or solar panels, just a plain white business card. I withdrew the card and flipped it over. On one side was a web address, and nothing more.

Shrugging, I slipped the card into the rear pocket of my jeans and walked into Cornflower Cottage.

Because my kind of luck was usually bad, Mitch was still upstairs, banging away. I dropped my purse on the dining table by the fireplace and plodded up the steps.

I stopped at my bathroom's open door. A bitter breeze blew from an open window. Mitch leaned from it, his jeans straining against the backs of his muscular thighs.

Embarrassed, I looked away. *Real mature.*

Mitch straightened and hit his head on the top of the window frame. "Ow." Turning, he rubbed his head, hammer in one hand. He winced, his bearded face screwing up. "You're back."

"Yeah. You done?"

"Just finished."

"Really?" My shoulders dropped, and I swallowed. "You got everything done?"

"Finished for today," he corrected. "I have to go pick up the insulation and a vacuum."

"Vacuum?"

"To suck out the old insulation. That job will take most of tomorrow, maybe some of the next day since I'm on my own. You'll probably not want to be here for it, between the noise and insulation dust."

My jaw clenched. This was my work space. Where else was I going to paint? "Do you *have* to do it while I'm living here?"

"If you don't want to freeze your assets off, I do. The temperature's supposed to drop this week. Besides, don't you care about the environment? All this heating is a waste of energy," he said with a mocking, grade-school grin.

"Fine," I said. "But don't come before ten o'clock."

"If I get here that late, I'll be at the cottage late into the night. I'll be here at eight."

"I need *some* time to get my studio work done tomorrow. Ten."

He shrugged. "Your funeral."

Biting back a growl, I stomped downstairs. But I'd won. Sort of.

Though I had a feeling it was a victory I'd pay for.

I dropped onto the bench behind the dining table and transferred today's photos from my phone to my laptop. There was a loud bang upstairs, and my gaze flicked to the beamed roof.

Finally, he jogged down the steps and ducked beneath the low ceiling. "I'm leaving my toolbox upstairs," he said. "I may need it again tomorrow, so don't mess with it."

"Why would I mess with your toolbox?"

"No idea. I—"

Someone knocked. I scraped back the wooden bench to answer. But before I could reach the door, Mitch opened it.

"Hey," Ham said. "I was looking for April."

"Why?" Mitch asked.

"I don't think that's any of your business," Ham said slowly.

I didn't think so either, and my mouth pinched. "I'm here," I said from behind Mitch and edged around his muscular form.

Ham smiled, his espresso eyes crinkling. His wheat-colored v-neck sweater accented his olive skin. "Oh, hey. I found this pen by the bonfire this morning. I thought it might be yours." He extended a black, Mont Blanc fountain pen with a silver snake on the cap.

"That's my uncle's." Mitch snatched it from his hand. "What was it doing at your place?"

Ham shrugged. "Your uncle must have dropped it the last time he stopped by."

"Why was he stopping by?" Mitch's green eyes narrowed. "The cottage you're staying in isn't one of his."

"Woodward passed the time whenever he was at April's cottage," Ham said.

"He came to this cottage often?" I asked, frowning.

"To read," Ham said. "He'd hike the trail here, read a bit, and hike back. It seemed like a regular thing, but I've only been here six weeks, so, what do I know?"

"Not much." Mitch slid the pen into the pocket of his flannel shirt. He strode past my neighbor and to his pickup.

Ham raised his brows. "Touchy. What's he doing here?"

The truck door slammed.

"Some repairs," I said.

"What sort of repairs?"

"The shower drips, a door sticks, and apparently some window trim was rotting and the insulation needs replacing."

His dark brows drew downward. "How did he know about the insulation? I'm assuming it's not something you complained about."

"No. He was up in the attic..." I crossed my arms. But why had Mitch gone up there to begin with?

"What was he doing up there?" Ham asked, echoing my thoughts. He watched as Mitch's pickup backed from my squat driveway.

"I don't know." It was almost as if Mitch had been looking for something. I shook myself. *Paranoid.* "Thanks for bringing the pen over, even if it wasn't mine." It was well out of my price range.

"Yeah. No problem. I'm having another bonfire tonight, if you want to stop by."

"Maybe," I said, noncommittal, but my mind raced. I'd conveniently left Mitch alone in the house for most of the day. If his uncle came to the cottage often...

Could Mitch have been looking for something related to his uncle? My insides compressed. Or was he looking for something related to his uncle's murder?

The problem wasn't only that I'd found Woodward's body. I felt an odd connection to the dead man. But if I somehow identified with him, I'd no idea why or how.

We said our goodbyes, and Ham left. I strode into the dining room. Nothing looked out of place. My arrangements of autumn leaves and pinecones seemed untouched on the fireplace mantel.

I walked into the living area, with its inset bookcases. A green-yellow pamphlet lay on a side table beside the couch. Brow crinkling, I picked up the cottage's copy of *Witchcraft in Pennsylvania is a Thing!*

I was certain I'd returned it to the bookcase last night.

Which meant Mitch had been snooping.

I paced through the rest of the house, but nothing else seemed out of place. Not that I would have noticed in my bedroom. The bed was still unmade, and I'd been slapdash with the clothing I'd jammed into the bureau drawers.

Dissatisfied, I returned to my laptop at the wooden table beside the fireplace. I pulled the business card from the back pocket of my jeans and typed in the address: https://bit.ly/mysteryschooljoin . It led me to a landing page:

Seeker:

As societies grow increasingly fragmented, hopelessness, nihilism, division and despair are on the rise. But there is another way—a way of mystery and magic, of wholeness and transformation. Do you dare take the first step? Our path is not for the faint-hearted, but for seekers of ancient truths.

Beneath the text was a box to enter my email address and a button to send it.

I smiled, wry. *Karin.* I had to give her points for persistence. She must have put the card in my box this morning to scare up business.

Curiosity piqued, I typed in my email. I hesitated then pressed SEND.

SUBJECT: WELCOME

WELCOME SEEKER!

Thank you for your interest in THE MYSTERY SCHOOL. To take the first step and demonstrate your commitment, this week do something you've never done before. It could be something as simple as experimenting with a new recipe, going to a place you've never been, or trying a new activity.

If you choose not to cast this spell for beginnings, **THAT'S OKAY**. THE MYSTERY SCHOOL isn't for everyone. In this case, you won't receive any more emails.

If you **DO** try something new within the next seven days, you'll receive another email from us outlining the next step toward initiation.

Should you choose to proceed, your other "homework" doesn't have to be completed this week, or even this month. If you choose not to proceed, it may never be completed. We're giving you this magical contract now, because part of the process *prior to* initiation is figuring out if joining the school is what you really want.

So take your time considering what type of magic you'd like to bring into your life, and what type of magic you'd like to practice. Then work on the spell for self-initiation, which you can download from the below QR code. If you're reading on paper (some students like keeping a binder of lessons), scan the QR code below to download the contract. If you're reading this on a computer, click the QR code. Your download is a sort of contract with the universe, designed to protect you and to set the direction for your magical growth.

When you've finished editing your magical contract, sign and date it, then get into a meditative state and visualize a powerful being (a warrior goddess, perhaps), cutting any detrimental energetic ties that bind you. You don't have to know where these ties came from—they could have been formed unconsciously or in past lives. Just have faith that the ties have been cut, and you are free to become the witch you were meant to be.

Jayce Bonheim
Doyle Mystery School

CHAPTER 7

WHIRRRRRR...

I yanked cotton from my ears. Throttling the paintbrush in my hand, I glared at the basement's varnished wood ceiling. *Mitch.*

He'd arrived at eight this morning. *Eight.* I'd thought of making him wait outside until ten, but it seemed childish. That said, I still hadn't bothered to make my bed—something I'd no doubt regret given the amount of dust flying around upstairs.

The noise abruptly cut off, and the space between my shoulder blades relaxed. His footsteps clunked above me. The insulation vacuum started again. I briefly closed my eyes, exhaling.

Shaking my head, I took my paintbrush to the metal sink and washed it out. Bloody red streamers of paint rippled through the pooling water. My stomach heaved. I dropped the brush and gripped the sink's cool edges.

Maybe I'd just avoid red paint for a while. Or forever. I returned to my canvas, an autumn night in Penn Dutch country, a fat full moon rising over curves of farmland.

Do you really think someone will buy that? My husband's ghost pressed close, squeezing the air from my lungs.

"Yes." I liked it. Someone else would too.

But I couldn't fool myself. It wasn't art. It was a distraction from my real purpose, from my thesis. So far I had only one example of someone who'd modernized hex signs into real, fresh art.

One example wasn't enough. I either needed to find a new angle or more modern hex artists.

The vacuum stopped again, and I glanced at the ceiling. Enough hiding. Enough avoiding my responsibilities.

I climbed the stairs to the dining room as Mitch emerged from the second story. He wore a mask over his face. Beige bits of old insulation flecked his dark, wavy hair.

"Something's jammed the vacuum," he said, the ends of the mask's rubber yellow straps jiggling behind his ears. "Probably a dead squirrel."

Ugh. "Good to know." I rolled my eyes. "Hey, you don't happen to know any modern hex sign artists? Any who are doing something original?"

"Zooks is gone, but they were doing trad stuff anyway."

"I know. Was the hex sign manufacturer related to Doctor Zook?"

Mitch laughed shortly. "No." He lifted the work mask from his face and snapped it to the top of his head. Flecks of insulation floated down to the blue rag rug. "There's Ryan Shaffer, down toward Babylon."

Folding my arms, I leaned against the back of the high kitchen counter. "I already met him."

"Then what are you asking me for?"

I ground my teeth. It was like talking to a sullen teenager.

It was like arguing with David.

Which was why I'd stopped arguing with my husband, stopped telling him how I felt, stopped communicating. A dull feeling clotted my chest.

I'd never been good at relationships. But I'd learned. At least, I hoped I had.

"Because I need more people to interview," I snapped and immediately regretted it. But I should have asked Ryan if he could recommend anyone else. "Did you move that booklet on Pennsylvania witches?"

"*Witchcraft is a Thing?*" Mitch snorted. "I didn't move it. I *read* it. Why?"

"That's what I was going to ask you." I straightened off the counter. "You said it was silly."

Mitch shrugged. "It's been a long time since I read it. I was curious. It seemed out of place."

It *was* out of place, the only booklet on the shelves. They didn't even hold paperbacks, only hardbacks and a few paper maps. I rubbed the back of my neck. "Maybe one of his renters left it."

"Probably," Mitch agreed. "You should ask your professor about it if you're interested."

"My professor?"

"Zeke Stoltzfus. He's written a book on hex sign history and one on *Braucherei*. I doubt they were bestsellers," he concluded dryly.

"You've read his books?"

"My uncle had two of them at his house. I don't know if he bothered to read them though. He was a big funder of your professor's work."

Zeke hadn't mentioned that. I bit the inside of my cheek. "He's my advisor, not my..." I shook my head. It didn't matter.

Mitch looked at me expectantly. When I said nothing more, he strode out the front door. It swung silently shut.

I clawed a hand through my hair. If Zeke had written an entire book on hex sign history, what did he expect me to add? But maybe he hadn't bothered discussing modern signs.

I exhaled through pursed lips. Of course he wouldn't have, or he wouldn't have put me on the track of those signs in the woods.

But why didn't he want to research them himself? Publish or perish, wasn't that the old saw in academia? I would have thought he'd be eager for a new angle for his own work.

Mitch stomped into the cottage. "Cleared it. Dead raccoon." He climbed the stairs to the second floor.

Raccoon? Nausea climbed my throat. I needed to get out of here. *Time for a walk.*

Snatching my phone and keys off the kitchen's gray granite counter, I dumped both into my slouchy purse, grabbed my running jacket, and hurried from the cottage.

Morning sunlight sparkled through the high branches. It had rained again last night, and the streets gleamed blackly.

There had been a map in the cottage which had indicated other, smaller hiking trails around Mt. Gretel. But they were likely dirt trails and muddy. And I didn't want to try anything new.

I strode past a yellow, 19th century cottage with gingerbread trim. I should never have subscribed to that silly newsletter. *Mystery school. Ha.*

As if they'd actually know if I'd tried anything new or not. They'd probably just send the next email a week from now, assuming that the gullible "student" had done *something* new.

Though no cars were coming to hurry my pace, I trotted across the highway and continued down a residential street. The spaces between the homes here were wider and thick with golden trees. Leaves lay damp upon the road, bright against the black pavement.

I found my way to the Rail Trail trailhead and studied the sign.

The King's Rail Trail is possible due to the generous contribution of Woodward King, who purchased the railway land and donated it to Babylon county. He also funded the removal of the tracks and creation of this trail. The King's Rail Trail is maintained by volunteers. Please take only pictures and leave only footprints!

Leaving footprints would be tough since the trail here was paved, but I got the sentiment. The rail trail continued in both directions. I hadn't taken the northern leg yet.

I glanced south, down the trail where I'd found Woodward King's body. The path vanished in a tunnel of trees. I swallowed.

I looked north. Setting my jaw, I strode down the southern trail. I wasn't going to be scared off it because of what—who—I'd found four days ago. It was better to get back on that horse, face my fears... and maybe come up with some fresh clichés.

Water dripped from the trees. Sodden, yellowing leaves dropped from their branches. There was more sky and sunlight today than the last time I'd been here, and I imagined the trail in summer, shady and cool.

I scanned the woods, hoping the breaks in the trees might reveal some traditional hex signs. But there were no barns on this stretch of trail. Only the drone of insects and the occasional distant house sheltering between the oaks and pines.

I rounded a bend, and there was the circle of stone. My footsteps stuttered to a halt. My pulse slowed.

I forced myself to continue forward. I forced myself to walk to the edge of the low stone edifice, swagged with yellow crime-scene tape. I forced myself to look inside.

The jumble of thorns and vines were matted. A puddle had formed near the center, where Woodward King had lain. I shook myself. *Stop thinking about it.*

A bird screamed, and I started. The sound of dripping water had subsided. My skin crawled, and...

And I was freaking myself out.

Jaw set, I walked around the circumference of the circle. What had the stone circle once been? Why was it here? The ruin had an ancient, arcane feeling... I shook my head. I was letting my imagination run amuck.

Briefly, I considered asking Mitch. Just as quickly, I discarded the idea. He'd only find a reason to sneer at my ignorance.

Of their own accord, my legs moved me forward to a narrow deer trail that formed a break between the blackberry bushes. I squelched through the thin layer of mud and pushed through the bushes. Leafy branches smacked wetly against my jacket.

I wended through more undergrowth, and the trail opened into a hushed clearing. My running shoes rooted to the earth, my scalp prickling.

The woods were still and silent, as if all life had fled, making way for something else, something other. A breeze rustled the trees, and a spiral of yellow leaves cascaded to the damp earth.

A strange hex sign hung on a pine. Its pattern was unfamiliar. This was it, one of the mysterious signs Zeke had mentioned. But I didn't feel elation at my find. I felt dread. Feet dragging, I walked closer.

The sign's colors were traditional—green and blue and gold. But it was definitely a new design—geometric but not abstract. Sweat burned my eyes, and I rubbed them. This was good. A discovery—maybe. So why were my limbs trembling, my breaths juddering?

I tugged my phone from my jeans. It slipped from my fingers and splatted wetly on the ground. Cursing, I picked it up and wiped the muck from the lens with the hem of my jacket.

I aimed my phone at the sign and zoomed in. Someone in blue brushed past, and I yelped, nearly dropping the phone again.

Karin strode to the sign. She lifted a hammer and swung.

CRACK. A third of the sign broke off and flew into the bracken.

My nails bit the palms of my phone-free hand. "What are you doing?" I shouted.

She swung again, and the other side snapped off and spun to the ground. "That should be obvious." Her thigh-length navy coat flared about her legs.

I gaped. "But *why*?"

Karin turned to me, her chest heaving slightly. She let the hammer fall to her side and jerked her chin toward the broken pieces. "The tree didn't like it." Beneath her coat, she wore a blue turtleneck and jeans.

She didn't *look* like a madwoman. She looked like a soccer mom.

"Do you... always carry a hammer with you when you go for a walk?" I asked.

"What?" She looked down at the hammer in her hand as if surprised it was still there. "Oh. No. Like I said, the tree didn't like it, so I went to the hardware store... It doesn't really matter." On tiptoe, she wedged the claw side of the hammer between the remains of the hex sign and pried it from the bark. It popped off the trunk and hit the ground by my feet.

Blood throbbed in my skull. "I would have liked to photograph that," I ground out.

"No," she said sharply. "You wouldn't have."

My jaw clenched. I think I knew what I wanted. "I needed it for my thesis. Do you know who made the sign?"

"No. I wish I did," Karin muttered. "Sorry," she said insincerely. "What drew you to this place?"

"No idea. The trail looked interesting." I smacked my head. I'd gone somewhere new. But this spot was only thirty feet off the main trail, so it probably didn't count. Not that it mattered. It's not like an automated email program would know.

"What's wrong?" she asked.

"Nothing."

She smiled brightly. "Which way are you going? I think I'm going to walk another mile or two toward Babylon."

I eyed the hammer in her hand. "I'm headed back to Mt. Gretel." Because witch or no, she was off her rocker.

"Oh. Too bad. Well, I'll walk you back to the trail."

We moved toward the opening of the deer trail, and I paused. "After you." I motioned.

She smiled and paced in front of me to the stone circle. Karin watched while I walked down the paved trail. I rounded the bend, glanced over my shoulder, stopped, and turned back. Carefully, I peered around a bush.

Karin was indeed continuing on toward Babylon. I waited until her navy coat had disappeared around a bend. Then I jogged back to the deer trail and retrieved the broken hex sign.

At my cottage, Mitch's enormous vacuum roared upstairs. I pressed the pieces together on the dining room's river table. They fit seamlessly, as if they'd never been broken.

Something about that disturbed me, and I pulled them apart again. Then I flipped them face down and opened my laptop.

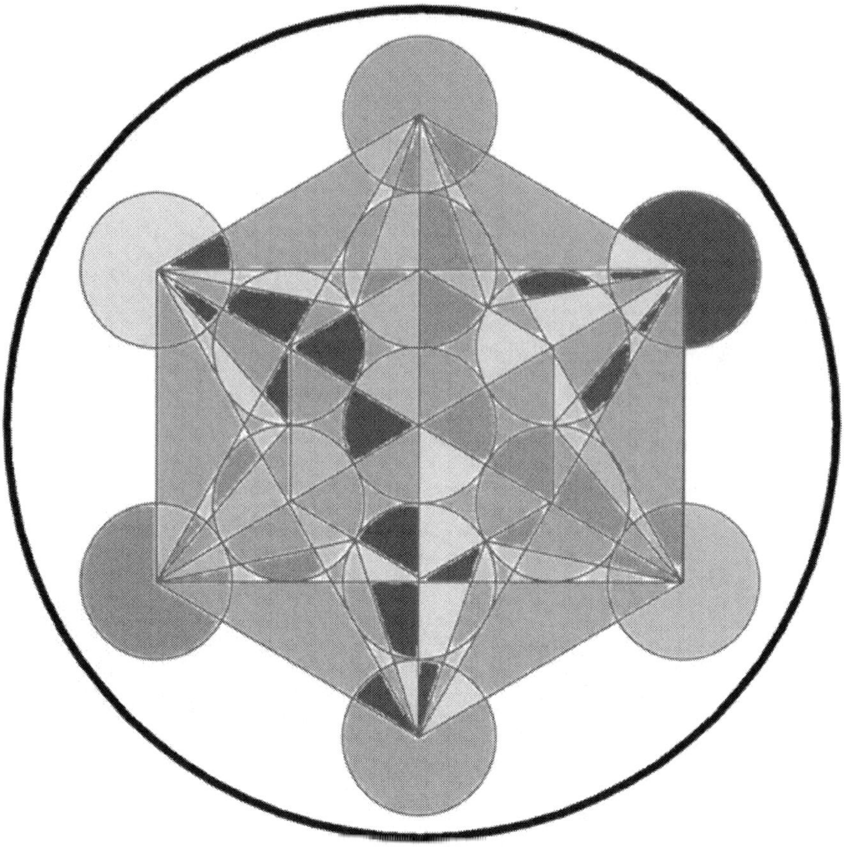

SUBJECT: CONGRATULATIONS

Congratulations, Seeker!

By doing something NEW, you've taken the first step toward initiation!

Initiation, fundamentally, is about transformation. In a mystery school like this one, the end point of this transformation is magic. And how do we make magic? By *becoming* the kind of person who can make magic.

- The witch is comfortable traveling between the shamanic realms of conscious, subconscious, and superconscious.

- The witch knows and loves her shadow side, so it doesn't control her.

- The witch seeks truth and beauty.

- The witch's base energetic set-point is happiness.

- The witch is in a regular state of mental and spiritual growth.

- Having changed herself, the witch sees the magic in the world around her, and by changing the way she sees her world, *she's able to change her world.*

You may grow impatient with the type of spells first taught by the mystery school. Initially, they may seem more "personal-growth" oriented than magical, and in a sense, they are. **But until you become the type of**

person who *makes* magic, spells and incantations are little more than curiosities for the armchair magician.

In your mail box you'll find your first UnTarot card, **The Seeker**. Contemplate this card and the questions below. When you're ready, you'll receive the next email.

But first, a little bit on the difference between contemplation and meditation. There are many ways to meditate, and we'll be discussing some of them in future emails. *Contemplation* is the act of turning over an idea or question in your mind. You don't need to "be present in your body" or to clear your mind. In fact, thinking is the *point*. (Though we do encourage you to find a nice, quiet place for this where you can be alone.)

You're seeking (it's why you're here), but are you seeking the right things? A witch needs to be able to focus, and that starts with knowing what to focus *on*.

Scan the QR code below, or if you're reading this online, click the QR code.

SCAN ME

Instructions:

    1. Contemplate what you hope to discover on your quest.

    2. Contemplate what you hope to achieve.

    3. Contemplate who you want to be.

    4. Distill each of the above ideas into ONE WORD and write the

three words down.

5. Create a spell from each word: "Let there be [WORD]. Thank you for making it so!" (We write these spells in the present tense, assuming it has already happened. And we end with gratitude, because that helps us build faith that it's happened, and because it's only polite.)

6. Speak each spell out loud every morning this week and feel gratitude knowing that your desires are manifesting. At the end of the week, stop, and don't think about the spells anymore. Trust your desire is being fulfilled.

Here's more info about THE SEEKER card:
SEEKER
The search for the Divine. Looking for answers. A quest. Pursuit of what matters.

Occasionally, we catch glimpses of the transcendent—the vaulted ceiling of a century's old cathedral, a sunset, a hummingbird. But we don't have to wait for a glimpse, we can go looking for it. We can live in this world and understand that there's more. But can we find it? The answer is yes, but we have to keep looking. We have to be open to the search, to stay curious, and to stay focused on what matters.

The symbols:
A woman meditates in a field of snow and contemplates a mystic universe. She is in the world but she sees more. An eye, representing seeking, forms a halo about her head. Cherry blossoms in the corner of the card represent spiritual beauty and a higher level quest.

The questions:
What should you be pursuing? Why does it matter?
Jayce Bonheim
Doyle Mystery School

What is my quest?

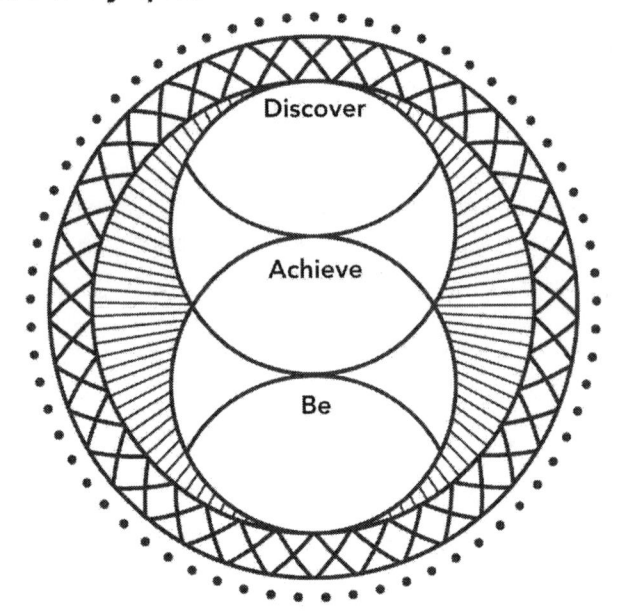

- Discover
- Achieve
- Be

Spells for manifestation:

Let there be _____. Thank you for making it so!

Let there be _____. Thank you for making it so!

Let there be _____. Thank you for making it so!

Chapter 8

In my mailbox? I walked onto the porch. A gray hose, nearly a foot in diameter, snaked from the bathroom window above me and into the bed of a truck with high sides. The vacuum hose jiggled and roared.

Beside the front steps was a blue metal box with a sunflower painted on its side. I reached inside.

THE SEEKER

CHAPTER 9

THE E-MAIL, THE CARD... Chest prickling, my shoulders curled inward. How did they know I'd done something new this morning?

On the porch, I turned the card over, as if its flamboyant fuchsia back would reveal the answer. Water dripped from the eaves in a hypnotic beat.

It had only been a day since the first email, and I'd been given a week to do something new. And yet the email had arrived today.

Above me, the insulation vacuum fell silent. I glanced at the hose extending from a window to Mitch's truck.

Karin must have put the card in my mailbox. She'd seen me on the deer trail, and...

How had she beaten me back home?

I scratched my cheek. There were likely all sorts of shortcuts through the woods that weren't marked on trail maps. It was a trick, and I'd figure it out eventually. But I returned inside to my laptop, my back to the cold fireplace, and reread the email.

What should you be pursuing? Why does it matter?

My stomach hardened. I should be pursuing my thesis and stop messing around with wannabe Tarot cards. My memory flashed to a Tarot reading David and I'd had at a wedding in Italy. David had thought it hilarious, mocking his reading in his usual sardonic, biting way.

Embarrassed by his sarcasm, I'd sat attentively when my turn came. I'd tried to look like I was taking it seriously and asked questions. The reader had explained Tarot had five suits and seventy-eight cards.

She'd also said that I'd have three lives. My third life would start in the middle, with the return of my power.

And how had I remembered *that*? None of that mattered. It was past.

One thing I *didn't* need to pursue was this silly mystery school. At least I couldn't accidentally do the latest assignment. They couldn't *make* me fill out their form.

The printer whirred, and I started. Clutching my arms to my chest, I hurried to the living room. The printer I'd set up on an end table by the bookcase spat a sheet of paper. Pulling it free, I hissed a breath.

It was the PDF attachment from the mystery school.

I gaped. I'd swear I hadn't... I *hadn't*. But I *must* have accidentally pressed print when I'd opened the computer file... Two minutes ago.

That didn't make sense. My printer wasn't that slow.

Heat zapped my veins. I crumpled the paper and tossed it in the nearby waste basket.

Returning to the dining room, I sat in a wooden chair at the table. Mitch's footsteps clunked upstairs.

I grimaced and forced myself to turn over the fragments of hex sign. The sense of wrongness pebbled my flesh. I reached to slide one piece against another and paused, one hand hovering above the three pieces. I withdrew my hand.

Rising, I bent over the table and studied the segments of sign. There seemed to be a second pattern behind the hex—a *pentimento*, in art terms. It appeared to be geometric too, but unlike the balanced, even lines of the hex, the image beneath seemed... asymmetrical.

I squinted. It was hard to tell exactly what was going on beneath the hex pattern. A fleck of insulation drifted onto the broken sign. I was probably inhaling the toxic stuff.

Grabbing my laptop and the broken sign, I fled to my downstairs studio. I didn't put the pieces together again, and I didn't emerge until evening, when the vacuum shut off.

Cautiously, I climbed the basement stairs. Through the window in the front door, I could see Mitch on the porch brushing insulation from his wavy hair.

I opened the door. "Finished?"

"With the vacuuming," he said. "I'll start spreading the new insulation tomorrow."

"Oh, goodie."

"You might be a little cold tonight," he said, ignoring my sarcasm. "You got somewhere else you can stay?"

"I'll use extra blankets."

He shrugged. "Or sleep downstairs. There's the space heater."

"I'm sure I'll figure something out."

"Figure what out?" The divine Ham ambled to the base of the porch steps. He motioned toward the pickup. A tarp covered the mountain of insulation in its bed. "Looks like quite a project. What's going on?"

"Insulation removal," Mitch said.

"I wouldn't even know how to start something like that," Ham said cheerfully. He jerked his thumb toward his shingled cottage. Two cars I didn't recognize sat parked beneath trees on the narrow street outside. "I'm barbecuing for some friends and have way too much food if you'd like to come over."

My stomach grumbled. Suddenly, I realized I hadn't eaten since breakfast. "I'm in. Thanks."

Ham jammed his hands into the pockets of his khaki slacks. "You're welcome too," he said to Mitch.

To my surprise, Mitch nodded. "Let me clean up, and I'll come by." He strode inside the cottage.

My mouth compressed. He was going to clean up in my bathroom, wasn't he? And no doubt he'd leave a massive mess.

The heady scent of smoke from a barbecue drifted past, and my mouth watered. "Can I bring anything?" I asked.

Ham shook his head. "Like I said, I went a little overboard shopping today. Come over whenever you're ready."

"Give me five minutes," I said.

He laughed. "I'll see you then."

Returning to the dining room, I grabbed my jacket off the back of a chair and stilled, my knuckles pressing against the chair back. A wrinkled sheet of paper lay flat on the dining table. The PDF from the school's email.

My muscles tensed. *Mitch.* He must have put it here. Who else could have? But what was he doing going through my trash?

The shower ran upstairs, and I glared at the ceiling. I'd deal with Mitch later.

I strode outside to Ham's sloped backyard, dotted with oaks. The doctor from the crime scene and the dark-haired mayor stood around the fire pit, cans of beer in their hands. Smoke rose from a wood pellet barbecue.

"Friends?" I asked beneath my breath.

Ham grinned. "New acquaintances." More loudly, he said, "Gentlemen, this is April Miller. April, this is Dr. Josh Zook and Santiago Morales, the Babylon mayor."

"We've met." Santiago strode forward, his hand extended. "How are you doing after...?" He motioned with his beer toward the woods, and his brown eyes crinkled behind his glasses.

"Fine," I said. "Having a hard time settling down to work, but I'm not sure I can blame that on what happened."

"Why not?" Josh smoothed his neat, dark beard. His long black coat gave him a funereal air. "It seems a natural reaction."

I stiffened. As natural as the hysteria the doctor had accused me of at the murder scene? *The best defense...* my mother whispered. "Did you complete the autopsy?" I asked him.

The doctor swallowed and looked away. A muscle pulsed in his jaw. "No. Woodward was a friend. Conducting it myself wouldn't have been appropriate."

My shoulders fell, my hands dropping to my sides. I'd been so concerned with my own offense, I hadn't stopped to consider that the doctor had reason not to be at his best at the crime scene. "I'm sorry," I said in quiet voice.

"But the county coroner confirmed my analysis today," he continued. "Woodward would have been dead in under two minutes with those wounds."

So either I *had* been hysterical... I felt the blood drain from my face. Or I'd barely missed the killer. Because I hadn't imagined Woodward's words.

The mayor studied his muddy boots. "At least Woodward went quickly."

"Do you still think he spoke to you?" the doctor asked me, his blue-gray eyes intent.

"I don't think it," I said, in a clipped tone. I was *not* a hysteric. "I know he did."

The doctor shook his head. "Trauma can play tricks on the mind. If you want to talk to anyone about it, I'm qualified."

My neck stiffened. Oh, the *hell* I'd talk to him. Of all the insufferable—

"Maybe you saw Woodward's ghost," Ham said lightly and handed me a glass of red wine.

I forced a smile, because I didn't *see* ghosts. I couldn't even be sure I felt them. "Ghosts" was the label I put on that close, airless feeling, the whispers in my ear. But maybe it was a delusion, a lie to make me feel better about my mistakes, to feel like my past cared and forgave me.

The doctor snorted, but the mayor cocked his head. "I saw a ghost once," Santiago said.

"Really?" Ham asked. "Where?"

"I was driving through Gettysburg with a colleague at night," he said. "We were coming back from a party. He'd been drinking, I hadn't. A soldier in gray appeared on the road in front of my car. I didn't have time to brake. I drove right through him."

"*Through?*" I sipped my wine and raised my eyebrows in appreciation. Ham had brought out the good stuff.

The mayor's smile was wan. "I didn't believe it either. I pulled over, sure I'd just killed a man. But there was no one there."

"Gettysburg is supposed to be one of the most haunted places in America," Ham said. "Maybe I should do one of those ghost tours. April, want to come with me?"

"Why not?" I asked and tossed him a smile.

"The Gettysburg ghost tours have all shut down," Santiago said.

Ham blinked. "Really? Why?"

"I'm not sure. Their mayor was complaining to me about it the other day. It hasn't been good for tourism. I'm sure it's only temporary. Probably a seasonal thing."

"There must be some ghost stories in Mt. Gretel," Ham said.

"Are there any ghost stories in Mt. Gretel?" Ham asked.

The mayor angled his head. "I'm sure all these cottages are haunted. They're old enough. But supernatural in Pennsylvania has always focused on witches."

Involuntarily, I glanced toward my cottage, and to Karin's beyond. "Witches?" I asked, edging toward a table laden with cheese and pretzels.

"Ignore him," the doctor said. "The old Pennsylvanians blamed everything that went wrong on witchcraft and hexes."

"Not so old," the mayor said. "It was still a popular belief in the twentieth century. And you've got Witch Hill here in Mt. Gretel."

"What's the story with Witch Hill?" I asked.

Santiago shrugged. "The usual. Midnight masses, that sort of thing."

Mitch strode to the group. His jeans and shirt were dusty, but his hair glistened with water and no doubt my conditioner. "That's not the story." He opened a cooler and pulled out a can of beer.

"Oh?" The mayor cocked his head. "What's the story?"

Mitch popped the can's top. "It's where the old *Brauchers* would discard the hexes and dark spells they'd drawn from their clients."

"*Brauchers*?" Ham asked.

"Folk healers," I said. "You remember, Karin asked about them?"

Mitch sighed. "Hex signs aren't magic."

"And folk healing is only wishful thinking," Josh said. "Or maybe an example of the placebo effect."

I sucked in my cheeks. I didn't disagree. But why was it so annoying hearing it from the doctor?

"I know," I said. "But... I found a weird hex sign in the woods. Zeke, my advisor, mentioned an unknown person was posting them. I don't suppose any of you know who that might be?"

The men shook their heads.

I rubbed the back of my neck. Of course they wouldn't know. Why should I expect my thesis to be easy?

"What did it look like?" Josh asked.

"It was a geometric design," I said, "painted green, blue and gold."

Josh's nostrils flared. "Where was this?" he asked me.

"Not far off the trail from where I found Mr. King." I glanced at Mitch. He stood stony faced.

"People are idiots," the doctor said. "Someone probably thought they were purifying the space after..." His mouth clamped shut.

After Woodward's murder?

"Woodward would have liked a little magic," the mayor said mildly.

"I understand he funded folkloric research at the college," I said.

"Yes," the mayor said. "Woodward was an avid student of local history and folklore. He didn't want the past to be lost. Will his estate continue to support the college?" he asked Mitch.

"Yes," Mitch said shortly.

"It must be tough." Ham waved away smoke. "Having to deal with all the bureaucracy and administrative details while grieving. Sometimes I think the kindest thing to do is make someone who *didn't* like you executor."

"We weren't close." Mitch slugged back his beer.

Ham blinked. "Oh. Sorry."

"So I guess my uncle picked the right person," Mitch continued.

A self-conscious silence spun out, twisted through the woods, a shroud spreading through skeletal branches. I didn't know where to look. None of us did. But we knew not to look at Mitch.

Santiago cleared his throat and met my gaze. "So what's your story? What made you decide to go back to college?"

"My husband died," I blurted, and my face warmed. This was the second time I'd done that—first about my parents, now David. Ham must think I was a drama queen.

Santiago polished his glasses. "Oh. I'm sorry. I didn't know."

"Of course you wouldn't," I said. "He had an overseas career, and I went with him. It didn't give me much chance to develop a career of my own bouncing from country to country. But wherever I went, I painted. And then when he died... It just seemed like a way to start over."

The silence grew even more awkward. Mitch studied the fire. Ham shifted his weight then stepped sideways. Smoke billowed toward him from the stone pit.

And now they felt sorry for me, and I felt like a fraud. I wanted to tell them it was all right. That yes, David's death had been a tragedy. His life had ended too soon, but I was all right. But that left out so much that mattered about David, about us, that it would be a lie.

The doctor met my gaze, his expression steady. I saw no pity in his brooding gaze, and gratitude closed my throat.

Now I was the one to scrutinize the fire. "I hear the historical association is turning the old canal into a haunted attraction for Halloween," I said brightly. "Do they do that every year?"

Topic successfully changed, Ham moved to flip burgers. We ate, we drank, and I staggered back to my cottage and forgot to put extra blankets on my bed.

I awoke shivering in the dark, my tongue thick and dry from too much wine, my breath steaming the air. With a groan, I stumbled to the closet and tugged extra blankets from the high shelf. They tumbled into my arms.

I threw the blankets on my squeaky bed and slithered beneath them. Covers pulled to my shoulders, I slugged down the water I kept on the end table, lay back, and let my eyes drift shut.

Glass shattered downstairs. My eyes flew open, my heart thundering. It was probably a glass I'd left perched somewhere. Or—

Footsteps padded below, and the breath caught in my lungs.

Or someone was in the house.

CHAPTER 10

HANDS CLAMMY, I MOVED slowly, terrified of making a noise. I fumbled a hand across the darkened bedside table and found my phone. The bedsprings creaked, and I winced.

I dialed 9-1-1.

The phone's unnatural light threw weird shadows across the walls—the distended shape of the rocker, my open suitcase on the floor.

And for a mad moment I wasn't in my bedroom. I believed it *wasn't* my bedroom. That it had changed somehow. That the moonlit frost in the windows was wrong. That my hand holding the phone belonged to someone else, a corpse.

"Nine-one-one," a woman's matter-of-fact voice cracked the spell. "What is your emergency?"

"This is April Miller," I whispered harshly. "Someone's broken into my house, Cornflower Cottage in Mt. Gretel." I swung my feet off the bed.

The bedroom was morgue cold. A bluish glow from the bathroom nightlight slivered from beneath the door. I told her the address.

She repeated it back to me. "Someone's on their way. Are you in a safe place?"

I glanced at the bedroom door. There was no lock on it. "No," I whispered. "I'm in the upstairs bedroom."

Stealthy footsteps moved toward the stairs. I blinked rapidly, my leg muscles taut.

This was real. This wasn't a nightmare. This wasn't a ghost story. This was real. An intruder was below.

"Can you get to a safe place, April?"

The bathroom. There was a lock on that door. But it was from the 1920s, and I didn't think it could withstand a serious attack. "I'll try."

Wood groaned downstairs.

"Where are you going?" she asked.

"The attached bathroom," I whispered, standing. The floorboards made an odd squeak, and I froze. "There's a lock on that door."

"That's a good idea, April. The sheriff is only five minutes away."

Only five minutes. A lot could happen in five minutes. Woodward had bled out in two.

I took a step toward the edge of light creeping beneath the bathroom door. The floorboard creaked, and my breath stopped. He'd hear. There was no way he couldn't hear.

Footsteps ascended the stairs. Heedless of the noise, I hurried toward the bathroom and banged my toe on my open suitcase. It clattered loudly.

"You still with me April?"

"He's on the—" My throat closed.

A dark shape rose between me and the bathroom door. Oily, sluggish tendrils slithered along the floor, flowing inward, congealing toward a midnight center. And cold, cold, cold. I shook with the arctic chill, teeth chattering in my skull.

Something clattered to the floor. Distantly, I realized it was the phone.

I was seeing things. It was a trick of the light...

The light. The light from beneath the bathroom door was gone, blocked by the thing before me.

I had to get to the bathroom, with its locked door. But I couldn't bring myself to move, to get a centimeter closer to the darkness that was growing taller, growing form.

And then it simply vanished.

I dropped to the floor, my legs no longer able to support my weight.

Move, move, move. Get to the bathroom.

I scrambled to my feet. The dispatcher's voice came faintly from my dropped phone. There was a masculine shout, the sound of a body tumbling down the stairs.

I grasped the doorknob to the bathroom. The hairs on the back of my neck stood on end, a spot between my shoulder blades heating despite the icy air. Slowly, I turned my head.

A man stood in front of the window beside my bed. Moonlight streamed through his silhouette.

CRASH. I screamed. The figure beside the window blinked out.

A man shouted. "April?"

Footsteps thundered up the stairs. "April?" Mitch flung the door open and charged into the bedroom. He slammed into me, knocking me onto the bed.

Atop me, Mitch raised himself up on his elbows. "You okay?"

"That's... He..." I pointed a shaking hand toward the window.

He swore, rolled off me, and found the switch, flooding the room with light. I rolled off the other side of the bed and looked around wildly. "There was a man."

"I know," he said. "I ran into the guy."

"No, he was in here." I turned to meet his gaze. "Good God, your nose!" The words exploded from me without thought. His nose was swollen and already purpling. Blood trickled from his nostrils, staining his upper lip. "What happened?"

"Like I said, I ran into the guy." He touched his nose and winced.

"Let me see." I stepped over the open suitcase and reached for his face. He reared away. "It's fine."

"No, it isn't." It didn't look broken, but it didn't look good either. Gently, I touched the fingers of my right hand to the spot between his dark brows.

His eyes widened, and he stilled, his breath warm on my palm. Mitch grasped my wrist, and electricity jolted through me. But the sense of flowing energy wasn't real. Neither was my Penn Dutch healing trick, distracting him to draw out the pain.

My mother had used it on me when I was a kid. It was all psychological. The distraction from the pain, the sense of relief. Like kissing a child's boo-boo. But the pain receptors (or whatever) were in the brain, and the brain could be fooled. Trick or not, it *worked*.

Careful not to jostle his nose, I pulled my palm away. Mitch released me. I shook out my hand, as if ridding myself of something sticky.

"That's..." Mitch frowned. "It doesn't hurt as much. What did you do?"

"It turns out it *wasn't* as bad as it looked."

"What do you mean he was in here?"

"What?" I asked, confused.

"You said—"

The man by the window. I swore, dropped to my knees, and looked under the bed. There was no one there. I leapt to my feet and yanked open the closet door. Empty. "There was someone in my room."

"He's not here now."

A vein in my forehead pulsed. "I can see that. But—"

A siren wailed. Blue and red lights strobed across the wood-paneled walls.

"You called the cops?" Mitch asked.

"Of course I called the cops." I clawed a hand through my hair, inadvertently raising the hem of my t-shirt. It dawned on me that what I was wearing—sky-blue panties, t-shirt, and nothing else—wasn't entirely appropriate for a chat with my new landlord/handyman.

My face heated, and I crossed my arms. The t-shirt didn't leave much to the imagination.

To his credit, Mitch kept his gaze fixed on my face. "I'll talk to them. You get dressed."

He turned and walked into the hall. The light snapped on. "This is Mitch Black," he bellowed. "I'm here to help. I'm coming downstairs."

I slithered into a pair of jeans, put on a bra, and pulled the t-shirt back over my head. When I came downstairs, Mitch stood in the frigid dining room talking to the grinning sheriff. Mitch was tall, but the sheriff towered over him.

The sheriff sobered when he saw me. "You'd better put some shoes on," he said. "There's glass everywhere."

The window in the front door had been smashed. Glass sparkled on the wood floor between the kitchen and dining room. A glittering trail led into the living area and down the stairs to my basement studio.

"I'll be right back." I jogged up the stairs, slipped into a pair of sneakers, and returned to the two men.

"Uh, huh." The massive sheriff raised a skeptical brow.

Mitch's handsome face crimsoned. "I tell you, I was in my truck."

"What?" I asked. "What's going on?"

Mitch exhaled heavily. "I had too much to drink at Ham's place. After you went home, I decided to sleep it off in my pickup."

"Is this true?" the sheriff asked me.

"How should I...?" My face warmed again. He thought Mitch had been with me. "I have no idea. I was in bed, and I heard glass breaking downstairs, so I called nine-one-one. I heard someone coming up the stairs, and then I heard them falling down the stairs—"

"Falling?" the sheriff asked.

"The guy probably hit his head on the low ceiling," Mitch said. "He wouldn't have known that beam was there in the dark."

The sheriff grunted, and I frowned. There was something not-quite-right about that scenario. Mentally, I reached for the wrongness, but it slipped away from my sleep-deprived brain.

"And then?" the sheriff prompted.

"Then I saw someone in my room—or thought I did," I said. "There was another crash downstairs, and I screamed." At least I *thought* that was what happened. How could I have imagined someone in my bedroom?

Giving my head a quick shake, I moved to close the open front door.

"Hold on," the big sheriff said. "I want a deputy to get prints off that door before you touch it. And I don't think closing it's going to make much difference at this point."

I dropped my hand and grimaced. With the window gone, the door was useless.

"And then what happened?" the sheriff asked Mitch.

"I heard glass breaking," he said.

"Were you awake or asleep?" the sheriff asked.

Mitch's face creased. "I must have been half awake. I got to her cottage in time for the door to blast me in the face." His fists clenched. "The guy ran right past me. And then April screamed, and I ran inside."

"Why'd you scream?" The sheriff adjusted his broad-brimmed hat. "It seemed an odd time for it, after the guy had left."

"I... I thought there was someone in my bedroom," I admitted, shame-faced. And obviously, I'd been wrong. "Dammit. The dispatcher!" Pivoting, I raced up the stairs to my bedroom. I grabbed the phone off the floor. But she'd disconnected.

I retreated down the stairs again, phone in hand.

"I called the station," the sheriff said. "They know you're okay."

"Thanks," I muttered. Ridiculously, I still felt guilty. She'd been so calm and kind, and I'd just dumped her call.

"Mitch, you notice anything stolen?" the sheriff asked.

He shook his head. "The only thing of value is my furniture from the cottage, and I know he wasn't carrying that on his way out."

I stiffened. *My furniture*? His uncle had just died, the cottage been burgled, and Mitch was marking territory?

More deputies arrived, and the sheriff led me through the house to see if anything had been stolen. In my studio, I stopped beside the card table. My paints lay scattered beside *The Seeker* card.

My lungs hitched. The hex sign I'd found in the woods was gone.

I checked under the table. Had I left the pieces somewhere else? A sheet of wrinkled paper lay on the floor, and I snatched it up. I jerked upright so fast my head grazed the card table. It was the mystery school form, the homework.

And I'd filled it out. I'd even colored it in.

Damn. I had a vague memory of doing it, but how much wine had I drunk?

"What's wrong?" the sheriff asked.

"I—ah—found a hex sign in the woods, not far from where I found Mr. King. It was, er, broken into pieces." The story of Karin smashing it now seemed too outré to mention. "I brought the pieces home. They're not here anymore."

The sheriff arched a brow. "Your guy stole a broken hex sign?"

"It wasn't a normal hex sign. It had an unusual design..." I trailed off.

It sounded silly even to me. Who would steal a hex sign, much less a broken one? My laptop made a better target for a thief, and it was still open upstairs on the dining table. "Maybe I misplaced it," I finished lamely.

"Huh." He turned and climbed the stairs, filling the stairwell with his bulk.

Mitch found some plywood and boarded up the window in the door. The police left. Mitch went home. I swept up the glass and made a cup of tea. I could have gone back to bed, but I was too wired to sleep.

Returning to my studio downstairs, I reached for my paints. *The Seeker* card whispered from the card table to the linoleum floor. I picked it up and studied it.

Was I a seeker? It didn't feel that way. Sure, I was trying to nail down my thesis topic, and that entailed some research. But was I chasing the wrong goal?

And was it coincidence that I was huddling with my mug of hot tea in the room farthest from the upstairs bedroom, and that...

I dropped heavily into a folding chair. What *had* I seen? My memories of the night were already clouding. But I'd seen something. I wasn't a hysteric. Yes, the break-in had been terrifying. Yes, I'd been frightened, but *not* out of my wits.

But.

This hadn't been the first time this week I'd seen something impossible. Was this menopause? Was I losing my mind?

There was a rap on the window. I started, my fingers tightening, crinkling the stiff card.

Karin stood outside in a sweat suit, her auburn hair up in a bun. Rising, I opened the basement door.

She stepped inside. "Are you okay?" She shook her head. "Dumb question. I can see you're all right physically. I saw the police, but I didn't want to interfere while they were at your cottage. And then I saw your light on down here and thought I'd check in on you."

"I'm fine, thanks. There was a burglar."

"What?" Her hazel eyes widened. "That must have been terrifying."

"Yes..." I set down the card. "Have you ever seen something that wasn't there?" I blurted then bit my bottom lip.

Karin cocked her head, a fall of auburn hair cascading over one shoulder. "No," she said, drawing out the word. "Did you see something that wasn't there?"

"No. I mean, yes. But it must have been a trick of the light or stress."

She nodded, her expression serious. "That can happen. But sometimes we see things that others don't." She smiled. "At least I do. It can make me look a little crazy."

I hesitated. "And when you see things other people don't," I said, tugging at my t-shirt collar. "What do you do?"

"I check my assumptions," Karin said. "It usually means there's something I need to look at more closely. Or it was a trick of the light. Or stress."

"Well." That was... surprisingly sensible. For a witch. "Thanks for coming over."

She took the hint. "I'm glad you're okay. I probably won't go back to sleep. If you want to drop by and chat or sleep in one of my guest rooms, you're welcome."

"Thanks."

She let herself out. I picked up the Seeker card again. *Check my assumptions. Look more closely.*

I'd told the men I was starting over. But how could I do that if I was second guessing myself, or worse, losing my mind?

I nodded. Whatever was going on with me, it had begun when I'd found Woodward King's body. It was time to start seeking answers.

CHAPTER 11

ALAS, MY CRIME-SOLVING KNOWLEDGE was rooted in 1980s detective shows. Happily, we were well into the 21st century, and the world now had the blessing and curse of the internet.

But once Karin had left my cottage, the adrenaline that had kept my exhaustion at bay hit me like a wine-soaked mallet. I walked straight past my laptop on the dining table and up the stairs to bed. But not before making sure every door and window in Cornflower Cottage was locked.

It was ten o'clock when I finally woke. I stretched beneath the warm covers, checked the time on my phone, and realized Mitch—for once—hadn't arrived bright and early. I tossed the phone back on the bedside table.

He was probably sleeping in like I had. But worry niggled my gut. He didn't seem like the kind of guy to sleep late—post-burglar encounter or not.

And it wasn't my business. Mentally shrugging off Mitch's absence, I dressed quickly in my frigid bedroom and ambled downstairs. I brewed a cup of coffee and studied the cold fireplace. I'd need to go shopping for firewood before I froze.

I sat at the dining table, my back to the stone fireplace, and booted up my laptop.

A draft lifted the hairs on the back of my neck. I glanced at the board over the broken window in the front door. Rising, I got my jacket from the coat closet and slipped it on.

I typed *Woodward King Babylon* into the search engine. The story of the murder was top of the list.

A BELOVED PHILANTHROPIST AND A SHOCKING KILLING IN MT. GRETEL

He was a behind-the-scenes philanthropist, a beloved member of the Babylon community, and on Monday, October 8th, he was murdered on the trail he helped create and maintain.

While walking the King's Rail Trail between Mt. Gretel and Babylon, Woodward King was stabbed to death. His body was found by a shocked hiker.

During a brief news conference the day after the attack, Sheriff Joseph Yoder declined to comment on any suspects, name any witnesses, or speculate on motive.

"The motive in this case is still unknown," Sheriff Yoder said. "We're investigating all possibilities, and we're not going to speculate."

While the motive for the murder remains murky, what is clear is the impact that Woodward King had on the Babylon community.

"Woodward was a force," Babylon Mayor Santiago Morales said. "He was a board member of Babylon College and the Historical Society. Because of him, we have the rail trail, which has driven tourism dollars to the area. And he's made a personal impact on many, many people. He never wanted to take credit for that in life, but I think I can tell you my personal story now. When I was a student, I was in a car accident that left me with medical bills so high I was on the verge of dropping out. Woodward paid them so I could continue my education. I never forgot that."

The Babylon Sheriff's Department received a call around 1:30 PM about a body found near mile marker 2 of the King's Rail Trail. When deputies arrived, they found Woodward King dead of multiple stab wounds.

If anyone has information about the murder, they are asked to contact the Babylon Sheriff's Department.

I sagged against the back of my chair. The article didn't tell me much I hadn't already known, though I was grateful the sheriff was keeping my name private. I'd known Mr. King was a donor to the college. I hadn't realized he was on the board.

But that explained the remark about King funding Zeke's research. I massaged the back of my neck. Who had told me that?

Cradling the mug of coffee to warm my hands, I realized it had gone cold. I frowned. It hadn't taken me *that* long to read the article.

Shaking my head, I rose and went to the kitchen for a refill from the coffeemaker.

There was a knock at the front door. "It's Mitch," he bellowed, and I hurried to let him inside. "Morning." He stood holding a toolbox in one hand.

"Hi," I said. "Your nose looks pretty good." It was still reddened, but not swollen.

He lifted his free hand to touch it. "Yeah. I can't believe I thought it was broken. Can I come in?"

"Sure." I stepped from the door, an easy warmth filling my chest. "Mitch, thank you for what you did last night. I feel incredibly lucky that you were here."

He flushed. "It's nothing," he said.

"It's not nothing. It was terrifying. And I don't want to think about what would have happened if you hadn't been sleeping in your truck." I motioned toward the damaged door.

He clawed a hand through his brandy-colored hair. "Yeah. Well. Me being here may have dented your reputation."

"You mean the sheriff?" I laughed. "I'm only here temporarily. I don't care much about my reputation."

"You should," he said seriously. "You found my uncle's body."

But that was... The sheriff couldn't possibly think...? "Sheriff Yoder knows I just got here. My only connection to your uncle is this cottage." I pressed my hand against my jacket pocket, feeling the lump of keys and the thin, hard form of the hobbit-door keychain.

"I know that. And you know that. But the sheriff has to consider that might not be true."

Damn. Feeling a little sick, I hugged my arms against my stomach.

"I've got some glass for the front door in my truck." Mitch looked around. "It's freezing in here. Why didn't you start a fire?"

"Lack of dry firewood," I said absently. Had I actually made myself a suspect?

"I'll get some for you."

"You don't have to—"

"It's part of the rental deal." Careful to avoid the blue river running through it, Mitch set his toolbox on the dining table.

"Well, thanks." I hadn't remembered that being on the lease, but I hadn't read the papers very carefully either.

He walked around the table and drew back the fireplace's mesh curtain. Kneeling on the stone ledge, he stuck his head inside and opened the flue. There was a metallic, scraping sound. Black ash dropped onto his upturned face.

Mitch withdrew and brushed it off, leaving a sooty smear on his cheek.

I bit back a laugh. "You've still got some, uh..." I pointed.

But he wasn't looking at me. He studied my open laptop. "Investigating my uncle?"

Heat rushed to my face. "No. It's not like that—"

"I've been checking my assumptions about him too."

I started at the echo of Karin's words and of the UnTarot card.

"Growing up, I thought he..." Mitch shook his head.

"Thought he what?" I asked quietly.

He met my gaze. "Thought he was a hypocrite. Woodward helped everyone but my parents. My parents are bohemians, artists—or they like to think they are. It gave them an excuse to waste their money, time and talents smoking pot instead of working. And I inherited some of their attitudes. Not the drugs. I always hated the way the drugs changed them. But their entitlement." He laughed shortly. "Woodward set me straight on that. He wasn't going to give me a cent to help out, and my grades weren't good enough for a scholarship. I had to make my own way. So I made and sold furniture to get by."

"Furniture..." I ran my hand along the dining table's live edge, finally understanding. River tables with live edges had emerged in the 1960s. Since they'd recently returned to popularity, I'd assumed the furniture was new. "Not—?"

"Yeah. I didn't realize Woodward was the one who bought my things. Every one of his rentals is filled with the furniture I made. The son of a bitch put me through college, and I didn't even know it."

"*You* made this furniture?" That was why he'd seemed so proprietary toward the pieces. Mitch hadn't been grasping for his inheritance. The furniture literally was his.

"Don't look so surprised." Mitch quirked a brow. "I have *some* skills."

My lips parted. "*Some* skills? These are amazing. I thought you were a contractor. I didn't realize you made furniture."

"I am a contractor. The woodworking's only a hobby."

I stared, astonished. The furniture in the cottage had been made by a master craftsman. And he'd made it to put himself through college? "Please tell me you're still selling your work."

He shook his head. "Not practical. And now that I know Woodward was the one who bought it all, it's a damn good thing I didn't follow my *passion*." His upper lip curled.

He couldn't seriously believe these had been bought only out of pity? They were marvelous. "But these are—"

"Forget about it," he said curtly. "The point is, there was more to my uncle than I knew. And you're not going to find the answers online."

"Then where are *you* looking?"

He blinked. "I've got to get to work." He strode to the front door. "It's going to be noisy."

Surprise, surprise. Stuffing my laptop and purse into my denim-colored backpack, I left him rummaging in the bed of his pickup.

I drove to the college library. It was either the library or a coffee shop, and I tended to spend too much money and consume too many calories in coffee shops. But that wasn't my only reason I chose the Babylon College library. I wanted to read my advisor's books.

I worked through the day, breaking for a campus lunch, tweaking my thesis proposal, and searching for info online about Woodward King and his gruff nephew. My research would have gone faster if my mind hadn't constantly wandered. *Was* I on the right path?

And not just on the thesis proposal. On everything. It had all seemed so clear before I'd come to Mt. Gretel. I had tasks, a plan. I'd never stopped to consider whether it was a *good* plan.

A feminine giggle issued from behind a nearby bookcase. I glanced toward the librarian's curving desk. No one was there, and I smiled. The lovers had chosen their time and place well.

I found a few online ads for Mitchell's contracting business. He had rave reviews. How did he find the time to work at Cornflower Cottage?

As to Woodward King, I found mention of him at various events, but not much else. The Rail Trail had been big news. But aside from paeans to his hard work and funding, there wasn't much about him in the articles I unearthed.

The light shifted through the library's high windows. With an unpleasant jolt, I realized it was getting late. I found Zeke's two books in the stacks and returned with them to my carrel.

I skimmed the table of contents of the hex sign book and flipped to the history section. There were a few points I hadn't heard before. Zeke had been thorough. I doubted there was anything I could add.

Eyes burning, I returned to the table of contents, then skimmed the book. Nothing on the evolution of hex signs, nothing modern.

I turned the pages more slowly, studying photos of hex signs. There was nothing like the sign I'd found in the woods. Maybe there *was* space for me to research something new.

I decided to check out the book and set it aside. I opened Zeke's book on *Braucherei*.

"April?"

My hand jerked, wrinkling the corner of a glossy page. "Professor Stoltzfus," I stammered.

"Zeke," he corrected in a low voice. He wore a tailored gray suit, his white shirt open at the collar. The flash of a folded, silvery tie made a lump in a jacket pocket.

"Right." My cheeks warmed. "Sorry. It's just, in this context..." I motioned around the library. Only a few students remained, their heads bent toward the long tables.

He grinned. "Good book?" The overhead pendant lights glinted off the bronze threads in his hair.

My face grew hotter. "You're the hex sign expert. I wanted to see what you'd covered, and if I could add anything."

Zeke leaned against the carrel beside me and crossed his legs. "And can you?"

"Maybe. I talked to that artist you mentioned, and I found one of those hex signs in the woods. The design was geometric, but I've never seen it before."

He straightened off the carrel. "Where?"

"Near, uh, mile marker two on the Rail Trail, in the state game lands, I think."

"I need to see this. Can you take me there?"

"Ah, I found it in pieces." And there I went again, covering for Karin. Why was I doing that? Yes, her actions had seemed crazy. But what was that to me?

"Still," he said, "I'd like to see them."

"You can't. I brought the fragments home, but they were… stolen." It sounded ridiculous. Who would steal a broken hex sign?

He blinked. "Stolen?"

"Someone broke into my cottage last night. They probably grabbed the first thing they saw without thinking and ran. Kids."

His brows drew together. "Broke in? Are you all right?"

"I'm fine. By the time I got downstairs, they were gone."

"You—" Zeke lowered his head. "I've been asking around, trying to find you a new place. So far I haven't had any success. But I'll keep pushing."

I wondered what he'd stopped himself from saying. "No," I said, "it's okay. It looks like I'll be able to stay in Cornflower Cottage."

"Why would you want to? Mt. Gretel's far from campus. And the cottage is obviously unsafe."

"But I *like* Mt. Gretel."

He grimaced. "Let me know if you change your mind." He turned as if to go, then turned back. "We should talk more about your thesis. You free for dinner tomorrow?"

I hesitated. But it wouldn't be a date. He was my advisor. "Ah, yeah. Sure."

"Great. There's an old tavern between Mt. Gretel and Babylon I think you'll like. I'll pick you up at six?"

"Okay."

He strode away. I frowned at the books stacked on the table. Usually advisors didn't pick their advisees up for dinner.

Whatever. I was no naive co-ed to be seduced. It was just dinner.

I skimmed the book on *Braucherei*. Zeke's style was dry, academic, and a part of me preferred the silly pamphlet in the cottage. But Zeke had been thorough, interviewing living *Brauchers* and tagging along as they provided their services.

When my eyes couldn't take it anymore, I checked out both books. Zeke's were oversized and my backpack was the opposite. I had to work to jam them inside, and I tucked my laptop beneath one arm.

It was dark when I left the library, the stars dimmed by the parking lot lights. I wended through parked cars to my old Honda and almost reached it.

Something rustled behind me. I started, my shoulders rocketing to my ears. A blow struck my upper back, and I flew forward, banging against the Honda. My own car had become a weapon. Against me.

CHAPTER 12

"I DIDN'T SEE HIM." Stiffly, slowly, I shifted my weight so as not to set off more sparks of pain. And there was a lot of pain. Not severe, but quantity had made up for quality.

There'd been no elegant dropping and rolling for me. Just slam, bam, no thank you, ma'am, and my backpack wrenched from my shoulder, my head bouncing off the passenger window, before I could yell.

And after ricocheting off my car, I'd landed in a puddle. So in addition to the bruising, my left side was soaking wet. *Yay, me.*

Rain drizzled to the pavement, pooling in the potholes. My scraped hands, too hot with pain to jam into my pockets or grip into furious fists, hung loose at my sides.

The droplets on the campus cop's plastic-covered hat glittered like glass beneath the parking-lot lights. He frowned down at me. The man was at least as tall as the sheriff but beanpole skinny. "Did you get any sense of him at all?" he asked.

I shook my head. I'd been too startled by the mugging to notice much. "It happened so fast."

At least I still had my laptop. It had gone skidding beneath my Honda. I was itching to see if I could still boot it up, or if the hard landing had KO'd the device.

Anxiously, I glanced at the brick library. Had I backed up my laptop when I'd been inside? I couldn't remember.

The cop shook his head. "I'm sorry you got mugged. But you need to pay more attention to your surroundings."

There's nothing more annoying than a round of victim-blaming. But he wasn't wrong. If I *had* been paying more attention, I might have seen my attacker, might have been able to avoid this. So I guessed there was blame to share.

"What's going on?" Zeke strode toward us. His forehead creased. "April? Is that you? Are you okay?" Diamonds of rain glinted in his dark hair.

"I'm fine," I said. "I just got mugged."

"Are you kidding me?" My advisor shot the campus cop a black look, and his full lips compressed. "What did he get?"

"My backpack. My wallet was inside, and—I had two new library books in it. Yours on hex signs and *Braucherei*. What am I going to tell the librarian?" I burst out.

And yes, I *know*. Priorities. But this program was costing me enough without adding library fees.

"Is this it?" Another cop, a pudgy redhead, jogged toward us carrying my blue backpack.

"It is." I squealed like a tween girl, realized I'd done it, and grimaced. "Where did you find it?"

He wheezed, breathing hard. "Dumpster."

I winced.

"Is anything missing?" the first cop asked me.

The fabric was stained with something I didn't want to think about too much. But I rummaged through its pockets. The books were there. My wallet was not, which was predictable. I groaned. "My wallet."

My wallet, with my driver's license. My credit cards. I'd kept one of my cards back at the cottage, because I'd gotten in the habit overseas of *not* carrying everything on me. But my driver's license would take time to replace.

"Why am I not surprised he wasn't interested in my books?" Zeke said ruefully.

I stared at him, then burst into laughter. He grinned.

"Okay," I said. Losing a wallet was a hassle, but I hadn't been hurt. "Perspective. At least I won't be persona non grata in the library."

"I'm glad you can laugh about it," Zeke said, "but that doesn't make what happened acceptable. You deserved better." He turned to the cop. "Do you need anything more for your report?"

The tall man shook his head. "I've got everything."

"Then I'm sure she'd like to get out of this rain," Zeke said, "go home and relax." He turned to me. "Do you need a ride?"

"No, I've got my car..." My heart jumped. *My keys.* And then I patted the front pocket of my jeans, where my keys nestled. "And my keys," I finished, relaxing.

The mugging must have scrambled my brain more than I'd thought. For a moment, I'd thought the keys had been in my backpack, and I'd gone through it and hadn't seen them...

Zeke nodded. "I'll walk you to your car."

I aimed my fob, and the locks on the Honda beside him clicked open. Its headlights flashed.

His smile broadened. "Then I'll save my gallantry for dinner tomorrow. That is, if you're still up for it?"

"I will be. I'll see you tomorrow."

Moving carefully, I got into my car. Zeke closed the door for me, and I drove toward Mt. Gretel.

I'd only been shoved. It could have been worse.

My hands clenched, sparking pain through my palms, and I cursed. Relaxing them, I handled the wheel with my fingertips.

My headlights illuminated golden leaves flattened to the black pavement. I made the turn to Mt. Gretel and slowed, creeping past a pizza place, the yellow meeting house, an ice cream parlor shuttered for the season.

I pulled into my cottage's driveway. Two figures stood in conversation beneath the porch light, and my brows drew downward. Karin looked up at Mitch and laughed.

I growled low in my throat. What were other people doing having a good time on *my* porch? And yes, that was totally irrational. But still. It was *my porch.* For now, at least.

I managed not to slam my door shut. I might not have stomped up the porch steps either.

Karin straightened off the railing, her longish blue parka rustling. "Hi, April. I was hoping to catch you, but I caught Mitch instead."

"Oh?" I asked.

"You're late," Mitch said.

"A wizard's never late," I said lightly to cover my irritation. Though Tolkien's famous wizard wouldn't have bothered pretending he wasn't pissed.

"Why are you—?" His brows slashed downward. "What happened?"

"A campus mugging. They got a whole twenty dollars and a credit card, which I've already canceled."

"Oh, no." Karin put her hand to her mouth. "Were you hurt? No, don't answer. I can see. Your poor hands. My sister has a balm. I'm sure I brought some with me. I'll be right back." She jogged down the steps and to her Gothic cottage next door.

Mitch studied me. "A mugging," he said flatly.

Water dripped from the eaves. An acorn banged off the stair banister.

"They happen," I said.

A muscle pulsed in his jaw. "Yes," he said slowly. "They happen in downtown Babylon—such as it is. Campus crime is unusual. And crime out here even more so. And yet since you've arrived, you've found a murder victim, someone's broken into your house, and you've been mugged."

"When you put it that way, it does sound unlucky."

"And were you quoting *Fellowship of the Ring*? Badly?"

"You recognized the quote?" I asked, pleased.

"Sure. I watch the movies every Christmas."

'The Peter Jackson director's cut?" I asked suspiciously.

"What else would I watch?"

"His movies are good," I said, grudging, "but not as good as the books."

His face went blank. "There are books?"

I stared. No. He couldn't possibly think... "That isn't funny." I moved toward the door, with its plywood where a window should be. "And I thought you were going to fix that."

Mitch grasped my arm. "April." His voice was hard.

But when I met his gaze, I didn't see anger. I saw worry.

"I know," I said quietly. "I keep wondering if—"

"If it has something to do with my uncle."

"But I didn't know him," I burst out. "We'd never even met. The college handled everything to do with the cottage rental. It has to be—"

"What? A coincidence? I've lived in Babylon most of my life, and I've never been a crime victim."

He was also a well-muscled man. It would take a lot of nerve to try to jump someone who looked like Mitch.

The bushes rustled. Low to the ground, a black tail flicked and vanished in the undergrowth.

"Could there be something about the cabin?" I asked. "Your uncle used to come here to read when there were no tenants. Maybe... Could he have left something here?"

"I've looked."

As I'd suspected. He'd been searching my cottage. My mouth flattened. No wonder the new insulation was taking so long. "And found nothing?"

He released my arm. "Unless there's a secret panel in one of the walls I haven't found—and believe me, I've checked—nothing. Somehow, you've gotten caught up in this. The question is, are you an innocent victim, or have you been a part of it all along?"

For Pete's sake. "I should be offended, but I'm too tired. I had nothing to do with your uncle's murder, but of course you can't take my word for it. And I can't prove a negative."

He growled low in his throat. "You don't seem to be taking this seriously."

"Trust me. I'm screaming on the inside." I turned and reached for the door.

He touched my lower back. "April."

I stilled. We stood too close. I could smell the sawdust in his hair and the faint sweat on his body. It was impossible that I could feel his breath, warm on my neck. But I could swear I did, just as I could swear I felt an electric cord humming between us. I remembered the weight of his body pressing against mine on the bed, and my face heated.

"Got it," Karin called.

Mitch stepped away.

She jogged up the porch steps and handed me a small glass jar. "Put it on after you clean your hands. It will soothe the burn and speed the healing."

"Thanks." I jerked my thumb toward the door. "Sorry. I really just want to go inside and clean up."

"Of course," she said. "I won't keep you."

I heard her descend the porch steps as I stepped inside, flipped on the entry lights, and shut the door behind me. One eye on the door, I washed my hands in the kitchen sink. But Mitch didn't come inside.

I lowered my head, my chest tightening. After a minute or so, his pickup engine purred. He drove off, his tires whooshing on the damp pavement.

I opened the jar and sniffed the balm. It smelled like mint and... something I couldn't identify. Gently I spread some on the angry scrapes on my palms. The skin cooled almost instantly. Witchcraft or not, the balm was good for something.

My husband's ghost snorted. *Not.*

I went upstairs to change into dryer, cleaner clothing, and my calm rationality fell apart. On the edge of the unmade bed, I sat, breathing hard, swiping at the occasional self-pitying tear.

I was shaken—not just by the mugging, but by what Mitch had said, because I had thought it too. The coincidences couldn't be coincidences.

Pulling myself together, I returned downstairs and stumbled on the bottom step. The cat sat on the blue epoxy river running through the dining table.

I drew back a little on the stairs. "How did you get in here?" I shook my head. "Don't answer that."

The ebony cat sneezed and looked away.

My mother's ghost laughed. *Like you could tell a cat what to do.*

"Well, I've got work." I sat at the dining table. The cat watched, unperturbed.

Hardly daring to breathe, I pressed the power button on my laptop. The black screen came to life, and I sagged against the back of my chair.

It hadn't been broken. I hadn't lost any of my work. "At least today wasn't a total disaster," I muttered.

Yet, my father's ghost whispered, and the air grew close around me. My ghosts tended to come around when I was stressed. I wasn't sure how I should feel about that.

Out of habit, I checked my email. A message from a friend I'd met in Italy. A notice from my bank that a new statement was available. Half a dozen pieces of junk that had made it past my spam filters. Something from the mystery school.

I hesitated. This was silly. I should unsubscribe. But I opened the message.

SUBJECT: ALCHEMY

CONGRATULATIONS! YOU'VE COMPLETED ANOTHER task through your contemplation of the Seeker card. You even found a nice, quiet place to do it!

If right now you're telling yourself you didn't come up with any good *answers* to those questions, that's okay. The important thing is to continue to pursue those questions with openness and curiosity.

In your mail box you will find your next UnTarot card, **ALCHEMY**. Don't worry, we don't expect you to transform lead into gold. (At least not in this lesson, haha). But are you up for the challenge of transforming yourself into a witch?

Most people never change. Maybe that's why alchemy has been associated with wild magic for so long. Transformation is so rare it's hard to believe. But there IS magic in the alchemical process.

Though the history of alchemy is mired in wacky schemes to change literal lead into physical gold, it's really a psychological and spiritual practice of transmuting ourselves. Here's the not-so-simple three step process to magic(k) in the western esoteric tradition:

1. Transform yourself, so you can...

2. See the world through magical eyes, so you can...

3. Magically change your world.

Alchemy was not a simple practice. In fact, it was considered crazy-dangerous. Labs exploded. Alchemists went mad. At the Mystery School, we do **not** recommend actual lab work. It's dangerous and unnecessary. For the alchemists, the alembics and aludels and athanors were focal points used to exert their magical will, just as witches today use wands and candle flames to focus *their* will. The type of tool doesn't matter. The focus and the will is what counts.

Successful alchemists transformed themselves into beings capable of making magic. The work at the Mystery School is doing the same. And like the alchemical process, it takes time.

Also like the alchemical process, it has its ups and downs, or more specifically, cycles.

Alchemy describes a process of destruction, or burning to ashes, then reconstitution. The alchemical process goes deep into the dark and then rises up like a phoenix. This cycle repeats over and over again until the alchemist comes out with her spirit polished to gold, shining like the sun.

The alchemist is up, on top of the world, feeling like she's got it figured out. And then she's down, crashing, realizing she has so much farther to go. And it's frustrating. The alchemist wonders if she'll ever get there, if the cycles will ever end, if she'll ever be the person she was meant to be. The secret is to keep going, to push through, and to have faith that yes, she will get there if she just keeps going.

But the paradox is that the person we're transforming into is *ourselves*, or to be specific, we're transforming into our *true* selves. Our true self is already there, but for most of us, it's buried beneath fears, traumas, and false beliefs. But who would you be if you were free of fear, your false personas released, your unconscious made conscious?

You would be you, your soul self. And that is power.

Another common trope in alchemical lore is once you start the process, it takes on a life of its own. This is true, and this is where the real magic comes in. There's a tipping point in the journey, where Nature puts helpful people and information in your way. Revelations will start coming thick and fast, and they'll seem so obvious you'll wonder why you didn't understand before. But of course, you *couldn't* see or understand, because the understanding was hidden in the shadow.

Which is our long-winded way of saying, keep the faith. Your journey will have twists and turns and bumps in the road and all sorts of other eye-rolling cliches. But if you hold fast, there will come a time when you look back and realize you aren't the same person you were, and that the future before you is glorious.

Journal on this card and the questions below. Let Alchemy guide you to the truth. (Scan the QR code below, or if you're reading this online, click the QR code).

SCAN ME

ALCHEMY

Turning a bad situation to good. Confusion leading to truth. The spirit of transformation through love.

The practice of alchemy is surrounded by confusion. While some alchemists focused on internal transformation, others took the practice literally, believing they could turn lead into gold. Charlatans took advantage, tricking the credulous into paying for fake get-rich formulas. But despite all the deceit and misunderstandings, physical alchemy wasn't a complete waste. It influenced and inspired scientists like Isaac Newton to explore our reality.

But something else came out of that confusion. Alchemists discovered they could change their spiritual lead into gold through the power of the heart, knowing that love is the key. Love of others, and yes, the power to love ourselves enough to work toward our own evolution.

Like other spells, alchemy causes a change of consciousness. We have the power to self-reflect, to see the potential of who we could be, and to work toward becoming that person. We have the power to raise ourselves up, to transform.

Alchemy is also a process of creation. Artists, writers, anyone who creates is engaged in an alchemical process, taking an idea and turning it into something in the real world.

The symbols:

The geometric figure in the background—Metatron's Cube—is considered one of the most sacred of all geometric patterns. It holds the five key patterns the ancients believed made up all matter, the Platonic Solids associated with the five elements—earth, fire, water, air, and spirit. It is, therefore, an excellent representation for alchemy. It also represents the meeting point of body and spirit.

If you look closely, you'll see a heart beats in the center of the UnTarot card's design. Alchemical symbols float in the top corners of the card. Alchemical bottles filled with a solution of rose petals stand in the foreground, representing spiritual transformation through love.

The questions:

How can you live from your heart today? What change do you want to see in your life?

Alchemical Breakthrough

I love:
_____
_____
_____
_____

The change I want to see in me:
_____
_____
_____
_____
_____

What will I do to live from my heart today?
_____
_____
_____
_____

Today I intend:

Try this mantra: I open my heart to love

CHAPTER 13

I HURRIED OUTSIDE AND wrenched open the mail box, pulled out the card. Shocked, I stared, the cardstock cold in my hand. A gust of wind, an icy caress, rattled droplets from the oaks.

The symbol in the card's background was identical to the hex sign Karin had destroyed. I rushed inside the cottage.

Unperturbed, the ebony cat sat on the dining table and licked her paw. I reread the email.

Let this card guide you to the truth...

I did a web search for Metatron's Cube.

The symbol is considered a powerful energy conductor, capable of dispelling negative forces. Focus on the design and visualize it turning clockwise to draw in positive energy and repel the negative.

Everything serious I'd read indicated that hex signs were simply decorative. But the sign I'd found in the woods was not. Unless the person who'd painted it simply liked the design and knew nothing about its metaphysical properties.

I read the email again, and my throat caught.

You've completed another task through your contemplation of the Seeker card. You even found a nice, quiet place to do it!

Karin couldn't have known I'd been contemplating the last question at the library. In fact, she couldn't have known I'd been at the library at all. I told her I'd been mugged on campus, but not where. Unless she'd been following me...

My hands clenched, and my palms didn't burn, damn her magic potions that actually worked. *Enough.* Enough with the mind games. Enough with the magic shows. I was done.

I strode from my cottage and across the uneven ground. *Enough.*

Karin's was the perfect cottage for a witch. Gothic revival style, pale yellow with gables, and a wraparound porch with slender, decorative turned posts. Its steeply pitched roof was covered in near-black shingles and black gingerbread trim.

I banged on the front door. Its double-unicorn hex sign rattled.

After a minute or so, Karin opened the door. She'd shed her parka, the sleeves of her white blouse rolled to her elbows. "Hi. Come to return that balm? You can keep it. I've got plenty back in California."

"So at least you're not psychic," I said dryly.

She frowned. "No. I'm not a medium either. What's up?"

"You've been following me," I snapped.

Her hazel eyes widened. "Why would you think that?"

"That's not a denial."

Her lips quirked. She leaned against the door frame and crossed her arms. "Then I hereby formally deny it. I assure you, I haven't been following you." Lines appeared between her brows. "*Has* someone been following you?"

"How did you know I was at the library today?"

"I didn't."

"It was in your email."

"My email—?" She paled. "You subscribed to the mystery school. How did you...? It's invitation only."

"Please don't act surprised. I know you put your business card in my mailbox."

"Business...?" Her voice was a rasp. "Have you been receiving UnTarot cards? *Actual* cards? Not just the electronic versions?"

Enough. I struggled for calm. "You've been putting those in my box too. What I want to know is how you've been coordinating them. Because it's a neat trick."

"It's not a trick. My sister, Jayce, runs the email list. Well, she had some help setting up the drip sequence. But it's all automated."

"It *can't* be automated. It seems to know when I've... done things."

She bit her bottom lip. "Can I see it? The email?"

I hesitated, then drew my cellphone from my back pocket, pulled up the email, and handed her my phone.

She scanned the screen. "That's not my email," she said in a strangled voice.

"You're saying I subscribed to the wrong mystery school?" I asked, outraged. How many were there?

"No. No, I mean, it's similar. The address is ours." Her gaze flicked to mine, then back to the phone screen. "The email's just... changed."

Give me a break. "It's changed," I said flatly. "You mean someone at the mystery school changed it."

"No, I mean... It was complicated spell work," she said in a rush. "We had to have help. There's this metaphysical detective—" Karin shook her head. "I'm sorry, I can't explain it. But if you found our business card, it was for a reason."

The reason being she'd put the card in my mailbox. I folded my arms.

She grimaced. "I know. It's weird. But this email was meant for you, and you alone, I think. And I understand why you're skeptical, and you *should* be skeptical. There are a lot of frauds out there. The worst are the ones who tell you you're in danger, under a curse, and only they can help you... for a price."

My jaw clenched. Did she think I was that gullible? "Thanks for not trying to charge me, but I don't care about the fraud. I care that someone attacked me outside the library."

Karin straightened off the doorframe, and her arms dropped to her sides. "I see. If I was following you to the library, then I'm a logical candidate as your attacker." She nodded. "Of course. What time were you mugged?"

I hesitated. I'd just accused her of a crime. She was taking it better than I would have. "Just after six."

"I was here all afternoon, writing on the porch. Around six I took a break for a dinner of wine, cheese, and crackers. I invited Mitch to join me, and he did. He may have seen me earlier as well, writing. I don't know. You should ask him."

"I will. And how did you know about that hex sign in the woods?"

"I didn't, until you told us at Ham's fire. Then I allowed myself to find it."

Allowed herself? She'd gone looking for it. But why?

We stared at each other. I shifted my weight.

"Would you like to come in?" she finally asked.

"No."

A heavy silence stretched, smothering, surrounding our little world on the porch. I didn't know if I should apologize for blaming her for a mugging or tell her never to darken my door again. But the fear that had fueled my anger evaporated.

Maybe it was embarrassment. I knew part of my antagonism toward the woman had been finding her head-to-head with Mitch. And that was ridiculous.

"I still have half a bottle of that wine," she said. "It won't be as good tomorrow."

"Fine," I said ungraciously. "There's no sense wasting it." I still didn't trust her, but no Californian worth her salt would ruin a wine with poison.

"Porch drinking?" she asked, and I nodded.

Karin vanished inside the cottage. The screen door banged shut.

I dropped onto a cushioned wicker sofa. Offering the wine outside was tactful on her part. I didn't know if I could trust her alibi. And I *would* ask Mitch about it next time I saw him.

But I didn't really believe she'd attacked me, not anymore. That shove had been efficient, impersonal, brutal. I rubbed the sore spot on my forehead. My attacker had been male.

After a time, Karin emerged carrying a wooden tray with a bottle of red wine, cheese, nuts, and local meats. FYI, the Penn Dutch are excellent at making all but the wine, which was thankfully Californian.

Karin set the tray on the low wicker table in front of the sofa. "Have you learned anything more about the murder?" She straightened.

I stared, astonished. "How did you know, I...?"

She winced and sat in a wicker chair at the end of the table. "It's obvious, isn't it? You're poking and prying, and someone's not happy about it. Or you're a part of it in another way. I know the signs, trust me."

I squinted. "And you say you're not psychic?"

Karin poured a glass and handed it to me. "I grew up in a small town, where everyone's in everyone else's business. I have a nose for these things. Plus, you know. Witch."

Change the subject. "And your book research," I said. "Is it going well?"

She sighed. "Not as well as I'd hoped. And you? Are you getting what you want?"

I started. She was asking about my thesis, but the question seemed bigger than that somehow.

"What's wrong?" Leaning forward, Karin plucked a round of Lebanon bologna from the tray.

"Nothing. My work's going fine. It's just, for a minute, I thought you were asking about something else."

"About what?"

"About life, I guess."

"And *are* you getting what you want?" Karin asked.

"I suppose I'm getting what I deserve." I relaxed on the wicker chair and crossed my legs at the knees. "Don't we all?"

"Or what we *think* we deserve?" she asked shrewdly.

It had been a stupid, self-pitying thing for me to say. What did anyone deserve? What did deserving have to do with anything? "I'm sure you heard I'm a widow."

She nodded. "No one deserves that."

No. *David* hadn't deserved to have his life taken so soon. As for myself... "Our relationship... it wasn't perfect."

"I'm not sure perfection is possible. The best we can do is dance with love within the imperfection."

I sipped my wine. "Put that on a tea towel and sell it online."

She smiled. "It *would* make a good tea towel. I'd hate to deal with shipping products though. Are you lonely?"

"Yes," I admitted, surprising myself.

She nodded. "And how do you feel about that?"

How was I supposed to feel about feeling lonely? I felt *lonely*. And a little embarrassed about feeling lonely. So I guess it wasn't that bad of a question after all. I shrugged. "It is what it is."

"That's good. Acceptance of your loneliness is the first step."

"First step to what?"

"To not being lonely." She sipped her wine. "All right. Your relationship wasn't perfect. What would you like in a relationship?"

"What would I like?" My throat went tight, and my eyes went hot. "I want a relationship where we have each other's backs. I want a relationship where we support each others' dreams and goals, and we support each other being the best people we can be. I want a relationship where we can have the hard conversations, and we can hear what's being said because we know it's said with love. I want someone who shares that vision, who understands that love isn't just a feeling, it's an action. And the more action you take the stronger that feeling grows."

WTF? Why was I saying these things? Maybe she really *was* a witch. Absently, I curled my fingers to touch my palm, cool from the balm.

"Those are all reasonable," she said. "More than reasonable. Perfect."

And I hadn't understood any of that when I'd fallen for David. I had to believe that it wasn't too late though, even if it seemed impossible.

"Why did you smash that hex sign?" I asked, again shifting the subject.

Karin crossed her legs, her wicker chair creaking. "I'll tell you, if you tell me why you signed up for the mystery school."

Why *had* I signed up? A whim, or something more?

I took a slice of the Lebanon bologna. It smelled like wood smoke, and it was as tangy and delicious as I remembered from my childhood, when the cured beef had been a holiday treat.

My father had been particular about the brand—Weavers vs. Seltzers. One Christmas, my mother had ordered the wrong one and had never heard the end of it. The air thickened, and I closed my eyes, willing the ghosts away.

"I was curious," I finally said. "And you put that card in my mailbox." I sipped the wine.

She poured herself a glass, and I thought her hand trembled. "Was it the first time you were curious about the supernatural?" she asked.

"That's two questions now."

Karin set the glass on the table and leaned forward, elbows on her knees. "Humor me. It's important. Please."

"No, of course it wasn't the first. I'm human, and the supernatural's... fun. I played with Tarot cards in college. When we were overseas, I did my share of ghost tours and cemetery crawls. The supernatural is everywhere you look." And I had looked. "Those blue glass eyes in Turkey to ward off bad mojo, for example. Vampires in Romania. Shamans in the Baltics. It's interesting."

She nodded. "I've found that people who are interested in the supernatural frequently have some sort of ability. Mitch told me how you healed his nose."

"That? It was only a trick to take his mind off the pain."

"Was it?" She sat back in her chair, and the wicker rustled and creaked. "How familiar are you with *Braucherei*?"

"The practice of the local faith healers? I've heard a bit about it. Literally. I'm Penn Dutch enough to speak the language, though I didn't grow up here."

Her hazel eyes widened. "You speak... Seriously? But that's amazing. Hardly anyone our age speaks it anymore. I've been having a devil of a... Are you free Monday morning?"

"Why?" I asked, suspicious.

"I'm meeting an old *Braucher*. She doesn't speak much English. I figured I could just write down what she said as best I could and get the translation later. But knowing how to spell things would be nice. Will you come with me?"

I gave a short laugh. "You're out of luck with the spellings. I never learned to write Penn Dutch, just speak it."

"But will you come? I'll pay you in wine and herbal remedies."

Meeting a *Braucher* could be interesting. And Karin had already given me one herbal remedy that worked. "All right. Let me know what—"

"Hello, ladies." Ham seemed to appear out of nowhere, like a forest satyr. He braced an elbow on the stair railing. Droplets glistened in his graying hair and on the shoulders of his ivory fisherman's sweater.

"Come up and join us," Karin said. "I'll get another bottle."

"Don't mind if I do." He climbed the steps and sat in the wicker chair opposite Karin's. She strode into the cottage. The door shut gently behind her.

"How was your day?" Ham asked.

"It's over."

He laughed. "That bad?"

I shook my head. I didn't want to get into the mugging. "Cheese and wine might not fix everything, but it helps."

He leaned forward and took a piece of cheddar, popped it into his mouth. "Indeed."

Karin returned with an open bottle and another glass. She handed both to Ham. "How's the land acquisition going?" she asked.

"It isn't. Woodward King's death has brought everything to a standstill. Temporarily."

"I thought there were other areas you were considering?" she asked.

"King had parcels in every section we're looking at. We may have to go the eminent domain route."

Karin stiffened. "How the hell can the government force someone to sell to a private developer? That's not a public good."

Ham shrugged. "If we're increasing the tax base, it is."

"It's not fair," she fumed.

He raised his free hand in a defensive gesture. "Hey, I'm just following orders. If I don't do it, someone else will."

Karin's mouth compressed. "I don't see how replacing a farm with a more efficient one, one that presumably requires less employees, helps the town."

"Oh, we won't be reducing the personnel size," he said cheerfully. "We'll be increasing it."

Karin frowned. She looked like she was about to say something, but Ham asked, "Are you two going to King's memorial?"

"I didn't know there was one," I said. "When is it?"

"Sunday," he said. "Ten o'clock. I'm going. I can drive you both, if you're interested."

"Oh," Karin said determinedly, "I am. But I'll drive myself."

"I'd like to go too," I said slowly. Why hadn't Mitch mentioned a memorial? He had to be involved in it.

We finished the other bottle and most of the goodies Karin had brought out. Karin got misty talking about her children, back in California. Heat pricked the backs of my eyes thinking about David and what could have been, if only I'd had the courage.

Finally, Ham escorted me to Cornflower Cottage. He stopped on the bottom porch step as I fumbled my hobbit door keychain from my pocket.

"Have you ever wished…" he trailed off.

At my door, I turned. "Wished what?"

"That you could go back, warn your younger self not to make the mistakes…"

I wanted to tell him yes, and the wishing was torture. Yes, I'd go back, if only to stop my ghosts from tormenting me. Yes, I'd go back. I'd give anything, anything.

But I couldn't say it, because the wishing wasn't right. We couldn't go back. We could only go forward.

Ham's eyes were slightly unfocused, and I realized he was a little drunk, and I was not. He'd finished most of the wine. But I also felt that balmy lassitude that comes with too much food and drink and the steady drip, drip, drip of water falling from the leaves.

I swallowed. "Sometimes," I said. "But the mistakes make us who we are."

"But who would we be if we hadn't made them?"

I thought about the path not taken. If I hadn't married David. If I'd been smarter about relationships and love. If I'd been the sort of person who had known what she wanted and had found someone who'd shared that dream. That unknown path of who I might have become was suddenly more terrifying than the path before me now.

"I don't know," I said roughly. "But we can't go back."

"Can't we?" he murmured. Ham shook himself. "I've had too much to drink. Sorry. Have a good night." He turned and strode to his cottage, and his footsteps were swift and sure.

I opened my front door. The cat streaked between my legs and down the steps. I jumped and muttered a curse.

The poor cat. I'd left her stuck inside for over two hours. I watched the cat's black form vanish into the darkness.

A stack of fresh-cut wood sat beside the stone fireplace, and my insides warmed. *Mitch.*

I pulled the dining table away, moved the couch as close to the fireplace as I could and made myself a nest to sleep in. But my brain went on a manic thought-loop that kept me awake until past midnight.

Karin had never told me why she'd destroyed the hex sign. She'd distracted me with wine and cheese, and I'd let her.

I watched the shadows flicker on the rag rug. And I wondered what Ham wanted to change.

CHAPTER 14

SOMETHING ABOUT THOSE FLICKERING fireside shadows had given me an idea.

In the basement the next morning, I painted a Metatron's Cube, but I used fall colors—reds and golds and browns. When I'd finished, I stepped away from the square canvas and half lowered my lids, relaxing my vision.

I glanced out the windowed door, at the woods glowing Saturday morning fire.

My painting wasn't right. It wasn't the same as the hex sign I'd found, and not because I'd used different colors. It was missing... those lines half-hidden beneath.

The *pentimento* had changed something about the painting on top. My breath caught. *That* was what Karin had wanted to destroy—not the Metatron's cube but what lay beneath. And now the sign was gone.

I nodded and got to work. But it didn't feel like work. It never did when I got in the flow. I hadn't been in that flow state in a long time, and my sense of ease and concentrated joy veiled the shadows shifting on the floor.

There was a knock on the basement door, and my arm twitched. Ham waved through the window. Setting down my brush, I let him inside.

My neighbor coughed. "Wow. How can you breathe in this?" He braced open the basement door.

"Habit, I guess."

"What are you...?" He stopped in front of my canvas. "Whoa."

I'd extended the arcs within the Metatron's cube and turned them into rolling farmland dotted with barns and sheep beneath an indigo night sky. A fat, yellow moon hung above the scene, echoing the cube's circular design. The sky was half speckled with stars, because I hadn't quite finished.

"This is... Wow. You said you weren't an artist," he accused.

"I was just playing around." Dismissive, I motioned toward my painting.

"This is *playing*?" He turned to study the damp canvas. "It's like an abstract American primitive. Is that a thing?"

"There's a local farmer who does abstract folk art. Not like this though. His are real..." Art. I smoothed the front of my smock. "His are unique."

"So is this." He shook his head. "Hey, want to stretch your legs, go for a hike?"

"I'm not..." I was about to say *finished*, but I was nearly done. "Can you give me thirty minutes?"

"Sure." With one last, long look at my painting, he ambled out the door.

I finished with the stars, then trotted up the stairs to clean up. Since I hadn't eaten lunch yet, I jammed cheese, water, and granola bars into my backpack.

Ham arrived on my front doorstep exactly thirty minutes later. I shrugged into a lightweight jacket, and we wandered down the leafy street.

"Where are we going?" I asked.

"Have you been on the Witch Trail?" he asked.

I stopped short. He continued on a few paces before seeming to realize he'd left me behind, and he turned. "What's wrong?"

"The Witch Trail?" I tugged on one of my pack's straps.

"Yeah. Have you been on it? I haven't." He pulled his phone from the pocket of his khakis.

"No." I sucked in my cheeks. "Did Karin suggest it?"

"No," he said, studying his phone. "Has she been on it? The trail's on my hiking app. You don't want to do it? There are other trails."

Hell. Was I going to be able to go a single day without witchcraft in my life? I gave in and smiled. "I guess I can't fight the season. Lead the way."

We ambled past Queen Anne homes and crossed the highway to a narrow woodland trail. He double checked his phone. "Yep, this is it."

"After you," I said, eyeing the overgrown trail.

He laughed. "Don't worry. It wouldn't be on my app if it wasn't passable."

I followed him into the woods. "How are you feeling today?"

"After all that wine, you mean? The secret to hangover avoidance is hydration. I drank two massive bottles of water before I went to bed. Sorry I got a little maudlin. Wine and beautiful women do that to me." Ham grinned.

It had been a silly, meaningless thing to say, but still, my cheeks burned. "So what's the story of the Witch Trail? I'm assuming it takes us up Witch Hill?"

"Looks like it. Though from the stories I heard, it sounds like Demon Hill would have been a better name."

"Why?"

"Invisible attacks on people and animals? Unknown forces in the woods? It doesn't sound like witchcraft, does it? I know the stories were just projections of people's fears about Indian raids and living in the wild. I guess it's typical the old farmers would look for some poor humans to blame."

"But aren't humans mostly to blame?" I asked.

Ham shot me a startled look over his shoulder. "I suppose they are."

A thin branch whipped toward me, and I struck it away. "And in fairness to the Pennsylvanians, they didn't suffer the witch hysteria of, say, Salem."

He stopped beside a rotted tree stump riddled with mushrooms. "So you *are* interested in witches."

"I just feel the need to defend my Penn Dutch ancestors."

"Oh yeah, you mentioned you were Penn Dutch."

"My parents were. I'm not sure I can claim it since I didn't grow up here." It seemed more cultural than genetic. But I wasn't an anthropologist.

The trail tightened, branches and dried grasses grasping. And then the trail climbed, snaking uphill. The trees and underbrush fell away. We crested the bald top of Witch Hill, and a strange sense of déjà vu came over me.

I stood, huffing, my hands on my hips. The view was spectacular. Rolling hills and farmland dotted with barns spiraling out like... My breath caught.

Like my painting. And not slightly reminiscent of my painting. Exactly like it.

There, the uneven cliff breaking the smooth round hilltop to the west. There, the yellow house. There, the gray barn with the stone half-cellar. There, the red barn with the painted quilt on the side, and the three silos, and the line of trees...

My gaze darted about the scene, and I rubbed my arms. They were laid out in the same pattern as my painting. *Precisely* the same pattern.

But I'd swear I'd never been here before. Or had my parents brought me here when I was too young to remember?

Ham was saying something, but I didn't hear the words. My breathing quickened. I had to be imagining the similarities between the scene and my painting.

But I knew I wasn't. I had an artist's eye, when I cared to apply it. And I was applying it now.

Somehow, I'd captured the view spreading from the center of the hill—a hill I'd never been on. My stomach churned. I walked to the edge of the cliff and looked down.

Below was a neat stone house with a black shingled roof. Smoke spiraled from its chimney. Across the street was the weathered gray barn with the hex signs where Karin and I had stopped.

Was that how my brain had pieced the scene together? My visit to that gray barn? I gnawed my bottom lip. The answer didn't satisfy.

"April?" Ham asked.

I blinked and shook myself. "What?"

"You okay?"

"Yeah. Yeah. It's lovely."

"You look like you've seen a ghost."

"Just... déjà vu, I guess." I shrugged off my backpack. "I'm starving. How do you feel about a picnic?"

Ham smiled. "I feel like it's something I should have thought of."

We sprawled on the dried grass and munched companionably.

"Have you ever thought about all the decisions you made that brought you to this moment?" he asked.

"Not to this particular moment. But yes." I studied the sweep of fields and woods, bursting with color. "It's a good moment though."

"Yes." He bit into his granola bar. "But not every decision leading up to it was."

I nodded heavily. That, I understood. "Regrets?"

Ham didn't look at me. His gaze was fixed on the unfolding farmland. "Questions about things I took for granted as true. As right. Now I'm starting to wonder."

"About what?"

The hillside darkened, and Ham looked skyward. "I guess a sunny day was too much to hope for."

Thunder rumbled, and I glanced at the dark clouds massing overhead. "We'd better get a move on," he said. "Because I didn't bring a raincoat."

Neither had I. I strapped on my backpack, and we half-jogged down the hill, Ham in the lead. A few, fat drops fell by the time we reached the tree line. I turned up the collar of my running jacket.

We hurried through the woods, rain pattering on the leaves. Grayish sunlight struggled to penetrate the tall pines. The only sounds were our footsteps, our breathing, and the drumbeat of rain. The forest darkened.

"If I'd known it was going to storm," he said, "I wouldn't have dragged you out here."

"You didn't drag me. The trail is lovely." And it was. The woods had a certain eerie charm. It was easy to imagine gnomes and fairies and... other things. I hitched my backpack on my shoulders, pulling it more snugly against my back.

The day grew colder, but I began to sweat. Rain ran down the back of my neck, darkened the shoulders of Ham's v-neck sweater. And I realized the darkness wasn't only due to the clouds. It was getting late.

Ham stopped beside a lone fencepost and frowned. "I don't remember this."

"It's not very memorable." But I shivered.

He shrugged and continued walking. "So what do you know about Witch Hill?"

"I've... heard it was where the *Brauchers* disposed of the evil spirits they drew out of people. And your story about it being a meeting place for dark forces."

He studied his phone and handed it to me. "If you're curious, here's what my app says."

I stopped to look. *Uh, oh...* "Ah, Ham?"

"Yeah."

"This says we're off trail." Rain dripped down my face.

"What?"

Holding out the phone, I pointed at the screen. The dot representing us was in the middle of a whole lot of nothing.

Ham took the phone. "That's not..." He shook his head. "Okay. We must have gotten off the main track. It's to the west." He pointed. "Back the way we came?"

I nodded, and we reversed course. Fifteen minutes later, we reached a dead end of tangled bushes.

"That's not..." He consulted the phone again. "How did we miss the trail?"

"Where does it say we are?"

"It says we're on the trail, but we're obviously not."

I shivered. Rain had soaked through my jacket and top. My eyes stung, the mascara running. I blinked and wiped at them with the back of my hand. "It must be Witch Hill," I said lightly. "The same thing happened to my GPS when I was driving nearby."

Ham looked up, his coffee eyes widening. "What?"

"It must be a dead zone or something."

He blinked rain from his eyes. "Oh. Right. Yes, of course. Look, I'm sorry about this," he said. "I guess we go back the way we came until we find the trail. Here." He handed me the phone. "You can be Pocahontas. I'm obviously not a winning guide."

I nodded. Head bent to the phone, I walked along the trail until we reached a wider track. "Here it is."

He blew out a breath. "See? All we needed was for you to be in charge."

I laughed. "Flatterer."

We turned down the trail. I walked on, studying the map. It would have been impossible to navigate by landmarks. Everything looked the same. Trees crowded together. Low bushes nipped our ankles.

"Look out," he shouted.

My foot slipped from beneath me and into thin air. I plummeted downward, too startled to scream, to react. And then hard arms grasped me and swung my feet to safe, solid earth.

I gasped, my hands pressed to the hard planes of Ham's heaving chest, my elbows tight against my ribs. His chiseled face was slick with moisture.

"Are you okay?" His brown eyes crumpled with concern. "For a moment I thought I'd lost you."

"What…?" My voice died. Water trickled into a black-rock chasm inches from our feet. And I'd nearly walked right into it.

CHAPTER 15

It would have been a nasty drop, but not necessarily a deadly one. The chasm looked to be a mere ten to twelve feet deep. But jagged black rocks lay at its bottom. They glistened wickedly, golden leaves dampened by the rain molding to their bitter edges.

My fingers gripped the soft fabric of Ham's sweater. My hands relaxed, and I laughed unevenly. "I guess I'm not much of a navigator either."

His chest heaved. "When I saw you drop—I thought you'd slipped on something. I didn't realize... Damn." He bent his head, his breath warm against my jaw, and my pulse jittered at the feel of it.

Rain pattered on the ground, plopped heavily from the dying leaves. We stood there a long moment, just holding each other. Gradually, my pulse slowed. The warmth of his body, the firmness of his grasp felt safe and comforting and wrong.

His hold loosened. Clearing my throat, I stepped away.

Ham smoothed my wet hair, one broad palm cupping my jaw. "You are okay, aren't you?" He peered anxiously into my eyes.

I nodded and stepped away. His hand dropped.

"What's life without a little risk?" I said, my voice uneven. "A good scare every now and then just lets me know I'm taking them."

Look where that got Jake, my father's ghost whispered.

Ham grimaced. "It sounds like you've had more than your share of scares lately."

Something round and white on a pine caught my attention, and I sucked in a breath. "Is that...?" I walked toward it. But it wasn't a hex sign.

"Ah, that," he said. "Now I know where we are."

It was a logo in black and white, a broken circle with a crescent moon at the top, and the letters *GDF* inside. Someone had spray painted a red line through it.

"I've been making friends and influencing people wherever I go." Ham motioned toward the sign. "This area was part of a grant for watershed restoration. I wasn't involved with that project, but I've helped with some of GDF's other work in the area. Let's get back."

Ham's app behaved itself this time. Twenty minutes later we found the main trail. He clawed a hand through his graying hair, plastered to his skull. "How did we get off the trail in the first place?"

"It might have happened on Witch Hill," I said. "Maybe there are other trails leading off it?"

"But the woods were..." He shook his head. "It doesn't matter, I guess." He checked his watch. "This little hike has taken longer than I expected. I hope I won't make you late for anything?"

I started guiltily. *Dinner with Zeke.* "I'm meeting my advisor."

"Then let's get you back."

I made it back to my cottage with twenty minutes to spare. It was just enough time to shower, change, and dry my hair. The bell rang downstairs as I was putting on a pair of dangly silver earrings. I grabbed my heels off the bedroom floor and hurried down the narrow steps.

I let Zeke inside. My advisor wore a navy three-piece suit and no tie, the collar of his white shirt exposing his throat.

"I see I'm unpardonably on time." His gaze roved from my single earring to my hips.

My toes curled in my high-heeled shoes, and I jammed in the final earring. "No, I'm unfashionably late. I'm ready though."

Zeke offered his arm, and I hooked mine through his. He led me to his BMW and held open my door. It was an old-fashioned, gallant gesture, and I confess I liked it.

We drove to an old stone inn that had been converted to a restaurant. A plump waitress seated us at a corner table overlooking a cornfield.

"Rumor has it Washington ate here," he said.

"Washington covered a lot of ground," I said dryly. It seemed like every town on the East Coast had an inn where Washington had eaten or slept.

Zeke laughed and set down his menu. "How was your day? I'm guessing busy, since I caught you on the hop."

Heat flushed my chest and neck. I *had* been busy, with one man after the other. Not that Mitch counted. He was just annoying. But I felt a little guilty about hiking with handsome Ham earlier and dining with Zeke now. "Sorry about that. I was hiking and—"

"Find any more of those signs?"

"No." I sat up straighter, my ego jolted. So I wasn't the belle of the Mt. Gretel ball after all, I thought with a rueful smile. Zeke was interested in the hex signs, not me. And that was for the best. "Do you have any idea where I might find another?"

"A student of mine mentioned seeing one in the state game lands, near mile marker four in the Rail Trail." He glanced past my shoulder. "We should try to find it when the weather improves."

I set down my paper menu. "I get the feeling you'd really rather be doing this hex research yourself."

"No," he said vehemently. "Not at all." He leaned forward, his voice lowering. "I—"

A waitress in a black apron over her slacks and blouse appeared at our table. "Can I get you anything to drink?"

We ordered wine. The waitress left.

"What were you saying?" I asked.

"I despise research."

I blinked. "But you wrote two books."

"Three, and I hated every minute of it. I loathe the publish-or-perish model. It's teaching that I love. The rest of it, the politics, the backbiting, the what-have-you-published-lately mentality... I hate it all."

"But—"

He raised a hand. "I know. I was cringing inside when I told you you needed to do more original research. Though you do need to. But there's a point where it all gets ridiculous. The theories are getting wilder, everyone trying to one-up each other, and the things being researched today..." Zeke shook his head. "It's a game. I don't play it very well, which is why I ended up at a small college instead of a prestigious university."

"But I thought you loved all things Penn Dutch."

"I do," he said. "But let's face it, you can love Pennsylvania from Harvard. If you've got the connections and the political chops to work there. I'm not interested in any of that. I want to teach. I want to help students do things, not just write about things. That's why I was so excited to have an actual artist in the folk art program. I was really impressed with the samples you included in your application."

"I'm not—" *An artist. But... maybe I was.* "Thank you."

"I wish I had your talent. I'm surprised you decided to pursue a degree that focuses on theory and history rather than straight art or design."

"I think it's important to understand where folk art comes from." *So I can promote my degree when I sell my paintings.* I bit back a grimace. That wasn't the only reason I wanted a degree. It *was* useful to know the roots of the art. But I shifted in my seat.

The waitress returned with our wine. We scanned the menu and ordered. Thankfully, Zeke dropped the topic of my degree, and we spent the evening laughing about Penn Dutch life and habits.

"Saving old boxes cannot only be a Penn Dutch thing," I said. "Why *wouldn't* you save a box that a stand mixer or TV came in?" It was a familiar argument, one I'd had frequently with David. But it was fun with Zeke.

"Because it takes up space," he said.

"Someday you're going to move and need that box."

"That's exactly what a Penn Dutchman would say. Or woman. And they almost never leave the state, much less move."

"Not me. I moved every two years."

The corners of Zeke's brown-sugar eyes crinkled. "It must have gone against every one of your instincts."

"It did." I studied my empty wine glass. "But it was David's career."

He looked at the table. The waitress had cleared our plates. The restaurant was emptying out. "And now you're building your own career," he said.

"I hope so." I leaned close enough to smell his spicy cologne and rumple the red tablecloth.

"Don't ever doubt it." He laid his hand over mine. "You have talent and drive. It'll happen."

Would it? I almost told him about my real dream, about my business. But the words stopped in my throat. I pulled my hand away.

We finished our drinks and discussed Zeke's books. He drove me back to the cottage and walked me to the base of the porch steps. I paused to check the mailbox. A card lay inside, and I hissed an indrawn breath.

"Thanks for a great evening," he said. "It's been a long time since I've just been able to relax and not play the professor game."

"Oh." I pulled out the card and slipped it into my purse. "I should be thanking you. It was fun."

Zeke cocked his head and was quiet for a moment. He nodded. "I can live with fun." He stepped closer, and his eyes seemed to darken.

My heartbeat sped. So he wasn't just interested in hex signs. And it had been so long since I'd been kissed...

"April—"

A black shadow landed on his shoulder, and I gasped. He jerked away. "What the—?"

The cat sprang lithely onto the porch railing. She meowed, stretching, unconcerned.

"Is that your cat?" Zeke checked his shoulder and brushed at a damp pawprint.

Relieved, I shook my head, my hand going to my purse. "I don't know who she belongs to, but she likes to hang around the cottage. Thanks again for a lovely evening."

Climbing the steps, I unlocked the door and slipped inside, leaving both cat and man out.

SUBJECT: TRUTH

SEEKER:

You went deep with your contemplation of the Alchemy card! Good job! You have begun the process of alchemical transformation. But there is more work to do.

There is freedom and power in being true to yourself and in speaking the truth. As we become more authentic, we move closer to alchemical transformation and to our true selves. Maybe this is why the concepts of Truth and Beauty are frequently paired. Without truth, there can be no beauty. Your true self is beautiful.

Truth is also a core component of spellcraft, which requires conscious will. If you're not honest with yourself about your motivations and desires, your *subconscious* will derail your magic. The subconscious is a powerful tool when harnessed. But when you're in the grip of self-deception, your subconscious will harness *you*, leading to unpredictable outcomes.

Some say we're living in a post-truth society. But this is because many are failing to recognize that while there are objective facts, which we should strive to reach, our *experiences* are subjective.

This confusion between objective and subjective may partly explain why things feel so off-kilter. Without truth, we're left in feelings of overwhelm and confusion. Without truth as a guide-star for justice, love, and beauty, we're left with might makes right. Without truth, our own magic is weakened. And that's how the dark magicians of the world want it.

We can, however, make a difference by living through truth in our *own* lives. This takes courage, but it is far preferable to losing our identity by going along to get along, avoiding conflict, and ultimately obliterating our identity, losing the meaning in our lives and weakening our life force.

We need this life force for magic, for joy, for eudaimonia.

All this is a long way of saying your next UnTarot card is **Truth**. Contemplate this card and journal on the questions below. Scan the QR code below, or if you're reading this online, click the QR code. Contemplate the spell throughout your week. When you are ready, you will receive the next email.

SCAN ME

If we become what we give our attention to, let us give our attention to Truth:

TRUTH

Saying the difficult things. Facing facts. Standing up for what you believe in. Behaving with honor. Living up to your potential.

A lie is a betrayal of the self, an evil we do to ourselves. Every time someone lies to fit in, to go along, to avoid conflict, they sell a little piece of their soul. We can also lie through our actions in the moments we go against our own values. It's in these little slips that we go off track. All lies are also attempts at manipulation; they're a form of dark magic.

But sometimes the truth, like sand, seems to be shifting all around us. Is the video real or a deep fake? Is that person on TV bending the truth?

In these times (in *all* times), the best way to hold on is to be honest with yourself, to be truthful, to be honorable, while being aware that we see through a glass darkly. We don't have a perfect perspective on ourselves and the world, and we'll get things wrong. But by living a life grounded in truth, it's more likely the outcomes of our actions will be positive.

Speak the truth, even when it's hard. To do otherwise is a kind of little death. Stop accepting bad behaviors in yourself that steal your potential. Don't expect people to read your mind. Without clear and honest communication, you can't have a good relationship.

The symbols:

An owl, a symbol of truth and wisdom, prepares to alight on a mirror in the desert. The mirror only reflects what's there, without judgment or preconceptions that might cloud its vision. The trumpet shape of the daffodil symbolizes speaking fearlessly in a clear and honest voice.

The questions:

What truths are you avoiding? What truths do you fear speaking?

What is True?

Truths I'm Avoiding

_____
_____
_____
_____
_____
_____
_____
_____
_____

Truths I'm Afraid to Speak

_____
_____
_____
_____
_____
_____
_____
_____
_____

The false stories I've been telling myself are now destroyed in the fire of truth.

I am free from my old stories and live truth and authenticity in the present moment

CHAPTER 16

THE MORNING OF WOODWARD King's memorial shone obscenely sunny. Birds chirped in the chestnut trees along the Babylon trailhead. A brook babbled nearby, a whispered counterpoint to the minister's prayers.

A spot heated in the center of my back, and I glanced over one shoulder. A trio of oversized Dutchmen in ill-fitting suits glared at me.

The men had been shooting me dirty looks since I'd arrived with Ham, who'd quickly abandoned me for the doctor, Josh Zook. The latter, in a black fedora, looked like a melancholy 1940s private eye, despite his very un-forties-like beard.

Karin, in a navy blue jacket and dress, stood serenely beside the Dutchmen. I'd inadvertently committed the fashion faux pas of wearing an outfit almost exactly like hers.

Shaking myself, I faced the minister.

Our memorial was better, my mother whispered. *I had people who loved me.*

My shoulders twitched. Had people loved Woodward? Or merely admired him?

Mitch stood somber in a charcoal suit that strained against his broad shoulders. Shadows dappled his face and brandy-colored beard.

The mayor stepped to the podium and launched into a speech about Woodward King's contributions to the community. The Historical Association. The Rail Trail. The Agricultural Land Preservation Society. The college.

The list went on and on, and I stopped wondering at the sizable crowd. Woodward King had made a difference, and people cared.

Did you really think the killer would come to his victim's memorial? My husband hissed, sardonic. *That only happens in the movies.*

The Hex artist, Ryan, spoke quietly to Ham. The doctor cocked his head, intent on the two men's conversation.

Ham shook his head. Ryan's face reddened. The doctor's dark brows sloped downward.

The mayor cleared his throat. "If there's anyone who'd like to share their memories of Woodward, you're invited now to speak."

One of the big Dutchmen stepped up to the podium. Adjusting his tie, he squinted into the sunlight. "Woodward King cared about Babylon. He cared about our history, and he cared about the land. He wanted to preserve farming and our way of life."

He shot a look at Ham, and the Dutchman's jaw set. "And that's not going to stop now that Woodward's gone. We're not giving up our land for some bug farm. We're not growing the bugs, and we're not eating the bugs."

The other men in the crowd murmured an agreement.

Confused, I glanced at Ham. *Bug farm?* But Ham's back was to me, and he didn't see. He turned toward the doctor as if speaking. Josh shook his head.

The man behind the podium sneered at the mayor. "The hell with your lab-grown meat that's not real meat, and your chemicals, *and* your fake food. We're with Woodward. We believe in real food grown on real farms, the way it was intended." He stomped from the podium.

Ryan scowled and strode toward the parking lot.

I hurried after him. "Ryan?"

The hex artist stopped and turned. His mouth relaxed beneath his long nose. "April. Hey. What are you doing here?" His black suit didn't quite fit him right, and his thin hair had been combed awkwardly over his head.

"I just thought I should." But I hadn't known the murdered man, and my presence here seemed silly now. I tucked my hands behind my elbows. "I'm staying in Woodward King's house. I found his body."

He blinked. "My God. I had no idea. I'm sorry."

"Did you know him well?"

His gaze traveled to the doctor. "I knew he wasn't to be trusted."

Though I hadn't known Woodward, I felt myself bracing, as if defending against an attack. "What do you mean?"

"He liked the ladies. Even the married ones. I need to go." He strode toward the parking lot.

Well, that was... *Even the married ones?* I glanced at Josh and wondered about that look Ryan had sent the doctor. Had he meant that Woodward had been involved with... the doctor's wife? Shaking my head, I returned to the crowd.

A woman tottered to the podium and told a tearful story about how Woodward King had saved her dog, Samuel. My father's ghost snorted. But I was only half listening.

Expressions furious, half a dozen Dutchmen surrounded Mitch. Mitch folded his arms, his face impassive behind his beard.

Curious and a little worried, I made my way through the crowd toward the men.

"—can't make any decisions until I understand the estate better," Mitch was saying.

"That's a cop-out," the man who'd spoken at the memorial rumbled.

"No," Mitch said, "it's a fact."

The mayor intercepted me. "Hi, April."

"Oh. Hi, Santiago," I whispered and tried to edge past him, to Mitch.

"How's your research going?" the mayor asked.

Why did he have to get chatty now? "Not well."

"I was thinking, you might be able to find some hex signs at the Red Dragon. Have you been there yet?"

Oh, who *cared* about the hex signs? "No," I said. "Where is it?"

One of the men raised a finger, as if to jab Mitch in the chest. Mitch's look turned black. The man's arm dropped to his side.

"It's a farmer's market and flea market," Santiago said. "It's happening this weekend, and it's pretty big. There are craftsmen and artists there, among other things. My aunt has a stand. She sells longaniza there, a type of Puerto Rican sausage. It's where we're from, in case you were wondering about my lack of Penn Dutchness." He grinned, and I couldn't help smiling in return.

"I honestly hadn't been," I said. Puerto Ricans had been settling in Pennsylvania Dutch country for decades. "But I'll be sure to check it out."

Mitch's gaze met mine. "April," he said over the grumbling of the men. "Ready to go?"

Go? I raised a brow. *Go where?* We hadn't come together.

The group of men around Mitch parted silently, their stares hostile. Ah. Mitch wanted a rescue. And after all he'd done for me, it was the least I could do.

I smiled. "Ready when you are."

He strode through the columns of men and clasped my arm. My skin tingled beneath his grasp. "Let's get out of here," he said and marched me across the lawn.

My gaze flicked to the cloudless sky. "I'm happy to provide an exit," I said quietly. "But I came with Ham. He'll wonder what happened to me."

Mitch stopped and scanned the crowd. "Ham!" he bellowed. "I'm taking April home."

Ham stood speaking earnestly with a farmer. My neighbor turned toward us, his forehead furrowed. He opened his mouth to speak.

Before he could though, Mitch resumed walking, hauling me along beside him to the parking lot. He opened the passenger door of his pickup and helped me inside. Shutting my door, he let himself into the driver's side.

"What was *that* about?" I asked.

Mitch started the pickup. "They're farmers. My uncle's tenants. They want to know what will happen to their leases."

"What *will* happen to them?"

We bumped from the lot. "They have the option to buy their land," he said, gruff.

I ran my hand down my seatbelt. "How many of them can afford that?"

"It's complicated. Too complicated for me to explain to a crowd of angry men at a memorial service. My uncle was trying to create a conservation easement on his properties with a local land trust."

Mitch may as well have been speaking Orcish. "What does that mean?"

"It means the farmers could keep farming and the trust would be prevented from developing the land in perpetuity."

I exhaled slowly. "But that's wonderful." I hated the thought of the farms disappearing, of them being replaced by McMansions and mid-rises and mixed-use developments.

He heaved a heavy breath. "It *would* be wonderful, but the land trust doesn't exist yet. My uncle was in the final stages of creating it before he died."

And now that Woodward was dead... I pulled my purse tighter against my stomach. "Can you finish it?"

He glared out the front window. "It's complicated."

I leaned back in the seat. I was sure it *was* complicated. Land trusts. Conservation easements. I only half understood what those things even were.

His face spasmed. "I'll abide by my uncle's wishes." His broad hands clenched on the wheel, his knuckles whitening.

Lightly, I touched the sleeve of his gray suit. "I know how hard it is to lose someone, even when your feelings for them are complicated. Especially then."

He gave a bark of harsh laughter. "Complicated. At least..." He trailed off.

"At least what?"

"Nothing. Sorry." He shook his head. "My loss was nothing compared to yours."

My mouth twisted. My hands fisted in my lap. "Because I'm a grieving widow? Except I'm not."

No more lies. "I mean," I said, "I am. I'm a widow, and David shouldn't have died. He didn't deserve it. But things had been... bad between us for a long time. And then he died, and everyone assumed..."

I looked out the window and rested my elbow on the ledge. The curves of farmland blurred. "It was easier to let people think what they wanted. Or at least I *thought* it was easier. But every time someone gave me a sympathy hug, I felt like I'd sold a piece of my soul. David wasn't a bad man, but we'd stopped being good together for a long time. Maybe we could have fixed it. Maybe counseling..." My jaw tightened. "But that was my fault. I couldn't bring myself to be honest with him about how I felt. I was too scared to have a knock-down, drag-out fight. So I fantasized about leaving and made myself more and more miserable and then he died."

I'd been emotionally immature—acceptable in a twenty-something, not so much in a woman in her forties. And even though I thought I understood the whys of how I'd come to be that way, I couldn't forgive it. Not yet.

Mitch glanced at me. "You don't seem like the kind of woman who has a hard time saying what she feels."

"*Now.*" I propped my chin on my hand. Though speaking my mind didn't always come naturally. "I've had a lot of time to think since David's accident." And it hadn't been pleasant. Self-reflection rarely is.

I still wasn't the person I wanted to be. But what did I care what Mitch or anyone in Babylon or Mt. Gretel thought of me? I'd be here for a few months and gone. Telling Mitch or Ham or anyone else the unvarnished truth should have been easy.

Was changing a lifetime of bad habits like recovery? Something I'd always have to watch for? Struggle against? And inevitably fall off the wagon? Outside my window, the trees were a blur of red and gold.

"When did your husband die?" he asked.

The pickup lurched over a pothole, and we swayed in our seats.

"Two years ago," I said, relieved to be dealing again in cold facts. I changed the subject. "What was that about a bug farm?"

Mitch shook his head. "No idea. You should ask the mayor," he said dryly. "If you can believe anything he says."

"He's not honest?"

He's a politician, my husband said, the coolness of his form pressing between us. *Don't be naïve.*

"Have you checked out the GDF website?" Mitch said and answered for me. "Of course, you wouldn't have."

The fund Ham was helping out with? I pursed my mouth and didn't respond. We slowed for an Amish buggy, beetling along the narrow road.

"There's this question going around online," Mitch said. "If you had a choice between being given a hundred million dollars or going back in time to when you were ten years old with all the knowledge you had today, which would you choose?"

Startled, I glanced across the seat at him. The question was so similar to what Ham had asked. Were we all poisoned by regrets? Was that what happened when you rolled past forty-five?

"Back in time," I said. "No contest."

"But we can't go back."

"So, it's a stupid question."

"No, it's not. The point isn't the question. The point is the reminder we *didn't* have the wisdom we have now, so we couldn't have done much differently. I mean, yeah, there were some things I did which I knew were wrong at the time. But those moments aside, we were limited. The point of the question is to move on."

My hand clenched on the seatbelt. If only moving on was that easy…

The road widened, and Mitch sped up, passing the black buggy. The gray-bearded man inside stared straight ahead, reins gripped in gnarled hands, intent on his destination.

CHAPTER 17

THE CAT SAT EXPECTANTLY outside my cottage's blue door, ebony tail curled about her paws. Mitch waited while I let myself inside. The cat trotted past my ankles before I could stop her.

Mitch prowled through the house to make sure no intruders lurked. And then he left.

Unaccountably let down, I went upstairs and changed into jeans, tee, and a comfy charcoal cardigan. I trotted down the steps.

I found the cat on the rag rug in the living room. She spared me a glance over her furry black shoulder then returned to staring enigmatically at the wing chair beside the bookcase.

"Look," I said. "I don't know who you belong to..." There was no collar. Maybe she didn't belong to anyone?

I shook myself. I was not acquiring a cat. "But this isn't your house, and I can't be responsible for any damage you may do." What if she sharpened her claws on one of Mitch's pieces? "You'll have to leave."

The cat stared at the chair.

I opened the door to the porch. "Go on. Scat."

She ignored me.

"Fine," I said, feeling like a poor loser. "Go when you're ready." Leaving the door ajar, I stomped to the dining table, where my laptop lay open.

I booted it up and found the GDF website. The front page was filled with articles about childhood vaccinations, climate change, and privacy in the age of the metaverse. I clicked on the "About" section.

Mission

The Global Development Fund's mission is to enhance public-private cooperation to make our planet a better place. We do this by engaging leaders in politics, culture, and business, to shape the global agenda.

The GDF was established in 1966 in Geneva, Switzerland as a not-for-profit. The Fund is based on the principle that businesses should not only serve shareholders, but also those who have stakes in the community the business serves. The GDF acts as a global village focused on a business citizenship approach, enabling corporations to be active in addressing global problems through public-private partnerships.

I leaned back in my chair and laced my hands behind my head. It was all corporate nothing-speak. Which made sense since its members were banks and media companies and other mega-corporations.

But what did it have to do with the mayor? I clicked on the *Partners* section and was confronted with an alphabetical list. I scrolled to the M's.

Santiago Morales's name was there. I clicked it.

A smiling photo of the mayor appeared on my laptop's screen. Beneath was a short, succinct, caption:

As mayor of rural Babylon, PA, Santiago Morales advocates for sustainable agricultural development.

Huh. I scanned the rest of the list. Santiago must have been doing a hell of a job with his advocacy, because he moved in elevated circles. Politicians, sports stars, and human rights lawyers from around the world were on the list. How did a small-time, small-town Pennsylvania mayor get included?

I shook my head. It didn't matter. I needed to focus on my thesis, though I really didn't want to. Plus it was a Sunday. I drummed my fingers on the wooden table and grabbed my purse.

I strode to the living room. The cat hadn't budged from her spot on the rag rug.

"I'm leaving." I held open the porch door.

The cat glanced derisively over her shoulder.

I shrugged. "Your funeral." Locking the door, I left.

The Red Dragon market was three towns over. The drive through amber cornfields cheered me, even if I did get stuck behind another Amish horse and buggy for a mile before I could pass.

The market's parking lot was emptying out—a bad sign for shopping, a good sign if you didn't want to drive up and down dirt aisles searching for a spot. I pulled in, locked up, and headed into the vegetable stalls.

I bought some squash and corn, because I couldn't resist, then wandered past sheds and through low buildings jammed with everything from honey to donuts. There seemed a weird amount of peanut butter products in the market. Peanut butter cakes. Peanut butter pies. Peanut butter donuts...

I stopped in front of a glass case of chocolate-covered peanut butter eggs. My mom had made them every Easter.

In fact, my parents had put peanut butter in and on everything from pancakes to pretzels. I'd always assumed my parents had shared a peanut butter obsession, but maybe it was a Penn Dutch thing?

I bought a half dozen chocolate peanut butter eggs to see how they compared. The young Mennonite woman behind the counter smiled beneath her pale blue bonnet and handed me a bag.

"Do you know where I can find hex signs?" I asked.

"I think I saw some in Building B." She pointed.

"Thanks."

I made my way to Building B, filled with Amish-style wood furniture. A lone hex sign hung behind a display of living room furniture. It was a typical star design, and I sighed and moved on. I did another circuit of the building, in case I'd missed anything. But I hadn't.

Outside, a cold breeze whipped my hair, and I tugged my cardigan tighter. Another long, metal building stood kitty corner from the one I'd just abandoned. I walked inside to aisles of stalls selling a jumble of random tchotchkes—pillow cases, Autumnal wreaths, fabric pumpkins, jams...

I clutched my bags. Resolutely, I sped past that stall. I had a weakness for jam. Maybe I'd come back later.

Scanning for hex signs, I stopped short in front of a table stacked with colorful pamphlets. A man sat behind it on a high chair and read a newspaper. I plucked a familiar green and yellow booklet from a rack.

The bespectacled booklet-seller lowered his newspaper. Wisps of gray hair stuck out above his ears. "Interested in witchcraft, are you?"

"Not really, but I've read this one." I turned the cover to face him.

"What did you think?"

"*Witchcraft is a Thing*?" I laughed. "It's a little overwrought, but I learned some new stuff from it... if it's accurate."

The older man grinned, exposing yellowing teeth. "Oh, it is. I wrote it."

My face warmed. *He* was Elmer Fenstermacher, Jr.? "Sorry, I didn't mean—"

"No, no. You're right to be skeptical." He rubbed his chin. "I guess my title is a little flippant. It used to be more serious, but I wanted to attract younger readers. I researched that booklet, and you can trust it, though not everything you hear is true. I reckon most isn't."

"Like hex signs are magic?"

His grin broadened. "That's a little more complicated."

"Oh?"

He sat back on his high chair and folded his arms, rumpling his faded green shirt. "It's about intent. Most of the hex signs for sale were mass produced—at least they were until COVID. Even the hand painted ones were done just for nice. It's not enough to just paint a symbol and expect magic to happen. You need to put something of yourself in it."

"Like art," I said, surprised.

He scratched his balding head. "I don't know much about art."

"There are all sorts of arguments about what makes something art versus just... for nice. I've always thought the artist brings something of himself or herself to the work. Call it soul or originality."

He shook his head. "That's not enough. True art touches the viewer's soul. There has to be skill and beauty too."

I nodded. The modernists would disagree with us. But I guess I was old-fashioned, because I thought art should be beautiful too. Even shocking pieces like a Goya or a Bosch were saturated with truth and beauty.

Shifting my bags to one hand, I opened my slouchy bag, digging for my phone so I could show him the photo I'd taken. "I actually found an odd hex sign in the woods. I hear someone's been posting them."

His face shuttered. "Hex signs are for barns. I don't know anything about signs in the woods."

Taken aback by the hardening of his voice, I withdrew my hand from my purse. "The design was a Metatron's cube," I said uncertainly.

The old man shook his head. "Never heard of it. I've got a book on hexes though." He nodded to a pamphlet with a goldenrod cover.

I thumbed through the booklet. It didn't look like much, but it was only $2.99. I bought it, along with a pamphlet of Penn Dutch recipes.

"April?" a man asked.

I turned, my cash extended. "Oh. Dr. Zook. Hi."

The doctor reached as if to tip his black fedora, then his hand dropped to his side. "Call me Josh, please. I see you've met our local academic." He nodded to the man behind the table. "Afternoon, Elmer."

"Doc." The pamphlet seller inclined his head and plucked the cash from my hand. "How was the memorial?"

"Hard." Josh picked up the booklet on witches and flipped through its pages.

Elmer slid my purchases into a green plastic bag. "Murder always is."

"You still selling this junk?" Josh returned the booklet to its stack.

"As long as people are buying, I'm selling." Elmer handed me the bag. "Thank you for your custom."

"Thank *you*." I wandered down the concrete aisle.

The doctor ambled at my side. "Here, let me carry something for you."

"They're not very heavy." I handed him my bags. "But thanks."

"I still have a *few* chivalrous instincts left. My wife—" He swallowed. "She used to call me her white knight. She's dead now."

And he still mourned her. My throat tightened. What would it be like to mourn cleanly? Not to have complicated emotions attached? "I'm sorry," I said.

"You don't have to be. I know you understand after your husband—" He grimaced. "What did you buy from old Elmer?"

I looked away. The crowds in the aisles had begun to thin. "A booklet on hex signs and some recipes."

Josh snorted. "You know more about hex signs than anything in that tourist trash. You're a soft touch, giving an old man a sale."

"Sometimes you find interesting nuggets in tourist trash."

"Then I'm surprised you didn't pick up his book on witchcraft."

"I didn't need to. There's a copy in the cottage."

"Is there?" His melancholy face creased. "A tourist must have left it."

"You don't think Mr. King would have been interested?"

Josh barked a caustic laugh. "Woodward was interested in all things Penn Dutch. But he kept his feet on the ground. I heard you had some problems out at the cottage. A break-in?"

I swallowed a shiver. "Yes. Mitch scared him off."

"Mitch?" He stopped in the middle of the aisle, and shoppers flowed past.

"He'd had too much to drink at Ham's bonfire and was sleeping in his pickup." My jaw tightened. Why had I felt the need to explain?

"That's a relief," he muttered.

"Why?" I asked, defensive. A woman jostled me, and I tucked in my arms.

The doctor flushed. "That must have sounded like I... It's not you. I mean, it *is* you." He ran one hand down his close-cropped beard. "Mitch has a temper. His divorce got ugly, and... Not that I can entirely blame him. His wife had a disordered personality. She blew through all their money, bankrupted him, and left him for a poker player. She wasn't my patient," he added quickly.

My stomach sank. First Mitch had been let down by his flaky, artistic parents, then by a flaky wife. But we tended to repeat our childhood models. I know I had, though I hoped I'd finally broken that pattern. But Mitch... "Oh."

"He's a great contractor though," Josh said. "Totally professional on the job."

"He's been terrific at the cottage," I agreed, wooden.

"Did Mitch see the guy who broke in? At least, I'm assuming it was a guy."

"No, I didn't see him, and yes, it was a man." I walked to the jam stall. An Amish girl in a pale-blue dress and matching bonnet made change for a customer. "It all happened too fast," I said.

"Too bad. Mt. Gretel hasn't been leaving a very good impression, has it?"

"The problem isn't Mt. Gretel. Murder can happen anywhere. The problem is one person, the killer."

"You think the murder and your break-in are tied together?" he asked sharply.

"You mean do I think it's all about me?" I grimaced. *Yeesh.* Was I that narcissistic? "I think... I've never had peach-rhubarb jam before, and I'm all about new experiences." *Something new every week...* Wasn't that what the email had recommended?

His dark brows drew mockingly downward. "Peach rhubarb? Live a little." He took a deep purple jar off the shelf. "Try the blackberry jalapeno."

I laughed. "On cream cheese and a cracker?"

"What else?"

I bought them both, along with a jar of elderberry jam and cherry rhubarb. Like I said, it's a weakness. And then we found the longaniza stand, and I bought a quarter pound of the pork sausage from the mayor's smiling aunt.

Josh carried the bags to my car. He held my door for me. "I'm glad Mt. Gretel hasn't scared you off. Have you been to the George Washington pub? They've started selling their opera fudge ale for the holiday season."

I made a face. Opera fudge was a Penn Dutch confection. My mother's simplified version was a dark chocolate-covered cream cheese mixture. I couldn't imagine that flavor mixed with beer. "I'm not sure if I should be horrified or intrigued."

"I thought you were about new experiences? You free Tuesday night?"

"Ah. Yeah." And now Josh wanted to take me out? *Josh?* I wasn't that alluring. Or at least, I hadn't been before coming to Mt. Gretel. My mouth quirked. Was it witchcraft?

"I'll pick you up at seven. We can grab a bite and a beer, unless you'd prefer something else?"

"No, no. I'm committed. Now I *need* to try the beer."

Josh laughed. "See you Tuesday." He closed the door and watched while I backed from the parking spot.

I returned to the cottage with my loot. The cat was not waiting for me at the door. Shrugging, I unloaded my goodies in the kitchen, made a cup of coffee, and tried a peanut butter egg. It was crunchier than my mom's, and somehow lighter.

Curious, I sat at the dining table and pulled up a copy of my grandmother's recipe for the eggs on my laptop:

3 lbs. powdered sugar

2 C peanut butter

Butter size of walnut

Soften with milk.

Shape into eggs and refrigerate until firm.

Dip in melted chocolate.

Refrigerate.

It was a farmer's recipe, used so often it made sense to the original cook. I, however, had never been sure about that walnut-sized butter. Shaking my head, I rose from the dining table.

"Cat?" I needed a better name for her than *Cat*. But she wasn't mine, so it didn't really matter what I called her. I rubbed my arms. It was freezing in here, and I hoped Mitch finished up with the insulation soon.

"Cat?" I grabbed my mug of coffee. "Where'd you go?"

I wandered into the living area and pulled up short, swaying, my blood freezing in my heart, in my head, in my veins. Cat was staring at the same wingchair. But it was no longer empty. Sitting in it with slumped shoulders was a dead man.

CHAPTER 18

WOODWARD KING. AND HE was real. I could feel the warm mug in my hand, and that was real. And the space heater disguised as a woodstove hummed, and that was real. And the *Witches* booklet lay face down on the end table beside his chair, and that was real. *Real.*

Blood stained the side of his craggy face and his silvery hair and his canary raincoat. His wrinkled hands gripped the arms of the wingchair. His eyes were the blue of a shark's gaze. His mouth moved soundlessly.

My heart hammered against my ribs. Woodward was dead. He couldn't be here. He was dead. And I didn't *see* ghosts.

But the cat apparently did. Unwavering, unblinking, unperturbed, she studied the spirit. Her ebony ear flicked.

Woodward King leaned forward in the chair. *Look beneath... the Brotherhood.* His voice was a winter wind.

But he was *dead*. Another sound penetrated my awareness, an odd, high-pitched whine. The sound came from a distance—from my throat. My breath fogged the air. My legs wobbled. "You—"

And then he was gone. He didn't fade into a mist. He was just gone, blinked from existence. My legs collapsed beneath me, and I gracelessly hit the floor. Coffee splashed across the wood planks. I sat, gaping, gripping the slick mug.

The cat meowed, stretched, and came to rub against me. Absently, I petted her silky fur.

"That was... That..." I hadn't imagined it. The apparition hadn't been there long, but it had been there. I'd seen it. I'd seen the blood matting his hair, his mouth moving.

The cat strolled to the back patio door and meowed. When I didn't respond, she pawed at it and yowled.

Setting down the mug, I crawled to the door and opened it. The cat snaked onto the porch, squeezed through the railing, and vanished. I shut the door and sat against it.

A *ghost*. I'd *seen* a ghost.

My shoulders curled forward, my ribs caving in, my hands pressing against my chest. Cornflower Cottage was haunted.

I couldn't bring myself to sleep downstairs by the fire that night. Not when Woodward King had been haunting the living room. Instead, I loaded up on blankets, hauled the space heater upstairs, and went to bed in my sweats.

I awoke to gray morning light, rain on the roof, and the smell of coffee. Since the coffeepot wasn't on a timer and burglars generally don't make their victims java, I presumed the intruder was Mitch.

I dressed quickly—it was too cold to dawdle—and I hurried downstairs.

"Did I wake you?" Mitch ambled through the front door, a toolbox in his hand. His brandy-colored hair was neatly combed, and he smelled of soap. His plaid shirt looked like it had been ironed.

"No." I walked into the kitchen and pointed at the coffeemaker. "Thanks."

He shrugged. "It looked like I was the first one up. I figured I'd get the coffee going."

"Do you want a cup?" I moved to the cupboard.

"No, I don't drink the stuff."

"You're a better person than I." I laughed, my chest warming. Making coffee had been a thoughtful gesture, especially since there was nothing in it for him.

And now I was about to ruin the moment. I rubbed my damp palms on the thighs of my jeans. "Can I ask you something personal?"

Expression wary, he turned at the base of the narrow stairs. "Okay."

"About your uncle."

His shoulders relaxed. "Not much I can tell you. Like I said, we weren't close."

"Did he have any special connection to this cottage?"

He raised a brow. "Special connection? Why do you ask?"

"Just..." I poured a mug of coffee. "You heard Ham. He said your uncle used to come here to read."

"My uncle had a connection to Mt. Gretel. He supported their local history museum."

"Do you think..." I swallowed. Unfinished business, wasn't that why ghosts hung around? "Is it possible his murder wasn't random?"

"Of course it wasn't random."

I blinked. "It—"

"He was killed for a reason, a personal reason, just like this cottage was broken into for a reason." One corner of his mouth crooked up. "You don't really think I'm spending all this time here just because of your charms?"

My stomach hardened. I guess I'd kind of hoped he had been. Oh, well. Another dream dashed. "You think I had something to do with his death."

"Not anymore. You just had the bad luck to find Woodward's body. What I don't understand is why that's made you a target." His green eyes narrowed. "Unless you know something you're not telling."

I didn't bother to respond to that. "Or the cottage is the target," I said coldly. "Your uncle spent a lot of time here. Maybe there's something here the killer wants."

"Then why go after you at the college?" He shook his head. "There's something about you that interests him, and you're in over your head. It's time to spill. What do you know?"

Heat bloomed in my veins. "Nothing," I said.

"Doc Zook said there was no way my uncle could have been alive when you found him. Why did you lie?"

Deliberately, I rested my elbow on the high counter. "The doctor was wrong. Your uncle looked straight at me and said—"

My breath caught. The ghost had looked straight at me too. Was that what I'd seen and heard on the trail? Woodward's ghost?

A lump hardened my throat. But if I *could* see ghosts, that meant... I wasn't haunted by my past. I'd been imagining the presence of my doleful dead all this time. Imagining their whispers...

Mitch folded his arms. "Told you what?"

I exhaled, blinking rapidly. *Get it together.* "To look beneath the brotherhood. And yes, I know that doesn't make sense. But it isn't meaningless."

"Why not?"

"Because—" Because the apparition in the living room ghost had told me the exact same thing. My mouth went dry. "Are there any brotherhoods around here?"

"Lion's Club, Odd Fellows Society, the Masons... Should I go on?"

"Was your uncle involved in any?" I asked.

"No."

"Are you sure? You said you didn't know him that well."

Mitch raised a hand in a *stop* gesture. "I didn't. But I've spent just about every night since his death going through his papers. There's nothing. And if he was in a fraternal order, I'd have known. It's a small town, and none of those are exactly secret societies. So whatever you *think* he told you, it was nonsense."

My hand tightened on the warm mug. I had to tell Mitch about his uncle's ghost. He'd think I was crazy. I half thought I was crazy. But I had to tell him. "There's something—"

Someone knocked on the door.

"Expecting company?" Mitch asked.

Setting the mug on the gray counter, I walked to the door without answering.

Karin stood on the dripping porch in a belted, navy raincoat. "Good morning." She brushed back her auburn hair. "Are you ready to go?"

I grimaced. *Dammit. Karin's local faith healer.* I'd forgotten about my promise to translate this morning. "Come inside." I stepped from the door. "Can you give me five minutes?"

She followed me into the cottage. "Sure. Hi, Mitch."

He grunted, turned, and stomped up the stairs.

"I don't think he's a morning person," I said apologetically.

Karin grinned. "Neither was I until I had kids." She sobered. "When I came here, at first I loved being able to wake up late. It seemed like such luxury. Now... I miss them, early morning wake-up calls and all."

"Hold that thought." I grabbed my purse, dumped my coffee into my tumbler decorated with hiking hobbits. Slipping on my tennis shoes, I followed Karin to her blue SUV.

The rental smelled of new car, which I loved, since I hadn't had a new car since ever. We backed from her driveway.

"So," I said. "You want to learn what the *Braucher* knows about knot magic."

"Knot magic," Karin agreed. "It's old. You can find it in all sorts of cultures, ancient and modern. There are European legends over a thousand years old about witches who could bind the winds into knots for sailors. Shakespeare even referenced it in *Macbeth*."

"How would a wind knot work? Theoretically."

The corners of her mouth tilted upward. "The witch binds the wind into a knot, and then when the sailor needs wind, he unties it."

"Huh."

She laughed. "Skepticism is a useful tool but a poor master. Knots were also used for love spells, binding lovers together. That spell was first described by an ancient Greek physician. But lover's knots were also used throughout the middle ages. Where do you think we got the phrase, 'tying the knot?'"

"I hadn't thought about it," I admitted.

"Not that I'd ever use a love knot in a spell," Karin said. "It would be unethical. Wind on the other hand..." She angled her head.

I wrinkled my nose. "So you're a witch. A real witch. Eye of newt, toe of frog, wool of bat and all?"

"Those are just old terms for mustard seed, buttercup, and holly leaves. So, yes."

I thought Karin would drive us into the country. But to my surprise, we drove into downtown Babylon. Its brick and wooden buildings had turned seedy, weeds sprouting through the sidewalk cracks.

A pang twinged in my chest. I knew from my parents' stories that a century ago, the small town had been thriving. Now many of the businesses were boarded up.

We took the bridge over the railroad tracks, driving past derelict warehouses with sagging roofs, and into a neighborhood of faded wood homes and unkempt yards. The gray skies and rain streaking the windshield amplified the general atmosphere of decay.

Karin pulled up at a small house with peeling yellow paint. The yard was neatly mown though. A cheerful display of pumpkins lined the window boxes, hex signs above their windows.

"Thanks again for this." Karin unbuckled her seatbelt. "Our first meeting was... well not *exactly* a disaster. The *Braucher* was very friendly. But communication was limited."

I raised a brow. Most Penn Dutch speakers I'd encountered spoke English too. It was hard to function in the modern world without it.

But I was curious about the faith healer. And though the hex signs on her house weren't special, I wondered if they were only "for nice."

Dodging raindrops (unsuccessfully), we hurried up the concrete walk. The screened front door opened.

The farmer, Ryan, stepped from the house, and I stopped short. What was the artist doing here? His thin, straight hair lay flat against his head. Over dusty jeans, he wore a burnt-red barn jacket, its shoulders darkened by the rain.

He turned and said something to a person inside the house. There was a murmured reply, and he nodded. He trotted down the steps. "She's waiting for you," he told Karin, then blinked at me. "Hey. It's you again."

"Hey back," I said. "I'm glad I ran into you. I wanted to ask you about a hex sign."

He shook his head. Rain dripped down his long nose. "No time now. Come by the farm. You know the hours." He jogged toward a silver SUV parked on the street.

An elfin, white-haired woman in jeans and a baggy sweater emerged from the house. She motioned us inside. "*Guder mariye! Kumm rei, kumm rei.*"

"She's inviting us inside," I said in a low voice.

"*That* much I got," Karin climbed the concrete step.

We followed the tiny woman inside, and I gasped. We'd stepped back in time.

Green wooden furniture with painted folk-art birds and tulips and hearts. Rag rugs. Shelves lined with hand-painted tin pots and plates and thick ceramics. A dowers chest with an American primitive-style couple holding hands painted on the front, and more hearts and flowers and distelfinks. Her home was an antique hunter's dream.

The old woman led us into a kitchen smelling of baking sugar and pumpkin. Copper pots hung from its dark rafters. Glancing at a stove and refrigerator that had to have been from the 1950s, I introduced myself.

"I just baked a pie," the woman said in Penn Dutch and pulled out a wooden chair. "Would you like some coffee and a slice?" She began to lower herself into it.

"It's a little early," I replied in kind, "but I won't say *no* to homemade pie."

The *Braucher* froze, hovering halfway off the chair, then she burst into laughter. She plopped onto the chair. "I should have known you would speak *Deitsch*," she said in the same language.

"Why would you have known?" I glanced at Karin. If communication had been as limited as Karin had said, how had she told the woman she'd be bringing a translator?

Karin's gaze, quizzical, bounced between the two of us.

The *Braucher* shook her head and smiled. "Because you were meant to be here."

Right. Like Karin, the *Braucher* relied on vague, mystical proclamations to make believers of her magic. I didn't know why I found that so disappointing.

I turned to Karin. "She's asking if we'd like some coffee and pie. Pumpkin, I'm guessing."

"I'd love some." Karin smiled at the woman, and I translated.

The *Braucher* rose and ambled to a wooden pie safe. She drew out a pumpkin pie and sliced us each generous portions, then poured coffee from a tin pot into blue clay mugs.

Inhaling, Karin cradled the mug, her eyes closed. She took a sip, and her eyes flew open. "Whoa."

"Egg shells," the *Braucher* said. "They are the secret to good coffee."

"Egg shells," I translated. "I think she puts them in the grounds." At least I hoped so. I'd rather not spend the morning picking eggshells from my teeth.

"Can you thank her for agreeing to meet with me again?" Excavating in her blue purse, Karin pulled out a notepad and pen. "And would you tell her I'm interested in the use of string or ribbons in her practice, or anything to do with knots?"

I translated, and the woman's blue eyes widened with astonishment. "But you know this already," she said.

"No," I said. "Karin didn't understand you the first time."

"Not her." She pointed at my chest. "You."

My forehead puckered in annoyance. Was this more of her magic shtick? Or was my Penn Dutch in worse shape than I'd thought?

"What's she saying?" Karin asked.

"Ah... Just a sec." I turned to the woman. "Sorry, I don't understand."

The *Braucher* tsked. "I will explain, but she cannot write anything down. The work must be memorized. The words are what matters. She must know the words, and they cannot be written."

I translated that for Karin. Grimacing, she returned the pad and pen to her navy purse and nodded.

The *Braucher* launched into an explanation of drawing out illness using red thread.

I translated for Karin. "First, you take red thread—it can't have been used for anything else. Measure the patient's height with it and cut the thread to fit. Then you pass the thread over the patient three times and sort of whisk it away from the patient..."

The old woman nodded and made a flinging motion with her hands.

I bit back a smile. *The hell she didn't speak English.* "Then you smoke the string. You repeat the entire process three times then throw the string into the fire."

The *Braucher* chattered excitedly.

"But not for all types of illnesses," I said. "Cramps need blue string and to be disposed of in running water."

Karin nodded. "I get it. Red string for fire and illnesses like fevers. Blue string for water and illnesses connected to the flow within the body."

I laughed shortly. "I'm glad *you* understand." I sure didn't.

"It's like attracts like," Karin said. "It's old magic, the concept of sympathies. But are there incantations to go along with the healing?"

I asked the *Braucher*, and she rattled off a spell.

I translated. "Red silk string—"

"Nay." The woman shook her head. "She must speak it like I did, in *Deitsch*."

My gaze flicked to the herbs hanging from the ceiling beams. *It was going to be a long day.* "I guess it only works if it's spoken in Penn Dutch," I told Karin.

Karin sighed. "Would you say it again please?"

I repeated the phrase, over and over, stumbling over the words. The *Braucher* ate pie and laughed at us, issuing corrections to Karin's pronunciation, until they were both satisfied.

I finished my pie. There'd been more than pumpkin, sugar, and evaporated milk in it. She'd liberally spiked the pie with alcohol.

The *Braucher* smiled. "Do you recognize it?"

I rubbed my cheek. *Recognize what?*

"What about knots?" Karin asked.

"Ah..." I translated for the *Braucher*, and she explained.

I turned to Karin. "For warts, you take strips of willow bark, tie a knot in the bark, and throw the bark in running water."

"The knot representing the wart?" Karin asked, and I translated. The *Braucher* nodded.

"You can also use string that you've removed an illness with and bind it to a tree," I translated. "The tree will... um..."

"Absorb it?" Karin asked.

"No," I said, "the trees are protective. They provide healing. The binding doesn't hurt the tree, they're too strong."

We kept at it for a good hour. Then the *Braucher* appeared to tire, her shoulders slumping, her papery skin paling.

Hastily, Karin rose. "Thank you for your time and patience and generosity. It's been wonderful speaking with you."

I scraped back my chair and stood. "*Gross dank.*"

In a shockingly quick move, the old woman reached across the table and grasped my wrist. "You are so like your grandmother. It does my heart good to see you again."

I drew in a sharp breath. "My grandmother?" To see me *again*? Had my grandmother brought me here when I was little?

She nodded. "She was a *Braucher* too, like your mother."

The words struck like a blade. *My mother*? "What?" I shuffled backward and banged into the cold stove. Something on it rattled. "No. Sorry, you must be mistaken."

"*Nay, nay.*" She rose. Walking to a shelf, she opened a recipe box, thumbed through it, pulled out a crisp white card. She handed it to me. "The pie recipe was your grandmother's."

I stared. My mother'd had a near-identical card. And the recipe was in my grandmother's handwriting.

CHAPTER 19

THE RECIPE SEEMED TO vibrate in my hand, and my fingers spasmed. The card fluttered to the *Braucher's* wooden kitchen table.

For Pete's sake. Get a grip.

Why was I so shocked? Babylon was a small town. My family was from here. It wasn't so outlandish that the *Braucher* would have known my mother and grandmother.

I stared at the recipe, face-up on the long, wooden table. Somewhere in all the moving David and I had done, I'd lost my mother's recipe box. Where had it gone?

But that wasn't the real question I wanted answered. "My mother and my grandmother were *Brauchers*?" I asked faintly.

The white-haired lady nodded. "Your grandmother was very well respected."

"What's going on?" Karin asked.

I turned to her. "Apparently, she was friends with my grandmother. This was her recipe for the pie. And... she was a *Braucher*."

Karin's expression didn't alter. "That explains it."

"It doesn't explain anything," I said, my voice rising. I moved to push the card across the table toward the *Braucher*.

She laid her wrinkled hand on mine and gently pushed it away, smiling. "Nay, nay. It belongs to you. She would want that."

"*Danki.*" I hesitated, then tucked the recipe card into my purse. Tugging my phone from it, I pulled up a photo of a Metatron's cube. I extended the phone to her. "I found a hex sign in the woods with this design. It looked like it was painted over something."

The *Braucher* reared away. "Leave it alone. It's too dangerous for you."

"But I thought the design was supposed to be protective," I said.

"It's what's beneath." The old lady shook her head. "Leave it."

I inhaled a sharp breath. *Look beneath...* Beneath the hex sign's final layer of paint? Could that symbol have been what the ghost meant when...? I grimaced. Dammit, did I believe I'd seen a ghost, that I could *see* ghosts now?

Muttering our goodbyes, Karin and I stepped from the house and into a depressing drizzle. Karin aimed her fob at the blue SUV, and it chirped, its fog lights flashing. "What was that last bit about?" she asked.

I opened the passenger door. "I asked her about the hex sign we found in the woods. The one you smashed before I could get a good look at it. Thanks for the Alchemy card, by the way. It was a nice hint."

"The Al...? Oh." She glanced toward the faded yellow house. "What did she say?"

"She said it was dangerous. Or what was beneath the hex sign was dangerous."

Karin sighed. "But she didn't paint that sign in the woods."

"Then who did?"

She climbed into the SUV. "I think you know."

My jaw tightened. I was fed up with her vague hints and innuendo. I lowered myself inside and slammed the door. "If I knew, I wouldn't have asked."

Karin started the car. "I can't help you if you're not honest."

I stiffened. "Honest about what?"

She checked her mirrors and pulled from the curb. "About everything that's been happening. Have you always had the ability to heal people? Or has it gotten stronger lately?"

"I don't—"

"Mitch told me how you fixed his nose. That was no psychosomatic healing. Have you seen any ghosts yet?"

I started in my seat. "How did—?"

"I didn't. I just suspected. I can see attachments, the invisible energies that connect people. It's part of my knot magic, I think. Connections, threads... I saw someone attached to you, and it had the feeling of a spirit.

But not your husband, not a loved one. And I got to thinking about what wandering spirit might have become attached to you. Woodward King was the first person who came to mind."

Steely numbness spread through my chest. She'd sensed Woodward. Not *my husband*. Not *my parents*. They'd never been with me. They'd just been gone. "Because I found his body," I said in a monotone.

"Doc Zook insists Woodward was dead when you found him. It could have been his ghost you spoke with then, though usually they have difficulty coming through immediately after death. I talked to my sister, and she says it's possible though."

We drove over the railroad bridge, and the SUV shimmied over a pothole.

"I'm not sure I believe all this," I said.

"You're going to have to find your way between faith and skepticism. What do you know about your grandmother?"

"She died when I was little. I only have vague memories of her bringing me stickers. She actually died when she was visiting us in California." I frowned.

She'd had a stroke and survived several days in the hospital. My mom told me when she'd reached the parking lot one morning, she just... knew her mother was gone.

My mom was running by the time she reached the hospital lobby. But she was too late. She'd told me that story of some sort of... psychic connection. Why hadn't my mother told me she was a *Braucher*?

"These things often run in families," Karin said, turning the wheel. "And families can be complicated."

"No kidding," I grumped. "And what's up with your mystery school anyway? So far there hasn't been much magic and mystery. Just a load of psychobabble."

"What do you know about mystery schools?"

Not a damn thing. "Not much."

"They go back to the ancient world. The ones that we're aware of, like the Eleusinian and Dionysian mystery schools, seem to have been around a process of death and rebirth."

"An alchemical process?"

Karin's smile was quick, then she returned her gaze to the street. "You read the Alchemy email. Good. And yes. But we don't know much about them because they did a good job of keeping things secret. Hence the mystery. We know more about the mystery schools from the 19th and 20th centuries. They were secret societies that couldn't keep their secrets as well as the ancient Greeks. There were different levels of students. Beginners got the basic information and didn't learn the real magical rituals and spells until later."

I slumped lower in my car seat. "You're saying since I'm a noob, I have to wait." *How convenient.*

"I'm saying the psychology is important. You can't just recite a spell off the internet and expect it to work. You have to turn yourself into a witch first. And you're right, there *is* a nexus between magic and today's psychology. Both focus our conscious and unconscious to manifest our desires. Though in my opinion, psychology is only a weakened form of magic."

I raised a brow, and Karin laughed.

"And yes," she said, "that sounds like a cop-out. But stick with the school. It takes time to become a witch. The process is slow, but that slow process works, and it weeds out the unserious."

She dropped me at Cornflower Cottage. Mitch's truck was still parked outside, and I wasn't sure how I felt about that. But he wasn't on the ground floor, and I didn't look for him upstairs. At least he'd started a fire, which I appreciated.

I sat at my laptop, my back to the warmth of the stone fireplace, and looked up love knots. The fire popped.

Love knots really *were* a thing. I believed Karin when she said she'd never used one in a spell. But I was willing to bet she'd practiced at least *tying* the knot...

I found a piece of string in a kitchen drawer and returned to my laptop. Squinting at the screen, I fumbled my way through a lover's knot.

Lovers' Knot

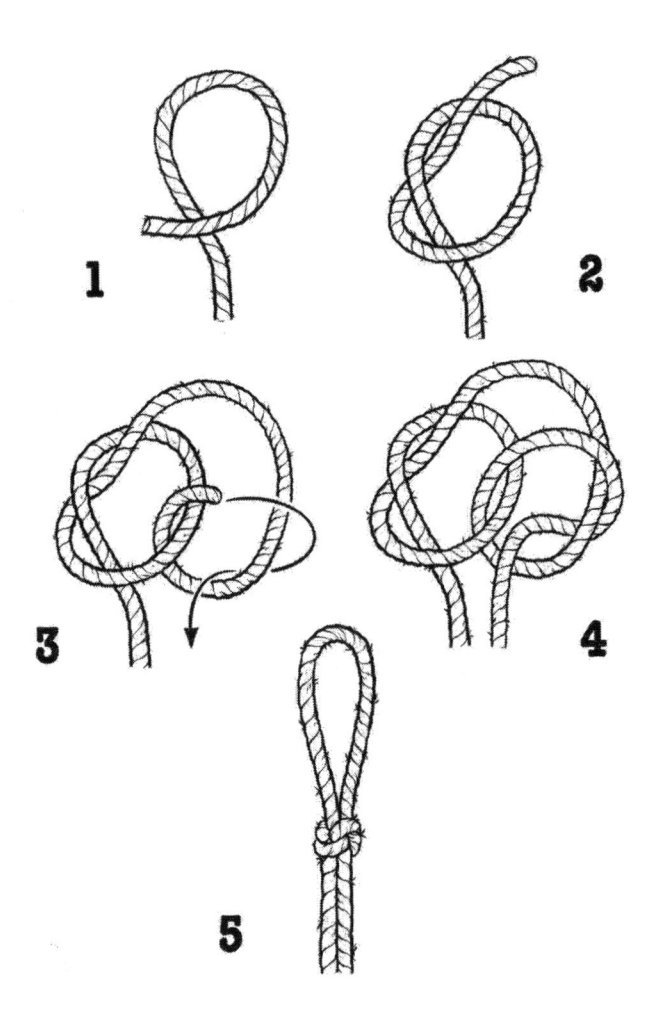

1

2

3

4

5

"A lovers knot?" Mitch asked. He held a broom with a dustpan clipped to its handle.

"Gagh!" I jerked in my chair. The man was as silent as the cat. "Where did you come from?"

"Upstairs. I just finished cleaning up. So are you joining the scouts or has our local romance writer inspired you to try a love spell?" He jerked his head in the direction of Karin's cottage.

"Neither," I said loftily. "Karin and the *Braucher* lectured me on knot magic, and I was curious. I was about to look up the wind knot next."

He grunted.

"And why do I suspect you've already done your own research into Karin?" I asked.

"Because she's been sticking her nose in my uncle's death too. At first I thought she was looking for material for a book. Now I'm not so sure."

I swallowed and closed my laptop. "Speaking of the supernatural..." *Say it. Just say it.*

"What?"

I pushed back my chair and stood, pressing my fingers into the table. "This is going to sound crazy. I *know* it's going to sound crazy, but I have to tell you, because it may mean something. Something about your uncle's death, I mean."

I drew a deep breath. The wood shifted in the fireplace. *Say it.* But I hesitated.

He cocked his head. "Well?"

"I think I saw your uncle's ghost yesterday," I blurted.

"What?" he said flatly.

"Here, in the cottage. He was sitting in the living room wingchair. The cat saw him. It was like he..." I trailed off.

Mitch stared with an expression of horror. I tugged my collar tighter. He thought I was crazy. What if I *was* crazy? What was I thinking? Why had I said anything?

He pivoted and raced down the stairs to the basement studio.

Okay. Saying I'd seen a ghost was admittedly weird. But I'd never sent a man fleeing in panic before.

He cursed loudly. "Open the door!"

I muttered a curse. *Open the door?* Mitch was downstairs. He could open the damn basement door himself. I walked to the top of the stairs. "Ah, you okay?"

He raced up the steps and pushed past me into the kitchen. "Go outside."

I jammed my hands on my hips. "*You* go outside."

He filled a pot with water. "I mean it, April. Outside." Grabbing the pot, he raced to the fireplace and dumped water on the flames. Steam hissed. Gray, ashy water splashed across the stone hearth.

I gaped. "What the hell?"

He dropped the pot on the rag rug. Grasping my arm, he hauled me, sputtering, onto the porch and down the steps. He peered anxiously into my eyes. "You need to see a doctor."

Furious, I shook him off. "Lots of people see ghosts. It doesn't mean I'm crazy."

He clawed a hand through his brandy hair. "The pilot light in the water heater was out."

I ground my teeth. "And?"

"There was a note on my uncle's desk about a faulty water heater." Mitch hung his head. "It didn't say where, and since I hadn't heard any complaints from tenants, I thought he'd fixed it. No wonder you were hallucinating. God knows how long this gas has been leaking. Stay here. I'll air the place out."

"But... I didn't smell gas." A gas leak—was that the answer to everything? To my growing paranoia? To the ghost? To the heaviness now spreading through my body? But I hadn't imagined someone breaking into the cottage. Even Mitch had seen him.

A bird cawed from a nearby oak. The leaves rustled, an acorn plunking to earth.

Mitch glanced at the blue cottage. "I'll put you in a hotel until I can fix this."

"I don't want to go to a hotel." I scraped my teeth across my bottom lip. "And how could the pilot light have been out? I had hot water this morning."

"Then it went out after that." Mitch stood mere inches from me. The beginnings of bronze bristles dotted his jaw. He smelled of smoke and sweat and sin, and I flushed.

"But I saw the ghost last night," I said. "The pilot isn't going on and off. Either it's been off this whole time and I've been gassed, or it just went off and it's a lucky thing you noticed."

A muscle pulsed in his jaw. "It sounds like you *want* to have seen a ghost."

"No. I want to not be crazy. I want to understand what's going on. And something *is* going on. You admitted it earlier. And I'm not sure I believe I can see ghosts, and yes, a gas leak is a much easier explanation to swallow. But I don't think it's the right one. It can't be. Either I'm crazy, or I saw something."

"There's a third option."

I folded my arms. "Oh?" I couldn't wait to hear this. What would it be? Female feeblemindedness?

"Or," he said, "someone's gaslighting you."

CHAPTER 20

I SHIFTED MY WEIGHT on the damp earth outside the cottage. The air was cool and sticky and gas-free, insects whining from the brush, water dripping from the oaks.

I should have been shocked. I should have been relieved he didn't think I was crazy. I should have taken a beat to consider the idea that someone *was* gaslighting me. The idea was preferable to insanity. Instead, I was pissed.

I was pissed, and I didn't know why my chest was heating and hardening. I didn't know why I was rejecting his idea.

It was a logical idea. Someone had been inside Cornflower Cottage. They could have used the time to turn it into a haunted house. Or turn off the pilot light on the downstairs water heater.

"How?" I demanded. "A hologram of your uncle projected into that wingchair?" I gestured roughly toward the blue cottage, its windows dark and dead eyes. A breeze shivered the branches, and droplets spattered the shoulders of Mitch's flannel shirt.

"If you'd been exposed to gas," he explained patiently, "a hologram wouldn't be needed. A hallucination would do."

My teeth clenched. "I wasn't hallucinating when I found your uncle's body. He spoke to me. Or his ghost did."

"Maybe Doc Zook was wrong about the time of death. Or maybe you were just under a lot of stress. Finding a murdered man—"

"I've seen bodies before," I snapped. "I know it sounds crazy. I know a rational explanation is preferable. But you're throwing the baby out with the bathwater. There's something going on here, and it's more than simple murder—if there's anything simple about murder."

"You've got a big imagination—"

"My God, you're so set on being practical and in control you've lost touch with your imagination, your art, your soul."

Mitch flinched, and I immediately regretted my words. Who the hell was I to play armchair psychologist?

"Yes," he said coolly. "I do prefer to take a practical, detached approach. Because most artists fail."

I felt the blood drain from my face and took an involuntary step backward. My heel turned on a stone. He didn't reach to steady me.

Most artists fail. David had constantly reminded me of that fact. And it *was* a fact. Few artists made a living at their work.

You bastard. Of all the insufferable, pompous... But I'd asked for this. I'd started it. My pulse thudded in my ears. I worked to slow my breathing. *Do not react. Do not react.* "Have you finished with the repairs?"

"Yes." He bit off the word.

I strode up the steps to the front door. "Then I guess I won't be seeing you."

He followed me inside, picked up the toolbox beside the dripping fireplace, and strode out. I managed not to slam the door after him.

My mother sighed. *Oh, April.*

My fingers curled inward, my throat thickening. I'd come so far in learning to set boundaries, to speak my mind. Now I'd gone too far.

Worse, I'd allowed myself to believe there'd been something between us—friendship, at least. Respect.

Oh, who was I kidding? I'd allowed myself to think of romance. And it had been an emotionally immature romance, because I'd been enjoying the company of the other men I'd met recently a little too much. Was that why I'd blown things up with Mitch?

"Idiot," I muttered, and I wasn't referring to Mitch.

I'd told myself not to rush into anything after David. I needed time to be on my own, to figure out what I really wanted, what really mattered. A part of me had thought I was ready now. Clearly, I hadn't been.

An ache squeezed my throat. Would I ever be ready?

Trying to burn off my emotions, I paced the cottage. When that didn't work, I cleaned up the fireplace, slipped my keys into the pocket of my jacket, and went for a run.

I hated my afternoon run even more than usual. But I felt slightly better after I'd returned to the cottage and showered.

I gulped water and checked the clock on the stove. Ryan would be at his barn studio by now. And I needed to lock down my thesis.

I drove to his farm. The sky made a feeble attempt to show some blue, then gave up and dumped buckets of rain. Naturally, this occurred as I pulled up to his studio beside the barn. I jogged to the door, running shoes squishing in the muddy ground.

Yanking it open, I hurried inside the lit studio. The hex signs leaning against the walls burst with color, a cheerful contrast to the sullen weather.

"Ryan?" I called and took a tentative step deeper inside. The door had been unlocked. He'd said he'd be around. But maybe he'd gotten distracted by a client or his cows.

I wandered past hex signs angled against the rough wood walls and stopped in front of a rainbow starburst.

The painting wasn't round. It was rectangular, split into two square pieces sitting together, to be accurate. It was bold and cheerful and *more*. And though it was simple, it wasn't "decorator." It had soul.

My shoulders collapsed. Did my work have soul? Did it matter? I *did* plan to make a living at my art, but was it even art? Was I deluding myself?

"Hey," Ryan said, and I jumped. Mud spattered his work boots and the cuffs of his loose jeans. His thin hair lay flat and wet against his head. Beads of water trickled down his angular face.

"Oh." I pressed a hand to my chest. "You startled me."

He rubbed his long nose and smiled, rueful. "Sorry. I was out with the cows. So you found our local *Braucher*."

"Karin did. How do you know her?"

He grinned. "Childhood wart removal. She needed some touch-ups on her hex signs."

"You do hex sign restoration?"

"I'll do anything to make a buck." His gaze scanned the cluttered studio. "These aren't exactly paying the bills."

It was the artist's lament. And one I didn't need a reminder of.

"What can I do for you?" he asked.

I pulled my phone from my bag and opened the photo of the Metatron's cube. "I found a hex sign in the woods. I was wondering if you'd seen this on a hex sign before?"

He took the phone and studied its screen. "Why are you so interested?"

"Like I said, I'm trying to find a new topic for my thesis—"

"And other people's hex signs is it?"

Why did that sound so... lazy? I crossed my arms. "My tentative topic is the continuing evolution of the hex sign. What you've done is amazing. You wouldn't mind being a subject, would you?" I asked anxiously.

Ryan grunted. "If it gets me publicity, I don't mind."

"I'm not sure how much publicity it'll get. Most theses don't go public."

"Huh. Your advisor'll make sure it will. He'll get his name attached somehow."

I shifted my weight. "I wouldn't mind if he did."

"Maybe you should." He returned my phone. "It's not a traditional design, if that's what you're asking."

"Do you know what it means?"

He shook his head. "Do you?"

"It's sacred geometry. It represents the meeting of mind and spirit."

Ryan grinned. "So it's *for nice.*"

"Did you paint it?" I dropped my phone in my purse.

He shook his head. "Nah. I don't leave my art hanging around the woods. I'd prefer to sell it."

That, I believed. And the Metatron's hex sign I'd found hadn't had the fine strokes of Ryan's work.

"And speaking of which," he continued, "is there anything here that interests you?"

"All of it." I laughed, rueful. "And I can't afford any of it."

I hesitated. "Can I ask you something non-hex related?" Maybe I was being delusional playing detective. But I couldn't forget Woodward King.

Maybe his phantom *had* been the result of a gas leak. But he'd felt as real as his rail trail.

"Shoot." Ryan folded his arms over his burly chest.

"The memorial for Woodward King."

"Yeah," he said, dark eyes wary.

"There seemed to be a lot going on."

"You could say that."

"What was that about bugs?" I asked.

"GDF wants to technologize agriculture. It's why they're trying to buy up the land."

"So the bugs... That was real? What do they want to do? Turn insects into food?"

"They say they're nutritious."

They said a lot of things. My brows rose. "Really?" I'd believed in the food pyramid for years, but recently that eating program had been turned on its head.

He shrugged. "They're probably not really using bugs, but it's going to be some sort of artificial or lab-grown meat. I don't know and don't care. I just want to sell this albatross of a farm and move on."

"So why don't you?"

"I can't sell to GDF unless the other farms around me do too. It's all or nothing."

"And Woodward King owned those farms," I said slowly. "Was he willing to sell them?"

"No," Ryan said shortly. "He didn't want to displace his tenants."

The phone pinged in my purse, and I dug for it.

His expression hardened. "If you're thinking I killed Woodward to force the sale though, you're way off base."

"I didn't—" My fingers touched my phone, and I pulled it out. I frowned. It was an email alert. My phone wasn't set to alert me to emails. It would be pinging all day.

I squinted at the message, and lightness fluttered in my chest. *Subject: Consciousness.*

SUBJECT: CONSCIOUSNESS

SEEKER:

You are progressing along the path. Congratulations! But are you awake?

Yes, you think, *I'm reading this, so obviously I'm awake.*

But are you?

We spend most of our waking hours sleepwalking. We allow ourselves to be lulled into a dream world by screens, by habits, by patterns. We live in our heads instead of our bodies. We eat food, but we don't taste it. We drive to work, but we don't see the world outside our window. We talk to friends and loved ones, but we don't really hear what they're saying or sense what they're going through. We let our unconscious patterns run the show, or we drift into our heads and lose awareness. And we miss a lot of the beauty of life.

But it doesn't have to be that way. We can make the unconscious conscious and create positive change in ourselves and in our lives. This process can be uncomfortable, but it is necessary. Magic is an act of conscious co-creation between the witch and the universe. But she can only co-create when she is living consciously.

Our minds are tuning-forks that are broadcasting and receiving. What are you broadcasting? This is an important question, because thoughts can become things. You can and do affect the outside world with your thoughts, so it is important that you become conscious, so you can magically direct them.

This week, throughout your day, ask yourself if you are awake. And after you do, really *notice* the world around you.

Bonus: Before you go to sleep every night, tell yourself that tonight, when you're dreaming, you'll ask yourself if you're awake. This is a lucid dreaming trick. If you can ask the question and realize the correct answer while dreaming, you'll come to consciousness in your dreams. Once you do, practice changing your reality in the dream. Change the colors of objects. Ask people what they symbolize. Fly (just for fun). Learning to come to consciousness and change reality in your dreams is an important step in learning to do the same in your conscious reality.

We invite you to journal on the next card in your UnTarot deck, *Consciousness*. Scan the QR code below, or if you're reading on a screen, click the QR code.

CONSCIOUSNESS

Call to consciousness. Self-reflection. Healing. Integration. Ego.

You are pure, divine energy. But it isn't always easy to be conscious of that, or of the effect you have on others. We're all acting from and limited by our current consciousness. We're also unconscious of what we don't know. For example, look back on who you were ten years ago—how much more are you conscious of now?

But there's another side to consciousness, or the lack thereof. When you act unconsciously, letting old patterns and stories run the show, you make yourself vulnerable to outside influence—magical and otherwise. You may even unwittingly cast spells on others.

You also get in your own way. This card is a call to examine past patterns, to let unhealthy ones go, and to consciously live in the present with love. It's a call to examine the egoic mind, to notice when it takes control (moments of embarrassment are a good sign your ego has kicked up), and why it has.

The symbols:

The pattern in the background of this card is the flower of life, representing consciousness. But patterns in general also represent the patterns in our own lives that we may be unconsciously living out. The meditating yogini, spending time in self-reflection yet acutely aware of the world around her, sits in a real-world flower, a trillium, its three petals representing integration of mind, body and soul.

The questions:

Are you aware in this moment? What are your emotional triggers? Can you notice when you're being triggered and say to yourself, "Oh, that's my old story/pattern kicking up?" Can you take full responsibility for how you're showing up? Can you forgive others when they've behaved unconsciously?

Am I Aware?

What triggers me?

What do I lose when I act unconsciously?

CHAPTER 21

Augh. Karin! I'd complained the mystery school was cheap psychology, and now a card turns up called *Consciousness*?

The cat's ears twitched. She lay curled on the cold hearth as if expecting me to light a fire.

Rain drummed against the cottage windows. Annoyed with myself, I tossed the card onto the dining table. The mystery school email confirmed what I'd suspected. It was all psychology, the "magic" of belief.

But I couldn't resist returning to the table and squinting at the image. It looked like there was another piece of sacred geometry in the card's background, not dissimilar to some hex signs I'd seen.

"Divine energy," I muttered. "Emotional triggers. Ha."

My thoughts flashed back to this morning, and how I'd reacted to Mitch's gaslighting comment. I'd overreacted, and why? It wasn't as if my husband had gaslit me. He hadn't.

"The hell with it." I printed out the PDF. And this time, I filled it out.

David had pointed out—correctly—that my art at the time had been a hobby, not a business. That it was almost impossible for someone to make a living with art. I'd agreed, because it was true. So I hadn't pursued my art the way I should have if I'd wanted to go pro.

Maybe I'd gaslit *myself* by downplaying the value of my art. I'd told myself stories that were sometimes but not always true. And I'd been a doormat. That wasn't Mitch's fault either.

The ebony cat stretched and rolled over.

"Easy for you to say," I told her. "Cats don't overthink."

There was a knock at the door. I opened it, expecting Karin.

But Mitch stood on the porch with an armload of books. His hair was wet—too wet to be explained by the rain, especially since his thick green vest was mostly dry. It looked like he'd just stepped from the shower.

"Hey," he said.

"Hey back," I said, wary. "What's all this?"

"Books."

"I get that. But—"

"Ghost books."

I stared. "For someone who doesn't believe in ghosts, that's quite a collection."

"And it's getting wet," he said pointedly. I stepped aside, and he walked into the cottage. "They're from my uncle's house," he said and turned to me. "What?"

I leaned against the wood-paneled wall. "Nothing. I'm just... surprised." And—I hated to admit—relieved he'd ignored my demand he stay away.

"Surprised my uncle had an interest in Pennsylvania supernatural?" He dumped the books on the dining table, and the cat started.

"That you're bringing these to me. Aren't you worried you're affirming my delusions?"

"You're not delusional," he said, "though you may be wrong."

"*Wrong?*" I asked, outraged.

"A rational skeptic is open to all possibilities. There's more in the truck."

"More...?"

But he'd already ducked outside. Three armloads of books later, I studied the stacks of hardbacks on the dining table. "What do you expect me to do with all these?" I asked, aghast.

"Help me discover a link between what's happening in this cottage and any local ghost stories."

Hm. He might be here only because he needed help, but he was *here*. "But— I *saw* your uncle. It's a recent haunting. What could these books have to tell us?"

"They might tell us about my uncle."

I shifted, pursing my lips. "You don't think he was killed because of his interest in the occult?"

"My uncle cared about it enough to fund your advisor."

"But what does Zeke—?"

Karin ducked her head into the cottage. "Ooh, are these the books?"

"You invited Karin?" I asked, voice clipped.

He shrugged. "Like you said, it's a lot of books. And she's got some experience."

Karin strolled into the dining area and picked up a fraying, cloth-bound book. She flipped to the front pages. "Wow. This is over a hundred years old."

"My uncle liked all kinds of history."

"I've got a sister who sells rare occult books," she said. "If you ever want to turn these into cash—"

"I'll think about it," he said shortly.

She rubbed her hands together. "Where do we start?"

"Look for any references to Mt. Gretel," Mitch said, "and any page he might have dogeared, underlined, or written on."

"I'll make the coffee," I grumped. Karin *was* the logical person to help. So why was I so annoyed? Oh, yeah. Because Mitch had ham-handedly taken over my dining room. Also, his determination to go through the books didn't make *sense*.

Why did he think his uncle's interest in the paranormal had anything to do with his death? Sure, there'd been a weird not-quite-hex-sign by the murder scene. But it was a good bet Woodward hadn't put it there.

But the books might tell me something about hex signs I didn't already know. And Woodward King had spent time in this cottage, *and* that booklet on witchcraft had been here...

I made coffee. Mitch made a fire. The cat curled into a tighter black ball. And we skimmed the pages. We couldn't possibly do a thorough read. The old typing was cramped, and it would take a month to go through them all.

Seated around the dining table, we marked likely passages with yellow sticky notes. Karin scribbled something in her blue notebook.

"Find anything?" I asked.

Her face flushed. "Uh, not for you. Just an idea for a book I'm working on."

"By the way, thanks for the new card," I said casually. A log popped on the fire.

Her hazel eyes widened slightly. "You got another—?" Her mouth clamped shut.

"You're surprised?" I jammed my hands in my pockets and ran my thumb across my hobbit door keychain. She *had* to have been the one who'd put the card in my mailbox.

"Yes, actually." She glanced at Mitch, his head bent over a leatherbound book. "They don't usually come so quickly. Either you're a magical savant—"

Mitch snorted.

"Or you need the information fast," she finished, her hazel eyes troubled.

"What information?" He looked up.

"About the nature of consciousness," I said.

"Huh," he said. "If you figure that out, let me know, will ya?"

Karin sighed, stretched, and pushed back her chair. "I've got a call with the kids. I've flagged all the sections that might be relevant." She motioned toward a short stack of books. Only a few sticky notes peeked from their pages. "It wasn't much," she said, making a rueful face.

"It's more than I expected," Mitch said.

Grabbing her notebook off the table, she walked outside. A gust of cold wind snuck through the door before she could close it behind her, and the dying fire flickered.

Mitch stood and arranged another log on the flames. The logs shifted loudly. "What did you find?"

"Someone—your uncle, maybe—underlined passages about a murder in the 1930s—not in Mt. Gretel or Babylon though. He also underlined a few references to *Brauchers* operating in the area. Nothing about Witch Hill."

And why *hadn't* I found anything on Witch Hill? Why wouldn't any of the books I'd read on local paranormal activity have mentioned the hill named for it?

He nodded. "I haven't found anything on Witch Hill either."

"I don't suppose absence of evidence can be evidence of... what? That the story behind Witch Hill is so dark it was buried?"

"It's not evidence of anything." He sat again, his back to the fire. "But it's strange."

"I should have asked Elmer where he got his information," I said absently.

"Elmer?"

"The man who wrote that little booklet about witches in Pennsylvania... The booklet!" I hurried into the living area. The booklet lay on an end table beside the wingchair, and my footsteps stuttered to a halt.

The wingchair. The wingchair where Woodward King's ghost had sat as if... reading. I hesitated, then snatched the booklet off the table and returned to the dining area.

"Someone underlined passages in here too," I said. "Here. *For while good witches can be solitary practitioners, both good and bad are known to work in groups to exert their will.* And there's a section describing an upside down pentagram, and that 1930s murder again." I quoted, "*Like so many accused witches, Susan just didn't get along with her neighbors. Her family had been feuding with another family since 1876 over a parcel of land.*"

"Let me see."

I handed him the booklet. Mitch skimmed it and grunted.

"We can't be sure your uncle was the one who underlined those passages," I said. "It could have been one of the cottage guests."

"I wonder why he kept this here?" He flipped to the back cover, then turned the booklet over and frowned.

"I haven't found any other books on the paranormal on the shelves. Or anything on hex signs."

"Speaking of which..." Mitch rose from his chair and strode outside.

Baffled, I waited. A few minutes later, he returned with a colorful, round sign.

I leapt to my feet. "That's the same design I found near your uncle," I exclaimed.

"I thought it might be." Face grim, Mitch handed me the circular piece of pressed wood. "I found it in the woods, not far off the highway."

I squinted at it. "There *is* something underneath the Metatron's cube. Hold on. And don't let Karin get her hands on this. She smashed the last one with a hammer."

"What?"

Leaving the sign on the dining table. I trotted downstairs and found my small cannister of paint remover. It was made to remove acrylic paint, which I guessed was what was on the sign. If whatever was beneath was acrylic too, there was a chance I'd end up removing both. I'd have to do a test spot first and be careful.

I returned upstairs with cotton and the solvent. Biting my bottom lip, I gently dabbed at the paint.

"Uh," Mitch said, "I thought you wanted that intact."

"I do, but I want to see what's underneath it." The top layer of paint dissolved, revealing a thick, black line beneath. I exhaled slowly. "The drawing underneath is in oil," I said, relieved, and worked more quickly.

When I'd finished, I set the pungent cotton on a piece of newspaper. The stained liquid darkened the paper around the cotton, smearing the print.

There was nothing demonic in what lay beneath the paint, beneath the symbol for balance and protection. But a chill rippled my flesh. If Mitch had asked me, I couldn't explain the creeping sensation along my spine, or why the image beneath—unbalanced and ugly—was also so, so wrong.

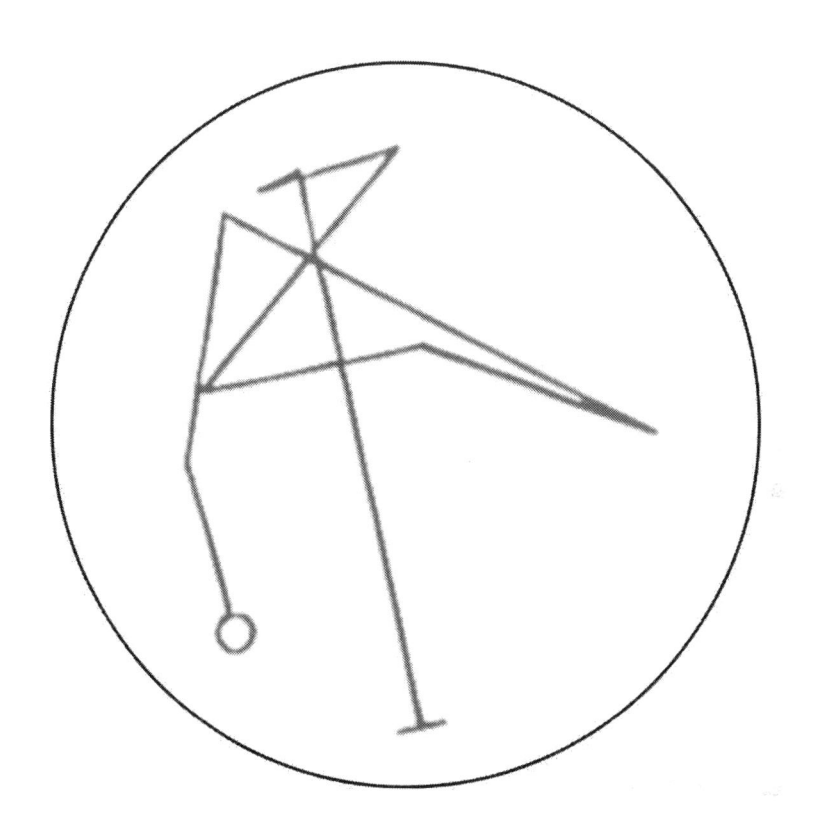

CHAPTER 22

MITCH GRASPED THE STRANGE hex sign with both hands. CRACK. He drove his knee through the thin wood and dropped the pieces onto the blue river in the dining table.

"Hey," I shouted. "I need that!"

The cat hissed and leapt to the floor. Casting an irate look over her shoulder, she prowled into the living room.

"Karin had the right idea," Mitch said.

My jaw slackened. And now Mitch was an expert on the occult too? "What do you know about that symbol?"

"Nothing."

My nostrils flared. "Then why'd you break that hex sign?"

"That's no hex sign."

I picked up one of the pieces. Mitch made a move as if to stop me, then jammed his hands in the pockets of his jeans.

Turning from the crackling fire, I held the piece to the light above the high kitchen counter. No, it *wasn't* a normal hex sign. Hex signs were balanced, geometric. This was... disturbing. The lines were wrong, uneven, unbalanced.

"I need to call Zeke," I muttered.

Mitch's brows drew together. "Why?"

"He was the one who told me about these signs. He's got an interest."

A muscle pulsed in his jaw. "You're thinking of your thesis."

"Of course I am. I've been floundering around, wasting time... If I don't get this degree—" I snapped my jaw shut. "Zeke's an expert in hex signs. And one of these, just like this—well, painted over, but you know what

I mean—was near where your uncle's body was found. It may not mean anything—"

"Since there haven't been other bodies found near them, it seems unlikely."

"But whoever broke into the cottage stole the pieces of the sign that Karin destroyed. And someone used oil paint on that... graffiti beneath the hex." I dropped it on the dining table.

"So?"

"Oil paint takes forever to dry. It's why I use acrylic. Why use oil on something so crude?" Reaching into my pocket, I touched the little silver hobbit door.

Mitch scratched his beard. "That *is* odd."

"Which?"

"All of it. Did Karin know you'd kept the pieces of the first sign?" He touched his thumb to his nose. It was no longer red, the blow perfectly healed. "No," he continued. "That was no woman who knocked me down the other night."

"Zeke may know something."

"Or he may be behind it."

"My advisor?" My voice rose. "Why?"

"My uncle set up a trust to fund Zeke's program. Now that he's dead, it's fully funded, and Zeke's named as the guy in charge. Your advisor benefited from my uncle's murder."

"Why didn't you mention this earlier?" I asked, annoyed. And why hadn't *Zeke* said anything?

"Because I didn't know if it mattered. But this is exactly the sort of weird crap an obsessed professor of hexology might do."

I huffed an uneasy laugh. "Hexology?"

"You know what I mean."

"Well, I've never seen anything like this. We need to talk to... Karin." And this time, I was getting a straight answer. Snatching up the piece I'd dropped, I strode into the rain, then ran back inside for my lightweight jacket.

Shaking his head, Mitch followed me to Karin's cottage and watched from the porch steps as I knocked on the door. A squirrel twitched at the sound and scampered up a nearby elm, its claws scraping against the bark.

After a moment, Karin opened the porch door, phone to her ear.

"We need to talk," I said.

She frowned and pointed to her phone. I raised the piece of hex sign.

Karin blanched. "I'll have to call you back." She disconnected. "I was on the phone with my kids. What were you thinking bringing that here?"

"The hex can get at them through the phone?" I asked, skeptical.

"You don't understand how energy works," she said huffily.

"So what is it?" Mitch leaned one hip against the banister.

"It's a sigil," Karin said.

"Not a spell?" I asked.

"A sigil is used to focus a spell," she said. "And that's a nasty one."

A breeze rustled the trees. The rain fell harder, drumming on the porch roof.

"So what does it do?" Mitch asked. "Allegedly."

Karin hugged herself. "Can't you feel it? It causes disruption, chaos."

"So we're dealing with anarchists," Mitch said, his voice flat.

She snorted. "Hardly. These people don't want anarchy for anarchy's sake. It's just a way to break things down to get what they want."

"They?" I asked.

"The GDF, the fund that's trying to buy up all this farmland." She motioned jerkily toward the woods. "Or the people behind them."

Oh, boy. She was a witch *and* a conspiracy theorist. And why wasn't I surprised those went hand in hand? "Hold on," I said, lifting my brows. "You're telling me the Global Development Fund, a non-profit, is run by a bunch of occultists?"

"Not all of them. Most are just useful idiots who believe they can remake the world. Or they're power-hungry idiots who think they can remake the world. But within the GDF is a group of occultists. They call themselves the Brotherhood."

I started and glanced at Mitch. "That's the phrase your uncle used," I said. "*The Brotherhood.*" Which either meant Woodward had been a conspiracy theorist too, or there was something to Karin's story.

Or it was all coincidence. But I was long past believing in that.

Mitch's jaw set. "And Ham works for ET, which funds the GDF. And you just happen to be staying two doors away from his place."

In the open doorway, Karin shifted her weight. "Ah, I didn't just *happen* to come here."

"You came here because of the GDF," I guessed.

She nodded. "When you mentioned the odd hex signs in the woods, I had a feeling they might be connected to… everything. I wasn't terribly surprised to find one near the old fountain."

"Fountain?" I asked.

"That stone circle where Woodward King's body was found," Karin said. "It's the remains of a fountain."

So much for pagan ceremonies.

"You got any evidence they're occultists?" Mitch demanded.

"Only the sort of stuff a wild-eyed conspiracy theorist would accept," she said bitterly. "We have a video of one of their ceremonies. The head of ET was there, along with the head of the GDF. But they were all wearing animal masks, so I can't prove they were there. But I know this group. I've encountered them before. They're dangerous."

"You kind of do sound like a wild-eyed conspiracy theorist," I said. There was a rumble of thunder, and I glanced at the canopy of trees and shivered.

"I know." Karin's voice dropped. "But haven't you felt that something's changed? That people are different? Not just online—though that's a major locus of their power. Offline too. People are meaner, more emotional, less… coherent. Things that would have been unthinkable ten years ago are now the norm. Demonic activity is way up. They had to cancel the Gettysburg ghost tours recently. They said it was because of a drop in seasonal tourism, but that's not the reason."

Mitch's face darkened. "A demon didn't kill my uncle."

"No," she said. "But I think your uncle knew something was going on. And he would know. He studied the occult. I'm willing to bet he had more books on it in his library that weren't about Pennsylvania."

Mitch folded his arms, his muscles bulging beneath his flannel shirt. "Maybe."

I started. The books on my table were only *part* of Woodward's occult collection?

"I don't believe your uncle was an occultist," Karin said gently. "I think he was an armchair magician—someone who read and understood but didn't practice. And sometimes knowledge can be dangerous."

Mitch pivoted and strode down her porch steps. We watched him stalk past my cottage, and I groaned.

"Where's he going?" Karin asked.

"To do something stupid, of course," I snapped. "He's going to confront Ham. You pointed the finger right at him."

"That's not what I—"

I turned and jogged after Mitch. He banged on the door to Ham's green-trimmed cottage.

"He's not home," I said.

Mitch turned and glared.

"His car's not here." I motioned toward the empty driveway.

Mitch tried the door. Naturally, it was locked.

"We only have Karin's word for all of this," I said in a low voice. And *she* was the one who seemed obsessed by the occult. But Woodward King had stood in the way of Ham's land acquisition...

"Ham really doesn't strike me as an occultist," I finished lamely.

"What does an occultist look like? I didn't think my uncle was interested in magic beyond local history. But Karin was right. He's got a whole room full of occult literature. British, Indian, Latin..."

"You read Latin?" I asked, surprised.

He growled, clenching his teeth. "I'm going to try the back."

I thought of telling him it would be locked too. I knew the ways of Californians, being one myself. But instead, I just went home.

The cat had vanished, which I chalked up to leaving the front door ajar rather than any feline magic. I locked it and made myself comfortable on the leather-covered couch with the *Fellowship of the Ring*.

Mitch didn't return to retrieve his books. I finished a chapter and closed the book. Wanting my dining table back, I stacked Woodward King's books in the living room, made dinner, and washed up.

I returned to Tolkien with a mug of herbal tea. When my eyelids drooped, I set the book aside, rose, and stretched. The rain had stopped. Shrugging into my crimson pea coat, I walked onto the back porch.

Ham had returned. His car was in his driveway, and a bonfire flickered in his backyard.

I sighed. It was better if I talked to Ham before Mitch did.

I opened the porch door and walked outside. The clouds had turned to haunting wisps. Between them, a full moon, fat and orange, hung above the trees. Entranced, I walked slowly to the bonfire, low and smoky.

It was a perfect night for magic, if I believed in it. If I believed in the sense of anticipation in the air. If I believed the silent woods were holding their breath, waiting. If I believed in my magic.

I shook myself, my chest flaming with embarrassment. Where had *that* thought come from? *If I believed in* my *magic.* Ha.

Besides, this wasn't about me. This was about asking Ham about the GDF and the Brotherhood. And if he asked me where I'd heard about the organization—if it even existed— would I tell him about Karin?

I'd play that by ear.

My feet seemed to glide across the steep hillside. I didn't need to look where I was going. I didn't stumble or hesitate.

And then, suddenly, I was there, at the edge of the clearing. And Ham was there, in his Adirondack chair...

I giggled at the rhyme. Or maybe at the charm of the scene. Ham's head was bent to his chest. The ancient god, Pan, fallen asleep. And hadn't the old gods all fallen asleep? Or did they still lurk in the woods and wild places, waiting and watching...

I swallowed.

I almost didn't want to disturb Ham. But he wouldn't want to be left asleep, to be awakened by the next burst of rain. "Ham?" I walked to his chair.

He didn't stir. Acrid smoke drifted across us. There was something unpleasant in it, and I stopped, head cocked, sniffing. A puff of smoke rolled from the pit and across us.

I coughed and flapped my hand in front of my face. "Ham?" I shook his shoulder. His head lolled, and I recoiled. He wasn't sleeping. Something was wrong.

Blinking rapidly, I reached to touch his neck, to feel for a pulse, but instead my hand went to his still chest as if it belonged there. "Ham."

The weave of his sweater was rough against my hand and had the musty smell of damp sheep. And it was cold, a cold that crept up my arm and slivered my heart. My body jerked away, but my hand remained pinned to Ham's chest.

And I felt the life leaving his body, and I felt the final chill of death, and the air compressed, squeezing my lungs. "No."

You can help him, my mother's ghost said.

And I knew how, the knowledge right there, in my mind, where it hadn't been before.

Whispering a word, I sent my own life flowing out my palm and into Ham, into that awful cold. And it didn't hurt. It didn't deplete me. And I realized it wasn't *my* life force. Something else flowed through me and into that void.

"Don't go," I whispered.

A strange lassitude lifted me, weightless. That was how it happened, wasn't it? Witches rose through their chimneys on the smoke...

I was going, and I was dying, and that was okay.

CHAPTER 23

My ascent is interrupted, roots sprouting from my feet
and digging into the cold earth.
Anchored, I sway above the forest, above the firepit, above the fire,
AND I TASTE bitter ashes. I need to move on,
but the only paths open to me are down or up.
Flaming leaves fall like cradles and anguish pulls me
down—the loss of children unborn, of loves unloved, of chances untaken.
Regret clogs my throat, knots my belly.
So many mistakes. Is it too late? Am I done? Burnt up? Over?
Up. I choose up, lifting past leaves in their last blaze,
my skin blackening in the smoke.
The dark clouds condense, seething, scorching, snaking,
terrible eyes glowing cinders.
I'm not alone. The thing clutches me in scalding claws,
talons piercing my crackling skin.
Give up.
I relax, and the pain retreats. It doesn't hurt if I don't struggle.
Flakes of my drying flesh
catch the upward drift of smoke and spiral, and I'm dying,
I'm dying, but I won't die, I won't be over, it can't be over.
Fear squeezes my neck,
choking, and
I scream...

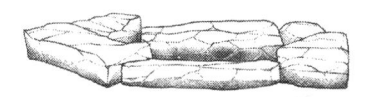

CHAPTER 24

AN ARCTIC WIND LASHED the trees, slapped my cheeks, snapped me into awareness. Fallen leaves tornadoed around me, obscuring my vision in a sunset blur.

Through the haze of leaves, I made out Karin striding into Ham's backyard, her navy trench coat flapping, her hands raised as if surrendering. I plummeted, my giggle at the visual was cut short, cut off, the wind sucking the smoke from my lungs.

I didn't feel it when I hit the ground. Later I wondered if I'd ever been airborne or had imagined it all. But that came later. For now, all I could think of was Ham.

I lurched toward him, but my legs wouldn't move. Dimly, I realized that was because I lay sprawled on the uneven hillside. And suddenly I was off it, my face pressed against a broad masculine chest. My head jounced against the soft fabric of Mitch's shirt.

He dumped me unceremoniously onto Karin's porch sofa. "Don't move." And then he was gone.

Ignoring his edict, I staggered off the wicker sofa and bent over the porch railing to peer past my cottage. Karin and Mitch emerged around its corner. They dragged Ham between them.

Karin and Mitch... My jaw firmed. Not my business, not my problem. But Ham...

Unsteadily, I made my way down the porch steps and to my blue cottage, where the two stood arguing over Ham's limp form.

"—quicker to drive him," Mitch was saying.

"I'll get my car." Karin hurried past me. "You're coming too," she said to me. "You did good."

I rubbed my forehead. "Coming?" I asked, but she was already gone.

"To the hospital," Mitch said, gruff. "You were exposed."

I shook my head, and the forest lurched. Dizzy, I reached for a nearby tree.

Mitch caught my arm. "You okay?"

"I don't feel so good."

Karin returned, her coattails flapping. "Did you call the police?" she asked Mitch.

Exposed? Police? Why...?

"Yeah," he said.

We were going to the hospital, and suddenly I realized what that meant. "He's alive." My knees wobbled. I grasped the porch railing. Making my way hand over hand, I tottered toward Ham, lying on the damp ground.

My legs folded, and I landed hard beside him. "Ham." I pressed a hand to his face. His skin was cold, and I gave an involuntary cry of distress.

Awkwardly, I shrugged out of my jacket and draped it over Ham's still form. I looked up at Mitch. His face was expressionless. "He needs a blanket," I said and heaved myself to standing.

"I'll get one." Mitch strode into my cottage, and I sat back down before I fell down.

The taillights of Karin's blue SUV backed toward us. She emerged from the car as Mitch exited my cottage, a blanket in his arms. Karin jogged to the back of her SUV and opened its hatch.

Together, we maneuvered Ham into the back. I didn't help much, though I tried. My muscles were oddly weak. Mitch tossed the blanket over him, then thrust me into the back seat.

"He should have a pillow," I protested, twisting in my seat to study Ham.

"He doesn't need a damn pillow," Mitch growled, slamming his door.

Karin pulled carefully from my driveway. Karin did everything carefully, I was soon to learn, including drive. We crept down twisting roads at a maddening pace.

"He may be dying," I snapped. "Can't you go any quicker?"

"It won't be quicker if we crash," she said.

Finally, we reached the hospital, a six-story brick building. Mitch sprang from the SUV and raced inside.

Karin turned in her seat to face me. "How are you feeling?"

My gut twisted. "A little sick."

"Physically or emotionally?"

"Both."

Her gaze met mine. "He should have been dead, you know."

I shuddered and looked away.

Soon, nurses were bundling me into a wheelchair and lifting Ham onto a stretcher. Ham vanished into the bowels of the grim building. The nurses abandoned me with Karin in the Emergency Room's waiting area.

I didn't know where Mitch was. It annoyed me that I cared.

After forever and an hour, a nurse wheeled me into an exam room, where a doctor in a white coat flashed a light in my eyes.

I winced and looked toward a pale blue wall. "I'm fine."

"I think you are." He dropped the flashlight into his coat's breast pocket. "Which is remarkable, all things considered."

"What happened? How's Ham?" I leaned forward, the paper on the exam table crinkling beneath me.

"I haven't been treating your friend. But he chose the wrong wood for his firepit. He was using manchineel."

I rubbed my jaw. "What?"

"Commonly known as death apple." The doctor leaned against a fog-colored counter. On it was a glass jar holding the largest cotton swabs I'd ever seen. "It's the most poisonous tree in the world. Even the smoke can kill you. The police want to talk to you when we're done."

And Sheriff Yoder did talk to me in the exam room. Not that I could tell him much. He seemed to assume Ham hadn't known what sort of wood he'd collected, and our near-death-by-firewood had been an accident.

"But... how do you accidentally collect poisonous wood?" I asked. "Is it from around here?"

"Florida," the sheriff said. The enormous man removed his broad-brimmed hat and swiped a paw over his round head. "One of my deputies is from Florida. Luckily for Mr. Powers, he recognized it immediately. The doctors know how to treat it."

"Then he'll be okay?"

"Eventually. Maybe."

"Maybe?" I gripped the soft cushion on the exam table beneath me. "But... where would he get it?"

The sheriff shrugged, his uniform jacket whispering against his bulk. "Someone who used the cottage before him probably left it there. You were lucky you weren't exposed for long."

Lucky. And luck was all it had been. I'd stumbled into toxic smoke, and if Karin and Mitch hadn't arrived...

I looked toward the counter with its gleaming sink. My throat thickened, my hands curling inward.

I'd been metaphorically stumbling around since David had died. And since I'd arrived in Pennsylvania, it had only gotten worse. I hadn't moved forward on anything—on rejiggering my thesis topic, on my art, on my business... On the murder.

But the murder had been another distraction, hadn't it? I'd been flailing. And I needed to get in gear, get organized. I needed to pull myself together and exercise some discipline.

The nurses wouldn't let me walk out of the exam room on my own. After filling out an ungodly number of forms, they insisted on wheeling me to the waiting area, where Karin sat reading a magazine.

Mitch paced the thin, gray carpet in front of her. "What'd they say?" he asked me.

"I'm fine." I stepped from the wheelchair and dropped into the chair beside Karin.

"I thought you would be," she said. The phone in her navy purse buzzed, and she pulled it out, glanced at the number. "My family. Excuse me." She strode through the automatic doors and outside.

Mitch glowered. "What the hell were you thinking?"

"Getting poisoned by toxic smoke?" I asked, incredulous. "Was I supposed to anticipate that?"

"Going to Ham Power's place by yourself."

"We're neighbors."

"Ted Bundy had neighbors."

"Ham isn't a serial killer. He's a..." *Victim.*

I blinked, surprised by the thought. A part of me had believed Ham might have killed Woodward King. But I didn't believe for a second he'd bought that poisoned wood—not by accident, not by intention. Someone—Woodward's killer—had left it for him.

"Idiot," Mitch said.

Fuming, I sucked in a breath to shout.

"Not you," he said. "Powers. Only an idiot would burn manchineel wood."

"Ham couldn't have known what it was."

"Couldn't he? It's typical of his type. It's not enough to end himself, he has to do it in a way that could take out the whole neighborhood."

"You think he tried to kill himself? That's ridiculous. Who kills themselves with poisoned smoke like...like some character in an Edgar Allan Poe story?"

"Someone who likes bonfires?"

"That's just..." I sputtered.

"He killed my uncle, he couldn't take the pressure, and he took the easy out. Or he tried to." Mitch scowled. "He couldn't even get that right."

"Sorry," I said coldly. "Are you complaining he wasn't... *efficient* enough?"

A nurse walked behind the curving counter. She shot us a glance.

"And you," Mitch snarled, "wandering around alone at night when you know there's a killer in the area. You knew someone's been in your cottage, targeting you—"

"Not Ham."

"Why did you even leave Cornflower Cottage?"

I sucked in my cheeks. *Of all the...* "Why shouldn't I leave? It's not a prison."

"I didn't take you for one of those too-dumb-to-live movie heroines, being chased through the woods in high heels and tripping over every root. Use your brains."

My face heated. And I'd actually been attracted to this man? It figured my first crush—and that was *all* it had been, a crush—would be with another man bent on telling me what to do.

"Mitch lost a tooth." Karin approached us and dropped her phone in her purse. She smiled. "My son Mitch," she explained. "Not *you*, obviously."

I snorted.

Karin turned to Mitch. "Do you mind giving us a moment?"

Without replying, he turned and strode to the nurse's station.

What now? I raised my chin, my muscles tightening. More witchcraft? More secret societies? More insinuations?

She grimaced. "We need to talk."

CHAPTER 25

Seriously? "No," I said, voice hardening, "we don't."

An alarm went off down the hospital corridor. The nurse at the desk ignored it.

Without responding, Karin turned and walked toward the glass exit doors. They slid open, and she strolled outside.

I muttered a curse. A part of me *did* want to talk to her, to understand what had happened tonight versus what my drugged-out brain had only envisioned. The wind that had blown away the smoke and confusion had arisen so suddenly...

The witch binds the wind into a knot... I swore again. Feet dragging, I followed her to a wide sweep of bricks with low bushes and a cement bench.

We didn't sit. The night was chill and damp. I imagined cold seeping from the bench, the way it had been stealing through Ham's still form, and I shuddered.

I buttoned the top of my crimson pea coat. "Well?"

"You saved Ham's life." Karin folded her arms over her trench coat, the fabric whispering.

I laughed shortly. "Me? You and Mitch were the heroes. I walked straight into that smoke and nearly passed out too."

She gave me a long look. "Is that all you think you did? Are you still in denial?"

"Denial of what?" I stared fixedly at her.

She studied the tips of her sensible blue shoes. "Maybe it's for the best," she muttered. "Maybe they won't see her."

"Who won't see whom?" I asked, exasperated.

She shook her hair. In the light from the hospital, auburn threads gleamed, snaking along the shoulders of her navy trench. "You found a murder victim. Your cottage was broken into. You were attacked. And now your neighbor nearly died under—let's say mysterious circumstances—and you got caught up in that as well. You're in danger. Even you, with your superior powers of mental evasion, can't deny that."

"No," I said dully and gazed toward the half-empty parking lot. I couldn't. But I'd known I'd been involved in this since Woodward King's ghost had appeared in the cottage.

Karin nodded. "I won't offer to ward your cottage. With your magic in the unsettled state it's in, I don't know how a spell against dark magic would react."

I stared, uncomprehending. And then I got it. Finally. "You think *I'm* a dark magician?" I asked, amused.

"I think you could go either way right now. It's the lies, you see."

I stiffened. "I haven't been—"

"Yes, you have. Mainly to yourself, it's true. But you've been lying to Mitch, and I suspect to others. And every lie—even the small ones—especially the small ones—creates a rift between you and your soul. That makes you vulnerable."

Bullshit. It was just more of her fake witchy wisdom. Everyone told white lies. Everyone lied to themselves about something.

And I hadn't lied to Mitch. There'd been omissions about my past, sure. But there was no law that said I had to bare my soul and my past to every person I met. Now, I was gladder than ever that I hadn't.

"It's late." I pulled my phone from my pocket. "I'm going home."

She sighed. "I can't stop the emails, you know. Believe me, we've tried."

Baffled, I moved a little away from her to call a ride share. When I hung up, Karin had returned inside the hospital, with Mitch.

I shook my head, my jaw hardening. Whatever was between them was their business, not mine.

I slept late the next morning and felt guilty about my lounging. After last night, I had every right to relax. But I'd already spent too much time unfocused. I needed to finalize my thesis topic, finish my degree, and get on with my life.

When I did get up, I painted in the walkout basement. The cat supervised for a time then curled up in the patch of sunlight beneath the windowed door.

After lunch, she followed me upstairs to the dining table. I checked my email and sipped coffee from my favorite LOTR mug. It read: MY PRECIOUS. Then I researched manchineel wood.

A tropical tree native to Florida, every part of the manchineel is toxic. Even standing under the tree during a rainstorm can cause symptoms. The manchineel is the deadliest tree in the world.

Also known as the death apple, the manchineel produces toxic, sweet-tasting apple-like fruits. While the native populations learned to avoid the tree, early visitors were not so lucky. Ponce de Leon was said to have died after being shot with an arrow tipped with manchineel sap. Early sailors come to shore for firewood were temporarily blinded when chopping down the trees. People have been known to die from the smoke of its burning wood.

However, uses have been found for the tree. Once dried to reduce sap, its wood is used in furniture making. It has been used as an herbal remedy to reduce excess fluids. And it reduces coastal erosion.

Today, red rings are painted around the tree trunks to warn people away. But they can also be identified by their glossy, oval-shaped leaves and cracked and furrowed reddish or gray bark.

My hands lifted off the dining table. *Used in furniture making.* Suspicion slithered in my gut. Did Mitch know about the wood? Mitch, who benefited from his uncle's death. Mitch, who'd been spending so much time at Cornflower Cottage, right beside Ham's...

No. Mitch hadn't been the man who'd broken in that night. Mitch had raced in to save me...

I pinched my bottom lip between two fingers. But had he saved me? I hadn't seen the intruder and Mitch together, only Mitch's busted nose. He could have done it to himself, running into something in the dark.

I rose swiftly, knocking back my chair hard enough for it to tip against the unlit fireplace. The cat started from her spot on the fireplace's stone hearth. I walked around the table and paced between it and the kitchen. The cat watched, her golden eyes wary.

The work Mitch had been doing on Cornflower Cottage had given him all sorts of time to snoop. But why? For what? If he wanted me gone, he could evict me at any time.

My college advisor had expected I'd lose the cottage after Woodward King's death. But Mitch had let me stay. Why?

I buried my head in my hands. My advisor. My thesis. I was letting myself get distracted. *Again.*

Returning to my computer, I worked on my new thesis topic until the cottage darkened. I checked the clock on my laptop. Josh would be here soon, and I didn't want to be late for my date with the doctor.

I jogged upstairs and changed out of my paint-stained clothes. My stomach fluttered. *Was it a date?* It had been a long time since I'd been on one. Should I dress up or keep it casual? Somewhere in between. *Nice, but not too nice...*

The doctor showed up exactly at seven in an overcoat over his dark gray suit and tie, so I was relieved I'd opted for a simple ivory sheath.

Adjusting his fedora, he smiled faintly behind his dark beard. "We may have both overdressed. But we can go somewhere else after the bar, if you like."

"Let's play it by ear."

He drove us into Babylon, and we parked behind a two-story brick building with peeling white paint. "I'm afraid old George would have been disappointed with what his watering hole became," Josh said, helping me from the car.

"Watering hole? Did Washington come here more than once?"

One corner of his mouth quirked upward. "I doubted he ever came here at all."

He took my arm, and we strolled into the dark, wood-paneled bar. Its grim interior still retained a modicum of revolution-era charm, copper pots hanging from graffitied ceiling beams. But the furniture was scraped and rough, and the bar had a seedy air.

Josh claimed a table in a quiet corner. Removing his hat, he ruffled his hair, clawing it across his forehead. We ordered opera fudge ales and appetizers and watched the waitress sashay toward the bar.

"I heard you had some excitement last night," Josh said.

"Yes." Stomach heavying, I sat back in my wooden chair. Of course the doctor would have heard. The story had made the morning papers, along with warnings about using manchineel wood. "Ham."

"Is he all right?"

"I don't know. I'm not family, so the hospital wouldn't tell me anything when I called."

Creases appeared between his dark brows. "And you're worried."

"I guess so. We weren't close, but we were neighbors." And I'd found him.

"Then I'll find out for you," he said.

I released a breath. "You can do that?"

"I spend a good amount of time in and out of that hospital. The staff knows me." Josh shook his head. "It's strange. I haven't heard of manchineel trees growing in Pennsylvania. Where did the wood come from?"

"Apparently, it's native to Florida and other tropical areas." Which Pennsylvania most definitely was not.

The doctor's expression flickered. "I had no idea. How did the hospital identify it?"

"I don't think they did. One of the sheriff's deputies was from Florida and knew about the tree."

His mouth tightened. "That's the problem with small-town hospitals. We don't have deep expertise. Ham was lucky. Very lucky."

"Yeah. I would rather not have learned about manchineel wood like this."

There was a shout and a crash, and we glanced toward the noise. A rough-looking man and woman, mid-twenties, obviously drunk, waved off a waitress.

Josh's expression tightened. "New Yorkers."

"Tourists? How can you tell?" Babylon wasn't exactly a tourist spot, despite Woodward King's attempt to attract people to his trail. Or maybe he'd had the locals in mind when he'd created it.

"Not tourists," Josh said. "Back in the eighties, New York made a deal with Pennsylvania to export their welfare recipients to Babylon and other dying small towns. I think the idea was revitalization. Towns like Babylon had empty houses, and the big-city poor needed places to live. But there were fewer jobs available than in big cities. The newcomers weren't able to get work. It ended up being a lose-lose situation. They were dropped into an alien environment, and the towns treated them like outsiders."

I pulled a face. "What's that about the road to hell being paved with good intentions?"

"Who said the intentions were good?" He dragged his gaze from the two and smiled wryly. "They must be second generation New Yorkers. And look at me, still calling them *New Yorkers*. I'm no better than the rest of Babylon. And I'm sure we can think of more interesting things to talk about than small-town culture."

"I find small-town culture fascinating. Especially Pennsylvania culture."

"Speaking of which, how's your thesis going?"

"I've rewritten my proposal," I said. "Now I need to submit it and hope it gets approved."

"It will be."

I smiled crookedly. "My last wasn't."

The waitress appeared with our drinks and a basket of beer-battered artichoke hearts.

Josh's intent gaze returned to the two drunks. "This town has had more than its share of bad luck, especially lately."

"Lately?" I tried the ale. It was darkly chocolate and sour, with hints of cherry. It didn't taste like opera fudge, but it was good.

"Woodward King's murder," he said. "Ham's accident. I wonder how that will affect the new processing plant?"

"Unless it wasn't an accident. Unless Ham's attack is connected to Woodward King's."

Josh's blue-gray eyes seemed to darken. "Using manchineel wood had to have been an accident."

"Are you sure?" I asked. "As you said, Ham's death might delay or even put a stop to the land purchases and the new processing plant."

"A plant Woodward didn't want." He sipped his dark ale. "The situation was complex. They were on opposing sides. I don't think there can be a connection."

"Was Woodward... active in resisting the plant?"

"Aside from refusing to sell his land? He wasn't leading protests or putting sugar in Ham's gas tank. Why would he?" The doctor's brow creased, his hair shifting, revealing a scabbed cut near his hairline. "Woodward's confidence was his fatal flaw."

I dragged my gaze from the cut. "What do you mean?"

"Woodward thought he could fix Babylon." He shook his head. "But he was at least a decade too late."

I hated to believe that. The town couldn't be over. Yes, things went in cycles, but at some point, the cycle had to be *up*. "We need to have hope, if only to piss off the people who want us hopeless."

Humor glimmered at one corner of his mouth. "Spite *is* an excellent motivator."

"*Did* someone put sugar in Ham's gas tank?" I asked.

"Ham didn't mention it?" He took a gulp of his ale. "Some farmers were responsible, no doubt. Probably the guys at the memorial. It was a rental car though. Ham just rented another."

"What exactly was Woodward's objection to the new plant?" I asked.

"Change. He wanted the farmland to stay as it was. It's impossible though," he said bitterly, his attention traveling again to the drunks, raucous at the bar. "The world has changed, and so has Babylon. All we can do is try to manage the descent."

"Descent? That's gloomy."

"I prefer to think of it as realistic," he said, tone sardonic.

My fingers curled in the cloth napkin in my lap. "But... We have to try, don't we? I mean, it becomes a self-fulfilling prophecy if everyone gives up hope."

"There's no point. People can't change." He nodded toward the two at the bar. The woman had fallen off her stool. She grasped the edge of the bar and clumsily hoisted herself up.

"Look at them," Josh said. "Do you think they're acting in their own best interests? That they know or care what's good for them or the community?"

"Not in the state they're in now, but—"

"Hey." Mitch appeared at our table. The collar of Mitch's flannel shirt was open, the sleeves rolled, exposing corded forearms. His wavy hair was mussed, as if he'd come from an assignation.

My face warmed. My mind had no business going there.

"What are you two doing here?" Mitch asked, voice hard.

Josh swiveled in his chair and didn't get up. "Just what it looks like."

"Then you're an idiot." He jerked his head toward me. "This isn't the place for April. Look around."

I stiffened. "I wanted to try the beer." Where else was I supposed to get opera fudge ale?

"April should be able to go where she wants," Josh said mildly.

"*Should?* What the world should be and what it is are two different things," Mitch growled. "You can take whatever risks you want, but don't drag other people into them—a lesson you should know."

Josh paled. He sprang from the table and cocked back his fist, swinging clumsily, so wildly Mitch should have been able to duck it.

But he didn't try. The punch connected, and Mitch took a step back, absorbing the blow, his thigh striking our table. Ale splashed across my dress, and I sucked in a breath, cold spreading across my torso.

Mitch rubbed his jaw. "Sorry."

What the...? Where had *that* come from? One minute we'd been sitting peacefully and the next they'd been chest thumping like two teenage boys.

"You're sorry?" My voice rose, and I struggled to lower it. "You two should both be... Oh, the hell with it." I whipped the napkin from my lap and blotted my dress.

Josh's shoulders crumpled beneath his suit jacket. He exhaled slowly, but his eyes blazed. "That was... I shouldn't have..."

I stood, because I was tired of looking up at them both and because the dark stain was spreading across my off-white dress. I was fed up with Mitch and murder and ruminating over my marriage.

"Don't come back to the cottage," I told Mitch. My voice trembled. "It doesn't need any more work. Not while I'm there."

Mitch blinked, as if surprised to remember I was there, or surprised I'd said anything at all. "You—" He pivoted and strode from the bar. The two drunks careened after him.

The look Josh shot after him could have smelted iron. The doctor lowered his head. "April, I'm—"

"I'm going to clean up." I stalked into the bathroom and grabbed paper towels from the dispenser.

Our waitress strolled inside. "Here." She handed me a white cloth towel. "This might work better than paper."

"Thanks." I ran the cloth under the hot water tap.

She crossed her arms and leaned against the tiled wall. "Don't take it personally. It was bound to happen someday. I just figured it'd be Mitch punching the doc."

Bound to happen? I paused, towel pressed against my dress. Water dripped between my fingers. "Why?"

"Because the doc dated Mitch's wife. After she divorced Mitch, of course. But still." She shrugged.

I scrubbed violently at the stain. "Is there *anyone* in this town who hasn't slept with someone else's wife?" I snarled. "Woodward King and the doc's wife, the doctor and Mitch's wife..."

"In fairness," she said, "it's a small town. Who else are people going to hook up with?"

I sighed. And here I'd been telling myself all my recent male attention had been due to my feminine charms. I was just a shiny new fish in a tiny Pennsylvania pond.

"I haven't slept with either of them." She straightened off the wall and grinned. "So there's that."

I huffed a laugh. She left me in the bathroom and I got most of the beer out of my dress. I returned the towels to the bar, then met Josh at our table.

"It's my fault," he said. "I lost control. I shouldn't have. My wife..."

I raised a brow. "*Your* wife?" *What about Mitch's ex?*

He exhaled again, more slowly. "She was stabbed by one of my patients, an addict. She was working as my receptionist." A muscle pulsed in his jaw. "I'm sorry. I'm no good tonight."

Stabbed. My God. I deflated, anger leaking from me in a regretful rush.

And Mitch—the idiot—had accused Josh of putting me at risk, of knowing better. That...explained why Josh had reacted so violently. Not that it excused it. But.

"No," I said. "It's fine. Let's get out of here."

Josh settled the bill, and we walked into the cool October night. Half the parking lot lights were out, but Josh had managed to find a spot beneath one that worked. We moved toward his Audi.

A screech of tires. A thump. I started, tensing. A woman screamed.

Mitch. I briefly clutched the soft fabric of Josh's sleeve. Unthinking, I ran toward the street.

The traffic light turned from green to yellow to red, bathing the slick street in garish holiday colors. The woman from the bar wailed over a crumpled figure, and it wasn't Mitch. Slowing, I covered my mouth with a shaky hand.

It was David. David in the street. David dying, alone. The red-light-runner speeding away from the crosswalk. I hadn't been there for David then. I'd gotten the details from the somber police officers at my front door.

The vision vanished. The man in the street wasn't my husband, and I drew a ragged breath. It was the young man from the bar.

A white-haired man clambered from his minivan. "He just walked in front of me," he quavered. "I couldn't stop."

Josh swore and grasped my elbow. "Stay here." Releasing me, he jogged to the fallen man.

I shivered on the sidewalk. People emerged from the bar to gawk. Police arrived. The woman's wails continued, desolate. Josh approached me. His hands were stained with blood.

"April, I've called you a cab. I'm sorry, but I think I'll be here a while. You should go home."

"Is he...?"

"Alive. But he's not in good shape. I need to stay with him."

I nodded. A yellow cab pulled up.

"That's yours." Josh bent. Careful not to touch me, he kissed my cheek. "Worst date ever?"

"Not quite," I said absently.

I climbed into the cab and returned to my cottage. At the base of the porch steps, I stopped, my muscles sluggish. They say you don't get over tragedies—you get through them. Maybe it's true. And maybe I hadn't completely gotten through my own.

The policeman who'd given me the bad news later confessed to me it had been his first next-of-kin notification. He'd been relieved, I think, I hadn't broken into sobs or hysterics. I'd just abruptly found myself sitting on my own doormat, the one David had bought that read: GO AWAY.

I checked inside the mailbox, my hands trembling. Somehow, I'd known a new UnTarot card would be inside.

SUBJECT: SPELLWORK

SEEKER:

You have begun to see new ways of acting and being, and this can be unsettling. It's time you begin learning to control the spells you cast, by combining your conscious intention with conscious *attention*.

Work with the attached form. Condensing your intention down to a word or two, write it down in the little finger of the illustrated hand. Then using only a word or two, write in the next finger what the successful spell will look like. How will your life have changed? In the next finger, write down how you'll feel. In the index finger (your magic wand), write down your spell as if it has already happened, e.g., Now I have/am_____. Finally, feel gratitude for having achieved your spell. Write down *where* you feel this gratitude in your body and *how* it feels (Warm? Fluffy? Pink?).

Below the hand, journal on what subconsciously may have undermined you in the past from achieving this spell. Know that by digging out any subconscious motivations NOT to cast a successful spell, you are gaining mastery over them.

Write down the spell at the bottom of the page and say it to yourself through the day this week, visualizing what it will look and feel like, and feeling gratitude for getting what you want.

We ask you to contemplate the next card in your Untarot deck, *The Spell*. Scan the QR code below, or if you're reading this online, click the QR code.

SCAN ME

THE SPELL

Magick. Empowerment. Illusion. False constructs. Entrapment.

There are many kinds of spells. The all-out, don-your-ceremonial-robes-under-a-full moon spell, the curse you cast at the guy who cut you off on the freeway, the curse you cast on yourself when you berate yourself for a mistake, and the "simpler" spells of our own positive and negative beliefs.

And then there are the spells others cast on you. They could be deceptions and false glamours. They could be words that boost or undermine your sense of self. Spells affect a change in consciousness, and we are all capable of casting them.

Spells influence how you see the world. If you don't believe you're worthy of a new job, you'll go into the interview projecting unworthiness, or maybe not work as hard as you could to prepare for it. If you start your day expecting to meet wonderful people, you'll be more inclined to act in an open and loving way, attracting reciprocal behavior, and feeling more charitable when others fall short.

Once your perception of the world changes, you change, and the reactions of the world to you changes. Spells are powerful things, so it's useful to consider what spells you may be operating under.

The symbols:

Clouds of illusion and confusion float at the top and bottom of the card as a woman casts a spell of intent, manifesting as a globe of raw energy. Hinted at around the circumference of the spell is an ouroboros, a snake eating its tail (or in this case, a dragon eating its tail. You can see his head in the upper left quadrant). In its positive aspect, the ouroboros is a symbol of eternity and endless return, the union of the earthly and the divine. In its negative aspect, it's a frame, a spell of confusion that keeps you trapped. The only way to break the spell is to break from the framing.

The questions:

What spells have been cast on you? What have you cast on others? What spells have you cast on yourself? Is it time to cast new ones?

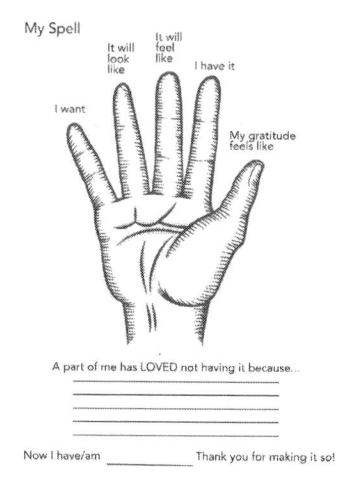

CHAPTER 26

A GHOST WOULD HAVE been welcome company that night. Wind whipped around the cottage, howling loneliness. I tossed in my lumpy bed and tangled in the cool sheets and thought of David.

We can tell ourselves we're whole and complete on our own as much as we want. And of course it's true—we are complete. But I couldn't deny my loneliness, or my longing for something more, for the type of relationship I'd confessed to Karin.

Or my dread that I could never have it.

Sitting up, I turned on the light, picked up the new card.

Had I cast a spell on myself? Was the idea I couldn't have that type of relationship only a belief, and a false one? Was there still hope?

Behind me were years of evidence to the contrary. My spell was too strong to break.

"Fuck me, I *am* some bad-ass witch." I tossed the card on the side table. It slid to a halt against the brass lamp. Downstairs, the printer whirred, and I stilled in my bed.

Dreading what I'd find—knowing what I'd find—I slithered into a robe and edged my way down the stairs. In the living room, a sheet of paper rested in the printer. I picked up the warm page. My *Spell*.

I might as well fill it out. It wasn't like I was going to sleep anytime soon.

Feeling silly, I sat at the dining room table and filled out the fingers on the hand.

I want... *a loving relationship.*

My pen hovered on the lines beneath the hand. A *part of me loved not having it because...* Hesitating, I wrote.

Because it kept me safe. It kept me from the pain of another loss. Because I could do what I want without answering to anyone. Because I was free...

Because you're scared, my husband whispered.

I leapt to my feet, the chair scraping backward. "Why can't I *see* you?"

No one answered.

Hugging myself, I shuffled onto the porch. Mitch's pickup wasn't in the street, and why did my heart sink at that? Of course it wouldn't be there. I'd told him never to darken my door again. And even if I hadn't, a sane man would be in his own bed.

Or in someone else's.

A light flickered in a window in Ham's cottage. Frowning, I gripped the porch railing and leaned over for a better look.

I checked the street. No cars drove along it. That hadn't been the reflection of a vehicle's lights.

My nostrils flared, my knuckles whitening. Someone was inside the cottage, and it wasn't Ham. Even if he'd returned from the hospital, he would have turned the lights on. He wouldn't be creeping around with a flashlight.

I should call the cops.

I kept telling myself that as I pulled on my sneakers and tossed a throw over my shoulders. Because what if it *was* Ham? These houses were old. There might be a wiring problem. His power could be out.

Call the cops. Phone in hand, I hurried down my stairs to the walkout basement. *Call the cops.* I quietly opened my back door. *Call the cops.*

I tiptoed across the wooded slope toward Ham's cottage. I'd just look and watch and see, and *then* I'd call the cops.

The wind tossed the trees. Dying leaves fluttered around me. The light shifted on the ground, the moon emerging from between the clouds.

BANG. I jumped.

The sound came again, the thud of a door in the wind. I moved closer, heart thumping. Ham's back door swayed open, and I froze.

Cold seeped through my bones. The wind stilled, and a compression of air molecules tightened my lungs. The moonlight took on a pallid cast, slithering through the skeletal trees. The stones ringing the firepit gleamed like silvered bone, and my teeth chattered.

A phosphorescence crept around the firepit. I swayed, sweat slick on my forehead. "David?" My husband's name died in my throat.

The mist congealed, forming something bulky and powerful.

Not David. David had been tall and slender.

"Woodward King," I whispered, sweat slicking my brow. "Is that you?"

A face wavered in the mist, taking on definition. The hard lines of his jaw. A straight, proud nose. But the eyes were inky horrors, and I backed away, my fists pressed to the sides of my head.

And it was *real*. I could see ghosts, and it was real.

His mouth opened as if to speak, but it kept opening, his jaw lengthening, his face elongating, a ghastly, rubbery horror. An unholy shriek ripped across the hillside, and I clapped my hands to my ears. The mist swept toward me.

I turned and fled. In my terror, I stumbled over a tree stump and nearly fell, but I made it to my basement and flew through the open door. Grabbing its edge, I swiveled to slam it shut.

The ghost was gone. The wind tossed the trees. The moon vanished behind the clouds.

I stood breathing hard, heart thumping against my ribs. *Too-dumb-to-live-heroine? Check*. Had I done it just to prove Mitch right?

A vehicle's engine started.

Emerging from the doorway, I jogged up the hill to the corner of my cottage. Taillights from a pickup flared. Pulling forward, they vanished from my view behind Ham's house and continued up the street.

Shaken, I backed to my door and returned inside. Nausea churned my gut. Mitch could have had a good reason, an innocent reason, to be burgling Ham's cottage. But why then, had his uncle's ghost driven me away?

CHAPTER 27

Five days later, I stood at the door to my advisor's office and didn't knock. Above me a florescent light flickered. The elevator door creaked open, and three chattering students emerged. The trio ambled down the hall without giving me a glance.

My hand gripped my purse strap. I'd been so certain I was on the right path. *Improve my skills. Get a credential. Start my business.*

Open my heart.

And I *had* opened my heart. I hadn't *thought* I had, but I must have. If I hadn't, the sight of Mitch's pickup that night would have inspired anger or horror, not this sick, disappointed dread.

If I hadn't, I would have called the police to tell them what I'd seen.

Inside Zeke's office, there was a shuffling sound and a soft clunk. I raised my hand and knocked.

"It's open," Zeke called, and I walked inside.

My advisor gave the window behind his desk a last tug closed, rattling the spider plant on the sill. He turned and smiled. "April. It's good to see you. Have a seat." He motioned to the chair in front of his desk.

I sat. The room was cold and damp, as if the window had been open all night, and I repressed a shiver. "So. My thesis."

He pulled a blue and gold tie from the pocket of his suit jacket and dropped it on the desk. "The plan you emailed looks good. I like the angle you've taken. It's fresh, it's original. It'll be a good contribution to the college's body of work."

"Thanks." I should have felt relief. Now I could get started on the actual research and writing. I could finish. But my stomach bunched.

He quirked a brow. "You don't look too excited about it."

"There's been a lot going on," I hedged.

"You don't have to get on this right away. Some people take years to finish their thesis."

My neck tensed, and I gave my head a tiny shake. *Years?* I couldn't afford that. "Not me."

He smiled. "No. That's one of the great things about you. You get things done."

"Then I guess that's my cue to get a move on." I pushed back my chair.

"I didn't mean for you to leave. Relax." He rose and walked around the desk, then sat against it beside me, his thighs straining against the rich fabric of his gray slacks. "Honestly, take a breather. You found a body, you were the victim of a violent crime. You can take some time for yourself."

"Thanks, but I like to work. It keeps my mind off things." Though my mind had rampaged out of control the last few nights.

I'd stayed awake thinking of all the innocent reasons Mitch could have been in Ham's house. I'd told myself the ghost's appearance hadn't been a warning, a way to protect me from the man inside. That I'd misinterpreted it, been tired, been seeing things.

"I get that," he said. "I think the work ethic is generational. I can't tell you how refreshing it's been to have someone my age as a student. Though I have to admit, it's had its challenges too."

"Oh?"

"You push back on me. The younger students don't."

I didn't remember pushing back that much. "I'm sure you deserved it."

He threw back his head and laughed. "And then there's that. What are you doing Friday night?"

"Working on my thesis, probably. No rest for the wicked." No fun, either. But I was long past the time when Friday nights were for parties and dancing.

"We can do better than that. Come out with me."

Oh. He was hitting on me. Yes, he was handsome and intelligent. But he was also my advisor. And my last so-called date had been a disaster. "Er, how will the other students feel about that?"

He grinned. "I doubt they'd even notice. Everyone's so self-absorbed these days, or they've got their heads in their phones."

Embarrassed, I rose. "Like I said, there's been a lot going on. I think I need some alone time this week."

"If you change your mind, let me know."

I nodded and left. *Awkward, awkward, awkward.* Had I been rude? Should it matter? He seemed to take the rejection well enough. Maybe he'd just been looking for friendship?

I strode down the hallway, my heels clacking on the linoleum. No. I hadn't been imagining it. He'd been hitting on me, and the fact that I was trying to downplay our conversation was just more proof that I wasn't ready.

It was better if I just steered clear and worked.

My good intentions fell apart at Cornflower Cottage.

In the basement I stared, brush in hand, at the blank canvas. Eventually, I gave that up and climbed the stairs to the dining room, where I switched to staring at my computer screen.

There were words on the screen. Pictures. Video. But they only dulled my senses and left no conscious impression.

A knock at the door startled me from my reverie. Pushing back my chair, I made my way around the table and opened it.

Karin, in navy hiking slacks and a matching jacket, beamed. A thick mist blurred the outlines of the oaks behind her. "Hey. Today's terrible. Want to go for a hike?"

I snorted a laugh. "*Because* it's terrible?"

She hitched up the pack on her back. "Because there's nothing better for shaking off terrible than going into nature, even if that's terrible too. I was thinking of checking out Witch Hill."

I folded my arms and leaned against the open doorframe. *Witch Hill. Of course.*

But... why not? I straightened. "Give me a few minutes to change. I'll meet you at your cottage."

She nodded, turned, and trotted down my porch steps.

I changed quickly into my running gear and a jacket, filled my hobbit tumbler with water, and met her beneath a tree in front of her cottage. Purring, the black cat wended around the ankles of her trail-running shoes.

Karin stretched, rising up on her toes. Without speaking, she walked down the road.

Followed by the cat, weaving in and out of the bracken, we huffed up the round hilltop. The cat vanished into a bush just before we emerged from the mist at the hill's top. A sea of white roiled around out little island. But above us, the sky was a blue ceramic bowl.

Karin jammed her hands on the hips of her hiking pants and wheezed. "That's a view."

The fog rippled like a slow moving ocean. "I'm not sure what I expected to see after all that fog down below," I said.

She glanced over her shoulder at me and grinned. "Clarity?"

I laughed shortly. "I never expect that."

Karin eased the pack off her slim shoulders, reached inside, and unfurled a microfiber blanket onto the dead grass. Dropping onto the blanket, she pulled a bottle of water from her navy pack.

I unscrewed the cap on my black tumbler and took a swig.

She pulled out a paper bag and unfolded its top. Holding it from the base, she shook it invitingly. Something rattled inside. "Trail mix?"

"Don't mind if I do." I sat beside her and grabbed a fistful of mix.

Cold seeped from beneath the blanket and into my bones. And suddenly I was a hobbit on the foggy barrows, and something lay below, something cold and cruel and waiting.

The tumbler fell from my hand. The sound of it striking the earth was unnaturally loud in the stillness of Witch Hill.

Hastily, I bent to retrieve it. Was that where I'd gotten my sense of déjà vu here earlier? From *Lord of the Rings*? But that didn't explain the landscape I'd painted.

"How's your murder investigation going?" Karin asked.

"Not well."

"Who are your suspects?"

"Everyone. Even Mitch benefited from his uncle's death. And... Someone was in Ham's house Tuesday night. I saw a pickup driving away." And Ham was still in the hospital. But at least he was still alive.

"Mitch's pickup?"

I hesitated. "I think so."

"Mitch couldn't have attacked you in the college parking lot though. He was with me that evening."

I met her hazel gaze. "Unless you two are colluding."

"I'm a stranger from California, like you. Why would I collude with a Pennsylvania contractor?"

Ham was from California too. Could he have another connection to Karin? "And we're assuming my mugging is connected to the murder and what happened to Ham. It might not be."

"Oh," she said, "it is."

I wrinkled my nose. "Is that magical intuition talking?"

She smiled and popped trail mix into her mouth. "Not intuition. My knot magic."

"Uh, huh. Oh, yeah, about the new card you left in my mailbox. It sure plays fast and loose with the definition of a spell."

Her smile faded. "You got *The Spell* card? Have you cast a spell recently?"

"How could I?" I snapped, my stomach hardening. "I don't know how."

"Were you around someone who cast a spell?"

"Really?" I asked, exasperated. "How would I know?"

A crow darted from the fog lapping against the hillside. The bird hovered for a long moment. A shudder ran through it, and it plummeted into the fog as if it had been shot.

Karin sighed. "I guess you might not. To answer your question, I can see the energetic connections between people. We fall in love, we're energetically attached. We get angry at someone, we're energetically attached."

"All standard New Age thinking."

She shot me a shrewd look. "Don't discount it. New Age thinking is a syncretization of deeper, older thought. Some of it—not all, but some—is helpful."

I grunted.

"Anyway," she continued, "what most people don't understand is that each attachment is unique. We all have our own energetic signatures."

My brows pulled inward. "And the signature of whoever attacked me in the parking lot is the same as Woodward King's killer?"

"I couldn't say. I'm not that good. But I can tell you that the signature was familiar. I'd seen it before. The attack on you wasn't random. It was by someone you and I both know."

I didn't respond. Again, her proclamation was vague enough to be useless, but tantalizing enough to put me on edge.

"Who else do you suspect?" Karin asked.

"I did suspect that farmer, Ryan Shaffer," I admitted. "He wants to sell his farm to GDF, but unless Woodward King sold his, it was a no-go. Now that Woodward's dead, who knows what will happen? But Ryan has an alibi as well."

She nodded. "Ryan's not our man. He's got some anger in him, but he's not connected to this. And his art's amazing."

I didn't think he was the killer either. "My advisor also stands to benefit from Woodward King's death. And he's been... paying more attention to me than he would a normal student."

Her lips trembled with mirth. "Did he hit on you?"

Heat crept across my cheeks. "Maybe. Yes."

"Well, he's single and you're single, and you're both attractive and share an interest in all things Penn Dutch. His asking you out could have nothing to do with the murder or the attack on Ham."

Or it might have everything to do with it. "He's the one who put me on the trail of the odd hex signs. What haven't you told me about those?"

"As I'm sure you already know, *Hexen* is the word for witches in German. To hex someone means to cast a curse. But what most people call Hex signs are believed to prevent curses—"

"They're just *for nice*." Yes, curse protection made a good story. But when the people who originated the signs tell you what they're for, it made sense to listen.

"I know," Karin said. "But let's go with what most people believe today. The original hex sign we found is like that. Someone painted over the Brotherhood's sigil as a way to block a curse."

"Yeah," I said dryly. "The Brotherhood. They've got their own secret sign and everything. Does your school have one too?"

"Yes." She flopped onto her back and stared at the blue sky. "I'm swimming in clichés, aren't I? I'm a witch with a mystery school, and our school's—humanity's—arch nemesis is a secretive occult organization hidden within—"

"GDF," I finished for her. We were back to her pet conspiracy. But that was how conspiracy theories worked, didn't they? They went round and round in confusing circles, like a snake eating its tail.

"Ham's Global Development Fund," Karin agreed.

"Not Ham's," I said sharply. "He doesn't even work for them directly. Not that I believe your story." I lay down on my back beside her. It was strange seeing blue sky and knowing everyone below could see only gray.

"Of course not," she said. "You'd be a fool to take it at face value. And yet, there's a Brotherhood member here. The energetic cords *they* cast are all uniquely the same. I just can't figure out who our villain is. I also thought it was your advisor for a while."

"Zeke?" My spine ached against the cold ground.

"His interest in magic makes him a suspect, and we've found that intellectuals make the best marks for the Brotherhood. They get so used to believing in their own high priests of academia, they're more vulnerable to buying into the high priests of black magic."

Well, that was just... *totally believable*. "But you said you thought it was Zeke, past tense. You don't think so anymore?"

"Let's say I'm less certain. I don't like that he pointed you toward those hex signs. If he's Brotherhood, then he's probably smelled magic on you like I have. And the Braucher said those signs make you vulnerable. But Ham made a more obvious suspect. His connection to GDF was why I got my cottage so close. And then someone tried to kill him, so it can't be Ham. Have you heard how he's doing?"

I shook my head. "Josh said he'd check in on him." And that had been five days ago. Why hadn't he called? More importantly, why hadn't I called?

"Hm." She cut me a sideways glance. "I didn't think you liked the doctor."

"I don't," I said, flustered. "I mean, why wouldn't I like Josh?"

She laughed. "Because he made you look foolish. You thought you were talking to a living Woodward King that day you found his body in the woods, but you were talking to his ghost."

I let that slide. "I was suspicious of the doctor," I admitted. "I thought he was obscuring the time of death. And he had reason to want Woodward King dead too. Woodward was... friends with the doctor's wife. There could have been an affair, or Doc Zook could have simply believed there was one. And he was on the spot when the body was found. But he wasn't lying about Woodward's time of death. My timing was wrong because I'd seen... something else. And then there's the mayor."

"Ah," Karin said, "yes. Small-town skullduggery. Santiago wanted Woodward to sell out and realize his dreams for bringing Babylon into the twenty-first century. Woodward was in the way. And of course, the mayor's a member of the GDF."

"Which is connected to the occultists."

"They're called a black lodge, actually. But they *are* occultists. The worst kind."

"And your mystery school? Is that the best kind?"

"I'd say it's the difference between doing good and doing bad, but most people in black lodges think they *are* doing good. The difference is black lodges teach people how to manipulate others. Their focus is primarily outward. This makes it easier to control their own members, because the more magic they practice, the more their dark subconscious urges and desires take over. When your conscious attention and intention aren't in the driver's seat, it's easy to be manipulated. The focus of our school starts inward, first to unravel the spells cast on you by yourself and others. To make friends with your subconscious. To recognize how the urges you don't want to admit to are influencing your ability to get what you want. Once you do that, once *you* change, the way you see the world will change, and magic becomes easy, second nature. And we never manipulate others."

Something rustled in the high grasses, and I edged from the sound. It was probably too cold for snakes, but I banged my heel on the ground, hoping to warn whatever it was away.

I rolled to my side and sat up. "Why are you telling me about this black lodge now?"

"Because you're not just involved in the murder. You're involved in what's going on with the lodge."

"No, I'm—"

"The UnTarot cards don't lie, April," she said, her fair brow puckering. "I don't entirely understand how they work either. But the email drip sequence has gone rogue. We set up a certain order for the sends, and instead, it's sending emails and cards in the order it thinks the witches need. *And* it's creating its own cards. We started with twenty-five, but we have fifty-two now. My sister Jayce thinks it will go to fifty-four, but we'll see. The point is, the cards think you're involved. Getting *The Spell* card when you're still a beginner... It's a warning."

I rubbed the hollow at the base of my neck. It had felt like a warning to me too. But I couldn't ignore that Karin was heightening my anxiety, playing on my fears. I couldn't trust her. "And Mitch's uncle had all those occult books in his private library."

She sat up, bracing her weight on her elbow. "Yes. You have to wonder if he knew..." She shook her head. "I haven't seen Mitch lately."

I winced, my chin dropping to my chest. "I told him not to come around anymore." And he hadn't. It had been five days. He was honoring my wishes. So why did I feel so terrible?

"Why?" Karin asked. "Because you saw a pickup that looked like his at Ham's?"

Looked like. I shifted on the cold ground. I couldn't be sure it had been Mitch's pickup. It had been dark, and all I'd seen was a faint outline of truck. "We had a fight. Or he had a fight with Josh." I told her about the scene at the bar.

Karin threw back her head and laughed. "And you told them both off? Fabulous."

I sighed, my heart contracting. "I liked Mitch. You know my grand ideas for what I want in a relationship, but to get what I want... Damaged people don't get that. Messed up people keep getting messed up relationships." I groaned. "Sorry. That was pathetic. I don't know when I became so... self-pitying."

"Yeah," she said, "it was kind of gross."

I huffed a laugh. I'd deserved that.

"On the bright side," Karin said, "it's also probably the most honest thing you've said to me." She sat up and took a sip from her water bottle. Carefully, she screwed on the top and returned it to her backpack. "Look, I'm not a psychologist."

"I know. I didn't mean to treat you like one."

"No, I only meant, take what I have to say with a grain of salt. It just seems... back home, I met a lot of messed up people, my family and me included. And it seems like we all think we're uniquely broken. But we're a lot more alike than we think. We're not unique in our brokenness."

Avoiding my gaze, Karin picked up the paper bag and tucked that into her pack as well. "Whatever you're going through, whatever you've failed at, you're still worthy of love. And that vision of love you shared with me doesn't seem broken. It seems pretty damn perfect to me."

My throat closed. Fog crested the hillside, phantom wisps of white gusting around us. I walked away from her, into the fog.

"Careful," she said sharply. "There's a drop-off on the eastern side."

I stopped and turned. "I thought you said you'd never been here before."

"Did I?"

My eyes narrowed, and she sighed. "I saw it from the barn on the hex sign tour," she said. "You were with me. It's just on the other side of the road."

"So aside from good witch/bad witch rivalry, why do you care about what the Brotherhood's doing here?"

Her jaw tightened. She stood. "Because wherever the Brotherhood goes, people die. Witches die, especially the unprepared ones. Witches like you."

CHAPTER 28

IT HAD ALWAYS TAKEN me a long time to learn the important lessons. Which might have been why I still couldn't bring myself to believe Karin. Not yet. Not until it was too late.

"Is that why you brought me up here?" I motioned toward the fog undulating against Witch Hill. "Because this is my place?"

"Witch Hill is where the *Brauchers* came to dispose of dark spells, isn't it? I wonder if archaeologists dug around here, if they'd find any remnants?" Karin mused.

On impulse, I said, "Can you see them?" I wanted to ask about the ghosts, and if she could see mine. But at the last moment, I changed the question to something else. "See the Braucher's spells?"

"I can see spells, but I don't see anything here. Your ancestors must have known their business. Whatever was once here was taken by the earth. Any curses or illnesses are gone."

No weird mists diverted us as we headed back to town. The cat hadn't returned to Cornflower Cottage ahead of me and wasn't on the porch. I told myself not to worry. The cat knew the woods better than I did. I worried anyway.

But the hike had cleared my head. I sat down to paint in the basement, and soon I entered that flow zone where time stopped and the images just came.

And when I'd finished, I had a hex sign. Not a traditional hex. My pattern was modern, a compass surrounded by moons in their march of phases. The colors were shades of modern blue.

Mine wasn't like Ryan's art though. It was still obviously a hex sign.

"Protection and guidance," I muttered. That was what a compass meant, wasn't it? If I was going to sell my own hex signs, they weren't going to just be "for nice." People wanted more than that. They wanted history. They wanted magic.

I smiled. A week ago, I'd been so sure I had no interest in painting or selling hex signs.

Ambling upstairs for coffee, I discovered the bag was empty. I rummaged through the kitchen cupboards, hoping another guest had left coffee behind. In a bottom drawer, I pulled out a glass jar filled with bottlecaps.

A familiar engine sounded outside. Setting the jar on the granite countertop, I deliberately removed my smock and rolled down the sleeves of my blouse. My phone rang in my pocket, and I answered. "Hello, Mitch."

"I'm calling to apologize for the night at the pub."

My lips pursed. "And you're honoring my wishes by calling instead of coming to the door?"

"I, uh, forgot about your wishes until I'd parked. Should I leave?"

I snorted. "No. Come in." But if he thought he was going to get off the hook with some sort of half-assed apology, he had another think coming.

I met him at the front door. A steady drizzle was falling. The cat lay curled on the porch sofa. I stepped outside, letting the screen door bang shut behind me.

Mitch grimaced. "I was a jackass. I'm sorry. I should have said something to you directly about my concerns instead of going after your date like a jealous teen."

It was as thorough an apology as I hoped to received. Statement of fact. Apology. What he should have done instead.

And it sucked the wind from my sails. "Thank you. I appreciate you saying that." I paused. "And it wasn't a date." Or at least it hadn't felt much like one. "So why'd you do it? Why not just warn me off Babylon's seedier spots?"

"I didn't know you were going to that bar. When I saw you there, I guess I just reacted. And I, uh, seem to have a hard time arguing with women."

"And you assumed any discussion with me would end in an argument?" I straightened. "What BS. And you've argued with me plenty."

"Yeah." He grinned. "I guess we have. My mother had a hot temper, and my ex did too. It was always easier to just let things slide and say nothing."

"Until you lost your temper with someone else?"

Mitch nodded sheepishly. "It's something I'm working on."

"Good, because it's dishonest." That was another lesson I'd learned too late with David. But I'd learned it. Finally. "If you can't tell the person closest to you how you feel, how can you have a real relationship?"

"We can't," he said.

Silence stretched between us.

"Oh," I said. *We*.

He reached for me, cradling my jaw with his broad hand, and my heart thundered in my ears. Gently, he drew me closer. He bent his head to mine, and my knees went weak like they hadn't for years, decades, and he kissed me in a dizzying, delightful swirl.

We broke apart.

"I expect we'll have arguments, you know," I gasped. "We'll both screw things up on a regular basis—or at least I will. And I want you to tell me when I do it, and I want to be able to hear it, because I know it's said with love."

He laughed softly. "Trust me, you won't be the only one messing up."

"But I don't like being told what to do or being treated like a child."

"No one does. No one worth knowing, at least."

He kissed me again. And again. When we broke apart this time, the black cat had discreetly vanished.

"Is that why you came by so late Tuesday night?" I asked. "To apologize?"

His brows drew downward. "After the pub you mean? No, I didn't come to Mt. Gretel. Why? Was someone here?" His grip tightened around my waist.

"Not at my cottage, no," I said slowly. "I saw someone at Ham's. They drove away in a pickup. I thought it was yours."

His jade eyes darkened. "What time was this?"

"Around ten."

He looked toward Ham's shingled cottage. "After the pub, I went to the mayor's house."

Why there? "Wasn't it a little late?"

"Definitely too late. But Santiago and I went to school together. I know his habits. Given the amount of land my uncle's giving to the town, Santiago made time."

"How much land?" I asked, alarmed. "Enough for the facility GDF wants to build?"

"My uncle put stipulations on how the land was to be used."

"Will the town honor it?"

"Santiago will." He cocked his head. "Why do you care?"

Why *did* I care? "I hate to see beautiful things go away, especially when they're replaced with…"

"Ugliness?"

"Yes. Babylon isn't perfect. The town's kind of a—"

"Dump?"

I winced. "Sorry. I can see it wasn't always this way." I rested my head on his chest, enjoying the feel of the hard planes of his muscles. "But the farmland, the rolling landscapes, they're beautiful. I *know* everything changes, but I don't see why this place has to."

"I'm with you. I hated Babylon growing up. Now I can't imagine it gone."

I didn't invite Mitch inside, and he didn't press the issue. It wasn't modesty on my part. But I knew if things went further, chemicals would take over and my common sense would leave the building. And there were good reasons for that not to happen.

I watched his pickup drive off in the darkness. And I tried to remember if it was the same silhouette I'd seen Tuesday night at Ham's.

I hesitated in front of the gleaming nameplate on Zeke's office door. My reflection wavered in the brass. Murmured voices inside the office rose and fell.

I didn't have an appointment, and I checked my watch. I could have—should have— called ahead or even emailed. But I was in too much of a hurry. Now that I'd made my decision, I wanted it over with and to move on.

I knocked. A florescent light flickered in the college's white-tile ceiling.

After a moment, a stocky man in flannels and baggy jeans opened the door. He nodded hello, his ruddy face pleasant, and strode past.

I edged the door wider. "Zeke?"

"April." My advisor rose from behind his cluttered wooden desk. The lamp above his desk shimmered golden in his hair. "I wasn't expecting you," he said, his voice neutral.

I swallowed. Considering what I was about to tell him, I'd have preferred a disapproving frown. The spider plants on the sill drooped. Outside the window, crimson leaves fluttered from the maple to the wide lawn.

"I know," I said. "I'm sorry to show up like this. But I wanted to tell you in person. I'm dropping out of the program."

Zeke's chiseled jaw sagged. He rose and swiftly came around the cluttered, wooden desk. "But I approved your thesis topic. Did you want to write about something else?" He flushed. "Was it because of the other day?"

"No. It's because I realized I was going for this degree for the wrong reasons, for the credential. And I don't need one to open my business."

"What business?"

My glance darted toward the bookcase. Why had I hid the truth for so long? My secrecy seemed stupid and petty now. "I'm starting up a Penn Dutch home decor store selling my own designs. It was silly to want a credential. I think it was just a crutch, a way to delay actually taking the leap."

"That's..." Zeke shook his head. "I had no idea. I wish you'd told me earlier."

"I wish I had too. I wasted your time, and I'm sorry."

"You didn't waste my time. Your exploratory research was fascinating. I'm just... If you'd told me, I would have given you the same advice. You don't need a folk art degree for what you want. What are you going to do now?"

"Take the money I would have used on the rest of this degree and put it toward starting my business."

"Where?" Zeke sat against the desk, his legs braced wide.

"I'm not sure." I'd assumed I'd return home. But my apartment in California had never felt like home, just a temporary place to live.

"You could start something here," he said with a hopeful note. "Be closer to Penn Dutch country."

"Maybe. I'd offer you my research notes on those hex signs, but I suspect you're already ahead of me."

He ducked his head and clawed a hand through his gold-streaked hair. "I wouldn't say that."

I raised an eyebrow. "Zeke. Confess. You're behind the strange hex signs in the woods."

Zeke paled. "That's—"

"It was all too pat. You didn't learn about the signs from Karin, but you knew their locations. The farmer you sent me to, Ryan, obviously hadn't painted them. They were too crude. But whoever painted over the signs had to know something about sacred geometry, someone like you. I don't think you did it for something new to publish on your own. Unless you were planning on jumping in on my dissertation later?"

His brown eyes widened. "Of course not."

"So it *was* you." As much as I usually enjoyed being right, disappointment heavied my chest. But had he created that creepy sigil beneath the signs?

He flushed. "Not exactly. It was a friend of mine."

"The man I just saw leaving?" I hazarded. He hadn't looked like a student or a professor.

Zeke nodded. "You may have seen his barn. It's got half a dozen hex signs on it. It's near Witch Hill, across the street from Doc Zook's house."

I'd been there with Karin. I'd *photographed* that ramshackle barn. I'd been so close to the hex painter, and I nearly laughed at the thought.

"He came to me with photos of strange signs in the woods," he continued. "Told me they had a bad feel to them. He suspected witchcraft and wanted to know what to do. Of course telling him he was being superstitious wasn't going to help. And he knew enough about *Braucherei* to know he couldn't just destroy the signs—any spell would leak all over. I wanted to set his mind at ease, so I gave him the Metatron's Cube pattern to paint over them." He shrugged. "It seemed harmless."

My muscles relaxed. I believed him. My advisor wasn't responsible for...whatever that sigil had meant—the sigil that disturbed me, even now. "And then he found more of those odd signs."

"Yeah."

"So why'd you put me on the trail of those signs? You must have known there was a risk I'd figure out the truth." The fact that he'd obviously considered that risk to be low was just insulting.

"I felt bad for you," Zeke said. "You were obviously struggling and... I guess I had a little crush on you too. I wanted you to succeed."

My cheeks warmed. "I'm flattered." *And still annoyed.* "But... I'm seeing Mitch Black."

"Ah. Well." He laid a hand against his chest. "Then congratulations are in order, I hope?"

Hope. The emotion flickered, fragile, in my chest. "I hope so too. Take care." I turned and walked out the door.

SUBJECT: CHANGE

SEEKER:

By now, you've begun to experience change, and that can be unsettling. This is where many seekers leave the school. They find the changes too destabilizing. It's easier and more comfortable to revert to their own ways and habits.

We won't give you advice on whether to stay or go. But before you decide, we'd ask you to consider not just what you're giving up, but what you're moving toward.

In order to move ourselves from mundane to magical, we need to change ourselves. We need to become magical people—witches.

This is a big ask.

Most people don't change because it's hard. Habits must be broken. Old beliefs and ways of seeing the world must be discarded. New habits and beliefs must be adopted. Practice is necessary.

It isn't easy. In fact, it can be overwhelming.

This is why we've broken the process into bite-sized tasks, repeated over time. When we start small, we don't get overwhelmed. We grow more confident with our small successes. And when we repeat these changes on a daily basis, the effects compound over time. They become habit. Our skills grow subtly but substantially. And one day, we will look back and realize we weren't the person we were. Our way of being has changed and our world has changed around us in response. We will see the magic in the world and in ourselves, and we will wield it easily with love and joy. Your ability to create change and to enjoy the changed world that you create is your source of power.

The incantations, the crystals, the candles, are all tools to focus our desires and intentions to make magic. But without the mental and spiritual foundation for the work, they won't do much. To make magic, first we must become witches.

But let's look at change from another angle. It's inevitable that the world will change around us. Relationships change. People more rarely. Resistance to this external change is often really an attachment to the status quo—to holding on to what we think *should* be rather than what *is*. In its positive form, it inspires us to change ourselves or to inspire change in the outer world. In its negative form, it causes needless suffering. These types of attachments will cloud your magic and keep you from moving on to a better situation.

What would happen if you let go of your desire to change a situation that you know, deep down, is really out of your control—or out of your right to control? (Dark magicians see no difference between what they want to control and what they have a right to control).

Journal on your next card, *Change*. On the PDF linked to the below QR code (scan or click the QR code to access it), write the situation that you care deeply about on the waxing moon. Contemplate how your attachment to a certain outcome is causing you to suffer.

Then write about the situation in the incantation below. For the next week, say it to yourself throughout the day. When the week is done, let it go and promise to stop thinking about the situation.

[QR code]

SCAN ME

And now, here is your next UnTarot card:

CHANGE

Change. The inevitable. Eternity. Evolution.

Nothing is permanent. The universe is eternally changing, and we need to evolve as well. Because if we stop growing, we're no longer *living*. We die inside.

But change can be stressful. Change means we're stepping into something new and leaving something old behind. But if we focus on the excitement of what we're becoming, if we can learn to be in the present, the process can be less traumatic.

The symbols:

Spirals represent the eternally changing nature of the universe. The fossil's counterclockwise spiral (from inside out) represents letting go to allow for creation. The spiral is also a natural fractal pattern, and spending time looking at fractals has been shown to significantly reduce stress, activating the part of the brain that helps regulate emotions. This spiral fossil reminds us that we can relax even as change is occurring.

Heather, another symbol of change, sprouts in the foreground of the card. In the background is a ruin, reminding us that everything ends.

The questions:

What ideas and habits do you need to evolve? How can you be present with change?

I Accept This Change

I accept _____ and trust everything is unfolding as it should. I will not try to influence it.

CHAPTER 29

My meeting with Zeke had left me unsettled. In search of retail therapy and comfort food, I drove downtown, past papered windows to the Babylon farmer's market, a two-story brick building in the center of town.

It was not comforting. It was depressing.

Rough-looking men lounged beneath the clock in the parking lot. Inside, the cavernous hall crisscrossed with steal beams was only half full of vendors behind red-painted stands. At this hour, the market should have been full of shoppers.

The building must have once been charming, the stalls once full. Comparing that prosperous past to Babylon's present made the day all the more bitter.

I bought meat and cheese and mustards, bypassed the candy stall, and hesitated at a bakery stall staffed by Mennonite girls in bonnets and long, pastel dresses.

"April?" Josh asked from behind me, and I turned. The doctor wore his long black coat. Beneath his hat brim, his somber, blue-gray eyes seemed resigned.

"Oh, hi." I jammed my hand in the pocket of my blazer and touched the cool metal of my keychain's hobbit door.

"I'm glad I ran into you," he said. "I wanted to apologize again for the other night."

"It wasn't your fault the evening was cut short by a car accident. Was the man okay?"

The doctor shook his head. "He didn't make it."

Briefly, I squeezed my eyes shut. *Just like David.* "I'm sorry."

"And I'm afraid I have more bad news. Ham's still in a coma. It's not looking good."

My heart plunged. *Dammit*. I'd hoped… But not all wishes came true.

"I'm ashamed I lost my temper with Mitch," Josh continued. "It wasn't a good look. I'm sorry you saw me at my worst."

"I'm glad you haven't seen me at mine." I smiled briefly. I was still embarrassed about moping to Karin. Maybe I could blame witchcraft. "But thank you for saying that."

He glanced around the market. "So you found our town's latest failure."

A silver-haired woman in a threadbare sweater clutched a plastic bag to her chest and scuttled past.

"It does seem a little… empty," I admitted.

"It wasn't always this way. For about two years it was the place to shop and run into friends."

"What happened?" The location was… okay, not ideal, but only because the entire downtown had deteriorated. Which I guessed answered my own question.

He shrugged. "People got tired of coming downtown. And can you blame them? I was surprised the market lasted as long as it did."

I stared down an empty aisle. The death spiral. Wasn't that what they called it? When crime scared away the customers, and then businesses closed and there was even less reason for people to come to town to shop.

Woodward King's dream of revitalization seemed even farther out of reach, and yet… Crime could be curtailed. And the infrastructure was here. There was still an old-fashioned appeal beneath the grime and decay.

The keychain turned slippery, and I withdrew my hand from my pocket. "What are you doing at the market?"

"My offices are on the other side of the building. I prefer walking through the market to stepping over vagrants." He shot me a quick smile. "Sorry. That must sound harsh. But there's only so much a person can take when your home's falling apart."

"I wonder if that GDF facility *could* turn things around," I said quietly. But turn them to what?

"At least Ham's accident hasn't derailed GDF."

"What?" I hugged my bags close to my chest. "It hasn't?"

"They sent someone else to take Ham's place in negotiations. I talked to her yesterday."

A bag slipped, and I juggled it before it could fall. "But I thought the farmers didn't want to sell?"

"Eminent domain," he said. "The local government will take the property, compensate the farmers, and sell it on to GDF."

"The mayor can do that?" I asked, aghast. Even if the facility helped the town, it didn't seem right to force people to sell.

"It's done all the time for the public good."

"But... How can they be sure it *is* a public good?"

He raised a Byronic brow. "I thought you said the facility could turn things around?"

"It might. I don't know. I hate to see the town dying, but the farms, the rural character, are what make Babylon special. There are other towns nearby that have kept their character, like Lititz. They're doing well with tourism."

"You sound like Woodward King."

"Maybe because he haunts me," I muttered.

Glasses crashed, and there was a feminine curse. We glanced toward the noise, but whatever had fallen was hidden behind the red-painted stalls.

"What were you saying about being haunted?" the doctor asked, face grave.

I blew out my breath. "Do you believe in ghosts?"

He scratched his neat beard. "I think there's a lot we can't explain," he said, surprising me. "I wouldn't discount them."

I braced an elbow against the bakery stall's high counter. "Woodward... Well he seems to be haunting my cottage," I blurted. "Or maybe he's just haunting me."

"What exactly do you mean by haunting?"

"I've seen his ghost. And yes, I know how that sounds. But it wasn't a trick of the light. He was there in his wingchair for a good ten seconds at least. Even the cat saw him."

The doctor started. "That's... disconcerting. Has the ghost tried to communicate?"

I rolled my eyes. "It's *all* he's been doing. Thanks for not making me feel crazy admitting it." I'd expected cynicism and wouldn't have blamed him if he had doubted. His reaction was a refreshing surprise.

Josh smiled, and the expression transformed him. "I've never met anyone less crazy."

"Wait until you hear my next question." I hesitated. "You haven't happened to find any old... remnants of magic on your property, have you? Someone told me *Brauchers* discarded their spells at Witch Hill and your house is right beneath it, isn't it?"

"Oh, yeah," he said. "I'm finding old bottles and nails all the time. Do you want one?"

Did I? They were curiosities, certainly. They'd probably sell well in my future shop. But the bottles had been discarded there for a reason. I tugged my jacket more firmly into place. "No, I don't think so. But thanks."

"Look, how would you feel about a do-over on our date? I can check out your cottage for ghosts."

"I can't, but thanks." I cleared my throat. "The thing is, today I quit my masters program. I have to figure out how to start my business sooner rather than later."

He cocked his head. "Are congratulations in order?"

"I'm not sure yet. It could be a giant mistake. But I don't think it will be."

"Congratulations then." Josh nodded and strode away before I could tell him about Mitch.

Someone brushed my arm, and I glanced over my shoulder. Karin's *Braucher* joked at the bakery stand with a Mennonite girl. The old lady bought a soft pretzel and took a bite.

"*Sis en shaynah dawk, gell?*" the *Braucher* asked.

I smiled. "Yes, it *is* a nice day," I replied in English.

Her blue eyes twinkled. "You should try the pretzels here. They're best with melted butter."

"Ha!" I pointed. "I *knew* you spoke English. You really gave my friend a hard time."

The tiny woman shrugged. "People don't appreciate knowledge unless they work for it, especially my kind of knowledge. And you? I hear you've given up on your degree."

I laughed. "You have sharp ears."

"And eyes." She nodded toward the doctor's departing back. "An unhappy man. Babylon is full of them."

"At least he's trying to make things better."

"Is he?" she said flatly.

I shifted my weight, and a bag full of jars banged against my thigh. "By bringing the new agricultural facility to town."

"Mm. Everyone's trying to make things better. The doctor, your boyfriend Mitch—"

"How do you know about my, er, friend Mitch?"

She grinned. "I hear a lot of things. I hear he's been buying up derelict properties and restoring them. But I don't think he'll be selling them to farmers."

I shifted my weight on the cold, concrete floor. "Who will he be selling them to?"

"City folk looking for more space than they could afford in the city, I imagine. It'll change things." She nodded. "The world changes whether we like it or not. We just have to hope the changes are for the better." She bit into her pretzel and walked away.

I stared after the older woman, my hands damp on the plastic bags with my purchases. Mitch had been buying up old properties? He hadn't mentioned that. Not that he had to tell me his investing plans.

But after buying a pretzel (with butter) I left the market, thoughtful. I finished the pretzel in my car. And instead of returning to Cornflower Cottage, I drove to Babylon's brick town hall.

As I pulled into the parking lot, a black pickup pulled out driven by the doctor. In the passenger seat, the mayor gestured animatedly. Josh shook his head, turned the wheel, and accelerated onto the street.

They'd seemed not to notice me, and I'm ashamed to say, I felt relief.

Their departure was also my good luck, because there was only one empty visitor spot in the lot, the spot the pickup had just abandoned. I zipped into it, locked up, and found my way to the records department, a gloomy basement room with pinging florescent lights.

A gray-haired clerk directed me to a bank of ancient computers in carrells for visitors. "Looking is free. To print, there's a fee." The bored-looking woman pointed at a credit card device and ambled back to her steel desk.

I sat at a carrell, took a deep breath, and searched for Mitchell Black's name. A list of records appeared, and my insides rolled.

The *Braucher* had been right. Mitch had been buying up derelict properties for a song all over Babylon. His investment seemed risky in the dying town. Unless he knew something I didn't...

I gnawed my bottom lip. There wasn't anything nefarious about the purchases that I could see.

But I thought back to that witchcraft booklet someone (Woodward King?) had marked up. He'd underlined a section on a land dispute being the root cause of a murder. It seemed... too on the nose.

Then I looked up Woodward King. He'd owned huge swathes of farmland on the outskirts of town, as well as cottages in Mt. Gretel and a few buildings in Babylon proper.

Yellow flags marked the farmland sites, and I clicked on the links. They took me to rezoning notifications. Six months ago, his farmland had been rezoned from agricultural to mixed use, including industrial.

I sat back in the metal and plastic chair, and it rocked slightly, squeaking beneath my weight. Agriculture was still allowed on the land, so the change wouldn't affect his current farming tenants.

Had King even known about the rezoning? I shifted. He *must* have known. By all accounts, he was active in town politics.

And the mayor most certainly would have known. I drummed my fingers on the narrow table.

Again, did it matter? The rezoning would make it easier for whoever got the property to do what they wanted with it. It probably increased his property's value. It certainly made it easier for GDF.

But if the town was going ahead with eminent domain and taking the land, it was unlikely that increase in value would reflect the price King's estate received. From what I'd heard of eminent domain, the property owners were typically low-balled.

And why not? They had little to no recourse.

So what would happen? The land would be taken. The industrial facility would be built. The local economy would hopefully be improved—more wage earners spending their hard-earned money.

And that would be good news for Babylon, and for the owner of all those buildings in town. Unless Karin was right. Unless a cabal of dark magicians really was behind GDF. How would *that* affect the town?

I reached into my pocket and scraped the pad of my thumb over the hobbit door. Mitch's investments might have been smarter than they looked.

Briefly, I closed my eyes. *Trust, but verify.*

I didn't print anything out at town hall, and I returned to Cornflower Cottage. With trembling fingers, I pulled another UnTarot card from the blue metal mailbox.

SUBJECT: FAITH

SEEKER:

Congratulations on your quick progress! Your next card is *Faith*.

Faith and hope aren't the same, but they complement each other, and both grow from the roots of gratitude, presence, and love. They're both practices, mindsets, muscles to be exercised.

Hope is future-oriented. It allows for potential and the possibility. Faith works in the present. When doubt threatens our present potential, it is faith that keeps us going. Change requires hope and faith.

The attached faith practice is ongoing (scan the QR code below, or if you're reading this on a screen, click the QR code). When you don't get what you want, note it down with the date. When you realize how not getting what you wanted actually made way for what you needed, write that and the date down on the line across from it. Over time, you will come to have more faith, as you realize the universe really is working in your favor.

SCAN ME

FAITH

Faith. Conviction. Hope.

Faith is a tricky thing. Too much, and you can be made a fool of. Too little, and you can't form meaningful bonds with others. The same is true of faith in magic. You need faith in the magic for it to work. But blind faith can make you credulous.

True faith isn't blind or closeminded. It's a decision to act with trust. Like love, faith is a practice, and it takes courage. But faith and hope and love also give us the courage to keep going and to stay in the game. And faith in something higher than us gives us humility—it keeps us from developing God complexes, a real threat to people with magic and other forms of power.

Have faith that life has meaning, and that we're all a part of that meaning.

The symbols:

The cairn is an old symbol of faith, something that guides us along lesser-used trails. In the background, two women swing in a dance, having faith that each will hold the other up.

The questions:

Where have you put your faith? Is it time to trust?

Faith: the Practice

The time I didn't get what I wanted.

_____
_____
_____
_____
_____
_____
_____

But I got what I needed.

_____
_____
_____
_____
_____
_____
_____

The Spell:

My heart overflows with love and gratitude, and my attention is focused on the present. No matter what happens, I know the universe has my back.

CHAPTER 30

SILVERY SUNLIGHT STREAMED THROUGH the gaps in my bedroom's thin curtains when I awoke the next morning. Stretching beneath the warm covers, I paused, arms above my head. I didn't feel my ghosts.

I felt... free.

I knew where I had to go and what I had to do. And with my path clear before me, nothing felt urgent. But I dragged myself from bed and dressed in comfy sweats and warm socks.

A thick morning mist had crept through the woods and pressed against the cottage. The lights were off in the cottages next door. I was alone on an island in the fog, but I didn't feel lonely.

In the living room, I curled up on the leather couch with *The Fellowship*. Frodo had just awakened in Rivendell after being injured in a dire pursuit by the servants of the enemy.

The wizard sat by his bedside, keeping watch. It was ten o'clock on October 24th, and they were in the house of...

My gaze drifted to the black clock on the bookcase. Its minute hand clicked forward. Ten o'clock. And today was October 24th...

I frowned and shook myself. *Coincidence.*

I kept reading. Frodo was so certain he'd reached safety and the end of his adventure. But nowhere was safe, not for long, and his trials were just beginning...

Something thudded against the window, and my head jerked up. A bluebird fluttered against the glass. After three more bangs against the window, the bird flew off.

After I finished the chapter, I rose, stretched, and descended the stairs to the walkout basement. My sense of frantic do-*something* might have evaporated, but projects awaited.

I painted. Entering the flow state, I painted another compass hex sign and then painted miniature versions on the bottlecaps I'd found in the kitchen.

"April?" Mitch asked.

I started and dropped a bottlecap. It rolled beneath the card table.

Mitch stood at the base of the stairs in a flannel shirt and jeans, his brandy hair in damp coils against his neck. The light outside had faded. The cat had come to join me, curled in front of a space heater, and I hadn't noticed.

"What time is it?" I asked, stooping to retrieve the bottlecap.

"Five o'clock," Mitch said. "The door was open. I knocked, but you didn't seem to hear me, so..."

I wiped my hands on my smock. "It's fine. I'm glad you came inside."

Astonished, I studied the rows of bottlecap hex signs lining the table. How had I painted so many, so quickly?

"What were you saying when I came in?" he asked. "It sounded like Penn Dutch."

"Was I talking to myself?" I didn't usually. *Weird.* "I guess I was so absorbed in my work, I wasn't paying attention."

"What are these?" He moved closer to the card table.

I handed him one of the dry bottlecaps. "Hex sign charms."

He grinned. "Are you a *Braucher* now?"

"Only genetically." And that didn't seem to be worth much. Unless... did *Brauchers* see spirits? I hadn't heard that was one of their talents, but there was a lot I didn't know. "I hope you don't mind me using the bottlecaps. I found them in a kitchen cabinet."

He shrugged and made to hand me the cap. "I don't need 'em."

"Keep it." I curled his fingers around the charm. "For good luck."

Mitch smiled down at me. "I think I've got all the good luck I need." But he slid the charm into the front pocket of his jeans.

Mitch and I lounged on the back porch with the cat. Bundled in sweaters, we watched barbecue smoke coil from my cottage's grill in the sloping backyard, and I told him about yesterday.

Mitch swigged his beer and chuckled. "I haven't seen Zeke surprised in a long time. And he actually admitted to setting you up with those hex signs?"

"It wasn't exactly a set-up. I think he believed he was helping."

On the railing, the cat stopped licking her paws. Her golden gaze bored into me.

He snorted. "Until it came out that Zeke was behind everything. No one would believe you didn't know."

I grimaced. I wanted to believe that Zeke had been genuine, that my advisor just hadn't thought that far ahead. But in a way it didn't matter. I'd made my decision, and I was done trying to prove my worthiness with a degree.

"So what next?" Mitch asked.

"Next I start implementing my business plan." I burrowed closer against his side, enjoying the feel of his hard warmth.

His brows drew downward. "You've already got a business plan?"

"I've had it for years. I mean, I've had to do some updates. But... I have friends with small businesses who helped me." They'd told me not to bother with my art degree, but I hadn't listened.

My insecurity had not protected me from failure. It had just held me back from success.

"Why *were* you so set on getting that art degree?" Mitch asked.

"Cowardice," I admitted. "It allowed me to delay getting started and taking any real risk." And starting a retail business was a big risk.

Rising, he walked down the porch steps to the barbecue and checked our burgers. Mitch looked way too smug when he returned and dropped onto the sofa.

"I do not like that look at all," I said, laughing.

"What look?"

"A man with a secret. What are you up to now?"

"I figured out a way to make sure the town doesn't go back on their word about the use of my uncle's land. Well, my lawyer did. The farmers will be able to stay. No eminent domain."

"The mayor agreed to that?" I tugged on my ear.

"Yep. I talked to Santiago yesterday afternoon. He's agreed there are better ways to develop Babylon."

"Oh?"

"I've been buying up and converting derelict buildings. It's been slow going, but I've found a group of private investors who are interested. With their funds, it'll speed things up."

Mitch didn't have to tell me about his properties, but I was glad he had. But uncertainty followed on relief's heels, and lightly, I bit my bottom lip. "So you're talking about... gentrification?"

He frowned. "I hope so. Babylon either gets worse or it gets better. I want better. It's not like I'm driving people out. I'm buying empty buildings."

I nodded, uneasy. An argument could be made that rising property values *would* drive people out.

But people had been driven out when the town had fallen on hard times too. And if Babylon could become a place where people wanted to work and live again, maybe that would create more job opportunities. But nothing was certain. Nothing was easy.

And that was the nature of the world. It was constantly changing, and we could just try to ensure those changes were for the better.

Change. Briefly, I closed my eyes. *That card.*

"What's wrong?" He sat beside me on the lumpy sofa.

I smiled. "Nothing. But you may have thwarted part of my plans."

"Oh?" He looped a muscular arm around my shoulders and pulled me closer.

The black cat sneezed and leapt lithely from the railing. She prowled down the stairs toward the smells wafting from the barbecue.

"I was hoping to sell your furniture in my shop," I said, keeping an eye on the cat. "But it sounds like you'll be too busy for furniture making."

"I'd *rather* be making furniture than working as a contractor. Maybe someday. But for now, I'm happy to keep my passion as a hobby." He leaned his head back and studied the porch's beamed roof. Straightening, he met my gaze. "What about you? Are you sure about this?"

"No. But I'm sure I have to move forward." I swallowed. And if this was going to work between Mitch and me, I had to be honest.

"My marriage with David wasn't good," I continued. "He wasn't a bad person, we just... A lot of the problem was me. I didn't have the guts to tell him what I thought, to tell him what I was feeling when those feelings were difficult. And since he wasn't a mind reader, it amounted to a lie. And even at the end, I was too... I was thinking of asking for a divorce when he died."

But I hadn't even had the guts to ask for that. "It seemed easier to run away than try to fix things," I continued. "And then... I lost my chance. It wasn't until he was gone that I started realizing my role in things, what mistakes I'd made."

And that was it. Everything. My shame, my regrets, my mistakes.

Mitch's gaze remained fixed on the barbecue. His profile could have been chiseled in granite, his close-cropped beard a craggy façade.

My throat tightened. Had I said too much?

He exhaled heavily. "So. If you were a different person, maybe you could have worked things out. But you weren't a different person."

I laughed mirthlessly. "It took David's death to *make* me a different person. And I'm still not sure... I'm afraid I'll make the same mistakes." But I hadn't been making them lately. Had I changed that much?

Mitch lowered his head. "You're not the only one. I didn't know how to confront my ex-wife, Rachel. So I didn't. And she went to someone else for connection. Or for... whatever. I guess you don't know what you don't k now."

I sighed. So she *had* taken comfort with the doctor. And I didn't feel indignant about that. I felt sad.

"I need to check those burgers." Mitch ambled down the porch steps. At the bottom, he jerked to a stop. Something in the rigidity of his figure, in the strange stillness of his form, prickled the hair on the back of my neck.

A greasy chill slithered up my spine. "Something wrong?"

A shudder ran through his muscular frame.

And then I saw it. The fog didn't drift, didn't swirl, didn't move. The woods had gone silent. Not a bird chirped. Not a leaf rustled.

I sucked in a breath. A tattered gold leaf hung suspended in the air, floating free and unmoving.

Unreasoning fear gripped my throat. I leapt off the sofa. "Mitch?" A bitter chill wafted across my skin.

He turned, his movements jerky. His fists clenched. "Run."

"What?" The air compressed, my breaths turning shallow.

He climbed the first step and swayed. "Run," he said, his voice hoarse.

I stepped backward. "Mitch, what's going on?"

His neck muscles corded. His face spasmed, and then it wasn't his face. It was someone else—some*thing* else, something cruel, something demonic.

I pivoted to run and squeaked a shocked gasp.

Woodward King stood between me and the porch door. The ghost was here, fully formed. No mists or half-formed shadows now. King was a beast of a man, tall and hulking, his craggy face gray with death, his eyes bottomless sockets.

And he didn't scare me half as much as what was behind me.

Jolting forward, I raced through the ghost. The impact of our connection was a shock of Arctic water, but I didn't stop. I wrenched open the door and ran inside. I locked the porch door behind me and backed through the living room.

The back of my thigh struck the dining table. The air was so tight I dizzied.

It was a spell. It had to be. That wasn't Mitch. My chest compressed. What had happened to him?

Karin. She was the witch. She would know. She could help.

I raced to the cottage's front door and yanked it open. The back porch door splintered, glass crashing, wood snapping.

I glanced over my shoulder. His uncle's ghost grappled with something.

A desolate shriek raised the hair on my arms. It wailed on and on, and I was screaming too, anything to block that awful, disembodied sound. And I ran.

CHAPTER 31

I HAVE A RECURRING dream where I'm running from something—a demon, a monster, a mob—and I can't get anywhere. My legs are lead weights. Familiar streets twist and turn in unfamiliar ways. And the demon is always there, always behind me, always too close.

The fog played the same eerie tricks on me that night. But it wasn't only the fog. It was the magic. It twined around me, tightening, teasing the air from my burning lungs.

I ran across the now unfamiliar hillside and banged on the door to Karin's cottage. No one answered. The gothic cottage was dark. In her empty driveway, a masculine figure loomed from the mist.

Dizzily, I retreated, shaking my head. *Mitch?* It had to be, but the shape seemed wrong.

I bolted down her porch stairs and kept running, stumbling more than once before my feet found the smooth street. Footsteps slapped the pavement, echoing my frantic steps. I headed downhill, toward the highway, past abandoned cottages, emptied for the season.

I passed the big yellow meeting house. The road would fork in a hundred feet, and the highway would be there.

Except the road didn't fork. It bent back on itself, taking me back toward the horror that had been Mitch. My breath rasped in and out. What had they done to him?

I skidded down a path between two dark cottages and hit another stretch of road. A heavy body crashed through the bushes. I ran as fast as I dared on the fog-slick pavement, a stitch of fear stabbing my ribs.

And the streets kept turning. In the mist, the Queen Anne cottages in their Gothic strangeness appeared and vanished just as quickly.

My limbs moved jerkily. Where was the damned highway? There would be cars there and the pizza parlor. It would be open at this hour, with people, life, normalcy.

The oaks fell away, the slope flattening, and I slowed, relieved. *The highway.*

A gust of wind parted the mist, exposing a mercury expanse of lake. Horrified, I stumbled to a halt. It was impossible. How could I have crossed the highway and not known it?

The footsteps behind me grew louder. I darted to the right. The pizza parlor was west of the lake, down the highway. I would *have* to connect with it soon.

My lungs burned, but the dryness in my mouth had nothing to do with this wild race. I was getting nowhere. The lakeshore went on and on, and that was impossible, because as terrified as I was, I knew I wasn't running in circles.

My fingernails bit my palms. By now, I should have been past the lake. The footsteps behind me grew louder. I could hear Mitch's furious panting.

He was too close. I wouldn't make it.

Blood pounding at the front of my skull, I darted through a break in the brush. Slender branches whipped my face.

I raced down an unfamiliar trail. But *everything* seemed unfamiliar. It was like that day on Witch Hill, when Ham and I had gotten turned around.

Branches cracked behind me. *Like that day on Witch Hill...*

I stopped and dropped to a crouch. Heart hammering, I felt for the ground in front of my sneakers.

There wasn't any, and I swayed, lightheaded. Lowering myself to my knees, I leaned forward, and the mist thinned. Beneath me, smoke spiraled from a chimney in a black-shingled roof. *The doctor's house.*

I blinked rapidly, my eyes stinging. I was on Witch Hill. And I was being driven over the cliff to Josh's house.

Josh, who had so many reasons to hate Babylon and the people in it. Josh, who'd been on the spot when Woodward King's body had been discovered. Josh, who'd been chatting with the mayor this morning after Mitch had wrangled a way to keep the development from happening. Josh, who'd been so helpful and curious about what I knew.

My head swam. It had always been the doctor.

"April?" Josh shouted. "Is that you?"

My muscles tightened, contracting, and I tried to make myself smaller.

And this strange mist, the changing roads... Was he some sort of magician too? I shook my head, still unwilling to believe. I'd just gotten turned around, that was all.

But how had I missed the highway? And what had come over Mitch? Because *something* had happened to him. I'd felt it, *seen* it.

"April?"

My fingers dug into the hard hillside, small stones scraping my flesh. And that man who'd been hit by the car, that look Josh had given him before he'd been killed... Had that been a curse? Was it possible Josh had caused the accident?

My thoughts fractured, impossibilities, conspiracies, madness tumbling together.

"It *is* you," Josh said, and I stood.

He waited in his long, black undertaker's coat, droplets of fog dampening his beard. And he looked... sane, normal, despairing.

Maybe I was the one who'd gone insane. I glanced over my shoulder. The roof beneath was a dark shore in the sea of white and too, too far away.

"What are you doing up here?" he asked.

"Stop." My voice shook. "What did you do to Mitch?"

"Did something happen to Mitch?"

"Stop it," I screamed. But the fog smothered the sound. My chest heaved.

"Stop what, April?"

"You're a member of that black lodge." My shoulders collapsed, my muscles slackening. I couldn't escape. I was powerless. "It's been you all the time."

"You know about the Brotherhood?" Josh lowered his head. "I'm sorry to hear that. How did you find out?"

"You've been leaving your damn symbols all over the woods," I sputtered, motioning roughly.

"You made that connection," he said tonelessly, his face expressionless.

"*Why*? Why is that factory so important to you?"

He shrugged. "Because the people I work for want it, and then this town and others will come to an end."

"What?" I raked a hand through my hair, damp with fog and sweat. "GDF's new factory was supposed to save Babylon."

"Only if you think a town is just a collection of buildings." He looked away. "Those will grow. More people will come. But the spirit of the place, of what Babylon was, will die. And it's time, April. Time for us to let it go and let something new take its place."

I swallowed. "Something...?"

"They've told me it will be modern." His head drooped. "More in keeping with the new man, whoever that is. Between us, I doubt the new man will be an improvement over the old."

Josh wasn't insane, I realized. He'd lost all hope, all faith, and that was somehow worse than lunacy. "That's why you killed Woodward King. You killed him, then took a trail through the woods to your car and doubled back to be on the scene when the sheriff needed a coroner."

"Close. I had to change my clothes. All that blood... But King's ending was quick. I was careful of that."

"I guess as a doctor, you knew exactly what vein to cut so he'd bleed out. Woodward suspected your partnership with the GDF, didn't he? He knew they were connected to the Brotherhood. That was why his library was filled with new books on the occult."

The fog twisted, phantoms forming and spiraling away. The air drew closer, tighter, and I struggled for breath.

"He warned me about the GDF's connection to the Brotherhood," Josh said. "He was intelligent, but he couldn't see what was right in front of him. I had to stop him."

"And me? You broke into my cottage." I stabbed a finger at him. "You cut your head banging into that ledge over my stairs. You wore a hat to hide it until you couldn't get away with it anymore."

He rubbed the spot. "Yeah. I was surprised you didn't notice sooner."

"Why? Why me?"

"Because you saw Woodward. You saw his ghost. He spoke to you on the trail, and I knew it was a matter of time before he told you everything. You have the gift. I thought I could scare you off, but you didn't scare. I saw you leaving the library and thought..."

Josh looked away. "Well. And then I thought I'd exaggerated the threat you posed. But you told me he was still haunting you."

I felt the blood drain from my face. "And so you came tonight. What did you do to Mitch?"

His smile was wintery. "Mitch has plenty of demons. Awakening a real one inside him was easy."

Good God. "And Ham?" My voice rose, my fists bunching. "Why poison him?"

"Because he was doubting, asking questions."

My chest collapsed as if I'd been punched. "Ham knew?" I'd been so certain he hadn't been a part of it.

"Not at first. But he started questioning things. He wasn't the company man we'd hoped."

Ham had hinted at having regrets. But he'd been attacked before he could tell anyone. Ham and I were more alike than I'd known. We'd both been afraid to speak the truth until it was too late.

"And so you swapped out his firewood for manchineel," I said, bleak. Something whispered at my side, and I shivered.

"You know how he was with his bonfires," Josh said. "He was bound to use the wood sooner or later. Fortunately for me, it was sooner."

"And the fact that other people could have been at that fire didn't bother you?"

"Of course it bothered me. But what could I do?" He raised his hands helplessly.

"Why?" Acid burned the back of my throat, and I swallowed. "Why do you hate Babylon so much? It's your town. You're Penn Dutch." The mist congealed at my side.

Josh's face contorted, his blue-gray eyes hardening. "It hasn't been my town since they imported those scum who murdered my wife." He shook his head. "Babylon's been dead for years. They killed it. They and all the other useless eaters." His lips compressed.

The molecules in the atmosphere condensed, heavying. A fist gripped my lungs, and I I pressed a hand to my chest, unable to breathe. The mist shifted, coalescing into a wraithlike shape.

"This is only one of many projects," he continued. "And things are speeding up. People are starting to understand the hopelessness of it all. And then they'll step aside, so we can proceed with our plans."

"Is that what all this is? A *demoralization* project?"

"Demoralization is a means."

"And the end?"

Woodward King emerged from the fog, and I gasped a breath. Josh didn't react.

If Woodward was here, was no longer battling whatever had taken hold of Mitch, was Mitch free? Or had Woodward failed? My heartbeat slowed, a cold fist gripping my heart.

In a swift motion, Josh grabbed my bicep. He shoved me toward the cliff's edge. One foot skidded into space. I shouted incoherently and clutched his arm. The ghost whispered in my ear, harsh syllables I didn't understand.

"Give up, April," Josh said quietly, peeling one of my hands free.

"Don't tell me what to do," I ground out. I grabbed him with my other hand and hooked my leg behind his, the beat of my blood thrashing in my ears. But I couldn't win. He was too strong.

"Use the hill," the ghost hissed.

A hysterical laugh escaped my throat. It was impossible. Hopeless. But that was how Josh wanted me to feel—hopeless. To give up. To make things easy for him. And if he wanted me to give up, then I had to have a c hance.

I had to have hope, hope and faith. I had to make the choice to believe.

"The hill is yours," the ghost whispered.

I chose hope, hope for the future, faith in my present. I opened myself to Witch Hill. Heat flowed up my legs and words from my throat, words that made no sense and all the sense in the world.

Josh wrenched my other hand free. Twisting my wrist, I broke loose and grabbed his long coat again.

Faces materialized in the fog. Somber German farmers. *Brauchers.* My mother. My father. David. A sob broke from my throat. And the words kept coming, a growing, guttural chant.

Josh and I grappled on the cliff like lovers. My heels scuffed the earth. Words filled my head. I was going to fall, to die. I'd crack open on the ground far below. But the words were already cracking me open.

I screamed, and words poured from my mouth. A tortured cry ripped from Josh's throat. A cold and greasy sensation slithered down my skin, and the hill wanted it, and I could *feel* its wanting.

I gave Josh to Witch Hill.

He shrieked, and I was falling. I hit ground—not roof, not rocks. And I was alone.

A breeze ruffled the dried grasses on Witch Hill. Panting, I jerked onto my elbows and I looked around wildly.

A gust of wind parted the fog. I crawled to the edge of the cliff and peered over.

Josh lay sprawled and still beside his stone house. A new wave of fog surged across the black roof, and he was gone.

CHAPTER 32

I SHIVERED IN MITCH'S jacket, and he held me closer. Red and blue lights strobed the fog beneath us, the small figures of sheriff's deputies taking photos, taking measurements, taking notes around Josh Zook's body.

The distance between us, at the top of the cliff, and the dim figures on the ground by the stone house seemed impossibly far. Or maybe it was just that I felt distant, disconnected.

Was it shock? I didn't think so. That had worn off quickly enough. Something had changed inside me. Now all my fears, my doubts, just seemed... unimportant.

"And you were where, exactly?" the massive sheriff eyed Mitch and adjusted his broad-brimmed hat, covered in plastic to repel any rain.

"At April's cottage. He must have drugged me somehow." Mitch's grip on me loosened, and his gaze slid away, toward the colored fog. He squeezed my hand. But I'd already seen the rough, pink circular imprint embedded in his palm. "When I came to, April was gone."

Sheriff Yoder's mouth puckered. He glanced over the cliff and then at me. "You were lucky. I don't know how a little thing like you managed to fight him off."

"Lucky," I repeated faintly.

"I guess it doesn't feel so lucky now." The sheriff jammed his meaty fists into his jacket pockets and cleared his throat. "I've got some good news. Ham Powers has woken up. The doctors think he'll make a full recovery."

Blindly, I reached for Mitch and felt his thick flannel shirt, the corded muscles beneath. *Thank God.*

"When did Ham come out of it?" I asked suddenly. "Do you know?"

"About forty minutes ago," the sheriff said.

I stilled. Forty minutes ago. When Josh had fallen to his death. The timing *had* to be a coincidence. But I remembered that smoke at Ham's firepit, and that sense that there had been something else in it—something not natural—and I shuddered.

"You might want to talk to Ham before that new woman from GDF does," I said. "Josh told me Ham was having second thoughts about the land purchase. That was why he tried to kill him."

The sheriff nodded. "And Doc Zook admitted to killing Woodward King?"

I forced myself to meet the sheriff's gaze. "The doctor said he took a path through the woods and doubled back after stabbing him. He said he had to change clothing, because of the... the blood."

There was a shout from below. A deputy emerged from the stone house carrying a plastic evidence bag.

The sheriff sighed. "Looks like we found Woodward's murder weapon." He ambled away.

Mitch rubbed the mark on his palm. "Are you sure you're okay?"

"Yes," I said in a low voice. "Are you? What really happened?"

"I'm not sure. It was like this red cloud came over me. I couldn't see. Couldn't think. I could only feel..."

I touched his palm. The angry pink mark was in the shape of a bottlecap.

His hand closed around mine. "Your hex charm. The pain was... clarifying. And then someone else was with me, and whatever came over me seemed to draw away. At first I thought it was you, but it was a man."

His uncle. I swallowed. I'd seen Woodward King at the cottage, and later he'd come to the hill to help me. Or to remind me of who I was.

A gust of fog crested the hilltop like a breaking wave. For a moment, I imagined phantoms in it. Phantoms of my past, my ancestors, my ghosts. The wave of mist hung suspended in the air. And then it dissolved into itself and was only fog.

"What really happened here?" Mitch asked me. "Because no offense, but I don't believe you fought him off either. Not on your own."

"I wasn't alone." Witch Hill *is where the other Brauchers came to dispose of dark spells... if an archaeologist dug around here, they'd find any remnants.*

I swallowed. Was that how I'd—or we'd—done it? Had I "disposed" of Josh Zook like a *Braucher* would?

But the doctor had been more than a dark spell. He'd been flesh and blood. And he'd been in the grip of something too, and for much longer than Mitch had been.

"I was arrogant," Mitch muttered.

I tore my gaze from the broken piece of cliff. "About what?"

"Everything. Laying down the law with Santiago like that. Of course he told the doctor." His mouth twisted. "And Doc Zook came here. He nearly—" He swallowed, his Adam's apple bobbing.

"We both made mistakes," I said. My past was littered with them. But it was the past. I didn't have to make it my future. The future could be anything; I'd let it surprise me. My chest warmed at the thought.

Mitch turned me to face him. "Would I be putting myself in a bad spot if I told you I fell in love with you when I first laid eyes on you in that cottage?"

My heart caught. And I didn't feel hesitation or anxiety or guilt. I felt free.

I glanced skyward. A pate of starry sky hung above Witch Hill. I hadn't expected the next surprise to come quite so quickly, and I smiled.

EPILOGUE

A CAMERA FLASHED, AND I blinked, blue-black dots floating before my eyes. Mitch pulled me closer and kissed me. He smelled of soap and his flannel shirt of sawdust, and I laughed from the sheer joy of being with him.

A woman edged past us in my shop. *My shop.*

The farmer Ryan Shaffer's work filled one distressed-brick wall. Mitch's furniture was set in groupings between shelves lined with Penn Dutch-inspired textiles and ceramics.

Intent, Cat stared out a front window at a bluebird in a blossoming plum tree. The cat had taken over my shop with the same self-assurance she'd once taken over Cornflower Cottage. And it hadn't surprised me one bit.

"Tell me more about your revitalization program," the reporter asked Mitch.

"We're going street by street," Mitch said. "This is our first."

Karin waved from across the well-lit room. I squeezed Mitch around the waist and left him with the reporter.

My shop's wasn't the only grand opening. The block was filled with new shops, thanks to Mitch and his investors. It was only one block, but it was a start.

I squeezed between a trio of shoppers and popped out beside Karin. I hugged her. "I didn't think you'd be able to make it." She'd returned to her home in California not long after Josh's death.

She brushed a hank of auburn hair behind one ear. "I wasn't sure I'd be able to either. But I wanted to come back. It's good to see a happy ending."

"Not an ending," I said. "Not yet, I hope."

Karin's smile widened. She glanced at Mitch, running his hand across a live-edge table he'd made. "A happy beginning then. Congratulations."

"Thanks."

"And your other talent? How's that progressing?"

I jerked my head toward the windows. "Let's get some air." I walked onto the brick sidewalk, and Karin followed.

Colorful banners lined the block. A police barricade had been set up, temporarily turning the city street into a pedestrian road. It was packed with tourists and locals, ambling in and out of new shops.

"I'm training with Mrs. Hocker's nephew," I said.

"Her nephew? I would have thought she'd train you herself."

"In the *Braucherei* tradition, *Brauchers* only train the opposite sex."

"How progressive," she said wryly.

"He doesn't see ghosts."

"Do you still?"

I nodded. My personal ghosts had moved on, but others had come, some for help, others just to talk. Seeing ghosts didn't seem to be part of the *Braucherei* magic. And yet, I had it.

"What do the ghosts tell you?" she asked.

"They miss pizza."

She laughed. "My sister Lenore told me the same thing. She sees ghosts too. They all complain about not being able to eat pizza."

"Maybe... Could I talk to your sister sometime?"

"Of course. And your other lessons?"

"As I'm sure you know," I said dryly, "I'm still working with the school's emails." They'd continued to be suspiciously helpful, the right hint coming at just the right time. "How *did* you create that email spell?" I burst out.

"At least you finally believe it *was* a spell." Crinkles formed between her brows. "If I could repeat it, I'd tell you. But our town's *anima locus* played a role, and things got away from us."

A red-haired woman walking a terrier squeezed past us on the sidewalk. The little dog yipped, and the woman pulled his leash closer.

"*Anima locus*... the spirit of the place?" I asked, slipping my hands into the pockets of my slacks. Josh had said something about the spirit of the place, and about ending that spirit.

"Exactly," she said. "I suspect Mt. Gretel's spirit is at Witch Hill."

Had the spirit of Witch Hill reacted to Josh's threat? "I'm not sure the *Brauchers* believe in an *anima locus*," I warned.

"Maybe not, but there's a reason that place was chosen as a depository for evil spells. I hear quite a collection's been discovered there."

I nodded. Last month, Zeke and a team of archaeologists had begun excavating the hill. He had enough material now for an entirely new publication on Pennsylvania folklore.

"But if a beneficent... spirit lived there," I said, "why did Josh make the spot beneath the hill his home?"

She shook her head. "I didn't say it was beneficent. An *anima locus* can go either way, depending on the location's history and people living there. If dark things happen, the spirit can twist. And there's power in that hill, power people would like to use."

I glanced down at my flats and frowned. "I don't think it's twisted," I said, remembering. *Something* had helped me when Josh had attacked. And it hadn't only been my ancestors or my own power.

"I don't think so either. The spirit of Witch Hill feels... neutral." Her eyes twinkled. "So. You and Mitch are really going for it?"

I flushed, my right hand going to the diamond on my finger. "We're engaged." And though this wasn't my first time, warmth rose in my face.

"Congratulations again. What changed your mind?"

"You know what changed it," I said.

She shook her head. "Honestly, I don't."

That night on the hill, when I'd come to believe in... not everything. I couldn't believe in everything. But I believed in more now. And I had faith in myself. I'd make mistakes, but I trusted myself to figure a way out of them.

The world hadn't changed, but the way I saw it had. And it was magic and full of potential. And Mitch was no mistake.

"I changed," I said simply.

"You signed your contract, Initiate."

So I *was* an initiate now. I'd filled out the spell for self-initiation, signing it that morning, and it felt... right. But I didn't want to know how Karin had known.

"I'm glad you and Mitch are together," Karin said. A green balloon floated above the street, and the witch followed it with her gaze until it vanished above a brick building. "The Brotherhood seems to have given up on this place for now."

"For now?" I asked sharply.

"They'll be back," she said. "They don't like to lose."

But they had lost this time. Mitch and his lawyers had made sure the land would stay in the hands of the local farmers. I shifted my weight. How long would that last? There were always work-arounds, and political winds shifted.

Across the street, the mayor held court with half a dozen reporters. The dark-haired man turned, his glasses flashing in the sunlight. Santiago's gaze met mine, and he nodded.

"When they do come back," Karin said. "Call me. You'll have help."

When. A breeze shivered the plum trees, and I crossed my arms, elbows tight against my sides. "I thought..."

"What?"

"That it was over. That I was free."

"I don't think it's ever over. The shadows are always there, and the darkness. And an initiation is a beginning of the work, not the end."

I glanced at my store window, bright with folksy home wares. My sudden burst of creativity—opening the store, building a relationship with Mitch— had that all been a way to hide from the truth? That the Brotherhood was still out there?

My mouth twisted. "I've been deluding myself, haven't I?"

"Have you?" Karin cocked her head. "I wouldn't know. I'm no mind reader."

Something in my glance must have given away my thoughts, because her lips curved upward. "But from where I stand," she continued, "it looks like you're doing just the opposite."

"By selling pretty things to tourists?" I asked, incredulous. Could anything be more banal? How quickly I'd turned from fighting the good fight to cultivating my own happy little world.

Karin hooked a loose hank of auburn hair behind her ear. "By spreading beauty and joy in your own life. And those things *do* spread. They're just as contagious as—"

"Evil?"

She hesitated. "I'd like to think they're more contagious, but I don't know. But don't discount what you've done here. Beauty matters. The little kindnesses, the love, count more than you think."

I caught my bottom lip with my teeth. "Thanks." Would it be enough though?

"The Black Lodge is everywhere. You saw GDF's website. But we're building a network now too.. We'd like you to be a part of it. If you're willing."

"Me?" What could *I* do? I laughed hollowly. "I don't think I'd be much help."

"You might surprise yourself. Again." Her smile was brief. "It really only takes one person to stand up, to do the right thing. Others always follow." She shrugged. "Like I said, good is contagious too."

"How big a network?"

"Not as big as theirs. But things are shifting. Can't you feel it? They've been spreading fear and anger, and it's contagious. But so are hope and love. And we need them both if we're going to win."

Mitch emerged from my shop and looked around. Spotting me, he strode through the throng on the sidewalk. "What have I missed?" he asked.

"Just some dull philosophizing," Karin said.

"About what?" He slung his arm around my shoulders.

"That even though times may feel dark," I said, "we don't have to be. We can put good things out into the world."

Karin nodded toward my colorful shop window. "And beauty."

Beauty was the UnTarot card I'd received this morning. In the bustle of prepping for the opening, I hadn't had a chance to read the email. "And beauty," I said.

"April's got a knack for creating beauty." Mitch smiled down at me. "I wouldn't have gotten back to my furniture making if it wasn't for her."

"Yes," she said. "Love will do that."

My heart expanded.

Love certainly would.

Note from Kirsten:

I've always enjoyed mystery, especially mystery with a bit of magic involved. So when paranormal women's fiction (PWF) became a thing, I thought I'd dip my toes in the water. Most PWF is lighthearted, but since this was a spinoff of my Doyle Witch mysteries, which are more serious, I decided to keep the tone. I also thought that PWF, where the heroine is going through some sort of mid-life change, was ripe for exploring more metaphysical changes—hence the mystery school emails and worksheets.

More books in the series are planned. Follow me on Bookbub or Amazon or subscribe to my email list at KirstenWeiss.com to stay updated on upcoming Mystery School novels. Watch for the next book in the series, *Shadow of the Witch*, and for the book of lessons from the mystery school: *The UnTarot—Witches' Wisdom Unveiled*.

And if you like spiritual growth and development with your mystery, I've also got a book on Tarot with a mystery woven through the footnotes you might enjoy: *The Mysteries of Tarot*.

A special thanks to Ralph Joachim, who inspired the more modern hex signs with his geometric abstractions. You can check out his other works on his website here: https://www.ralphjoachimartist.comAnd a hat tip to Patrick Donmoyer's excellent book on Pennsylvania *Braucherei—Powwowing in Pennsylvania*.

If you enjoyed this book, please tell your friends about it!

Click to share on Twitter!

Click to share on Facebook!

Or here's a sample post to copy and paste:

I just got done reading LEGACY OF THE WITCH and I loved it! If you're a fan of Alice Hoffman, Paolo Cuelho, or Amanda Flower, I recommend checking this book out. https://bit.ly/Legacy-Direct

SUBJECT: BEAUTY

Seeker:
When you come out the other end of the transformation, it's easy for elation to be quickly followed by a sense of loss. You've changed, and you've left something behind. That something will occasionally nip at your heels, and that's okay.

In times of great change, it's more important than ever to focus on the good and beautiful in life. The beautiful is a manifestation of the sacred, and it brings peace and inspiration.

But it's easy to be distracted from it. So become aware of the beauty around you. Create it as a vessel of the divine.

But what is beauty, and why does it matter for the witch?

In the Greek myth of Psyche and Eros, Psyche is so beautiful that people begin abandoning the temples of the goddess Aphrodite in favor of admiring Psyche instead. Aphrodite can't let that sort of thing stand. The goddess sends her son, Eros, to make Psyche fall in love with someone awful. But when Eros sees Psyche, he falls head over heels in love with her, and a grand adventure of the soul's journey ensues.

Why the soul? Because in Greek, "Psyche" means "soul," ad "Eros" means "desire." The story tell us that the soul is so beautiful, even the personification of love and beauty, Aphrodite, is nothing beside it. And like attracts like. Beauty points us toward our souls. And in this age of nihilism and "whatever," the reminder that we're something more, and that "more" is beautiful, matters. The desire for beauty is a natural imperative.

Technology has redefined and continues to redefine our perception of beauty in others. The camera turned beauty into what lies on the surface—the physical. Inner beauty rarely shines through a camera lens. But beauty truly is more than skin deep, and many of us have lost our ability to perceive it because we've been retrained—not only by the camera, but by the people behind it who tell us what is beautiful this year and what not the next.

But the witch is present and can see more easily beyond the surface. (Inner beauty does come through in classical art, however, which shows us the truth beyond the surface).

Beauty in our lives matters because it helps put us in a positive frame of mind and sparks our creativity. This, in turn, aids our spellcasting. It keeps us on a more energetically positive and loving path than we would be on if we didn't have beauty in mind. True beauty is transcendent and helps us feel our connection with the universe and with each other.

When performed with presence and love, any daily activity can be beautiful and connect us to Source. Or to the Artist. And when we are present and living in love, we are acting in accordance with this great energetic flow. When we do this, spellcraft is simple, and we can make our lives inspiring works of art.

One of the easiest ways to cultivate a magical eye for beauty is by studying works of great art. Classical art inspires us and expand our vision of our own potential. The older paintings also tend to hold a lot of magical symbolism in them—useful knowledge for the witch.

Fortunately, today the classics are accessible to nearly everyone. Great works of literature are available online. Museums display classic paintings, and if you can't get to them, many now offer virtual tours online. Classic cinema is available to rent.

And when we're present, we can find beauty in the mundane. It's everywhere. Focus on it.

Take 10 minutes every day to experience classic works of great beauty this week—whether they be literature, art, or cinema. We don't have to let our minds become cluttered with garbage media or surround ourselves with people who pull us down rather than lift us up. Beauty is everywhere—it's in all of us, if we cultivate it. By taking some time each day to actively look for it, the beauty within and without will become more obvious.

Bonus action: Listen to the Carole King song *Beautiful*, and really *listen* to the lyrics. (You should be able to find it on YouTube.)

BEAUTY

Inner beauty. Appreciating art. Creating beauty for yourself and/or others. Appearance. Harmony.

Too often we think of beauty as a luxury. But it's a spiritual necessity. Beauty helps inoculate us from dark spells of nihilism and despair. When we're surrounded by beauty, the path to wonder and the beauty inside us are clearer. Beauty makes us stronger and moves us toward the transcendent.

So beauty is not optional. Beauty is the *point*, because it's a manifestation of love, pointing to something higher. And that makes the creation of beauty a radical act.

But what seems to be beauty can be superficial and false. Beauty can be misapprehended and taken as appearance. Surface glam can dazzle without any substance behind it. This is why it's important to cultivate a beautiful mind. True beauty is based in love.

The symbols:

A transcendent ocean sunset forms the background of this card. Pearls of beauty and inner wisdom merge with the clouds, and a peacock, symbolizing beauty and immortality, struts along the sand. Butterflies, representing beauty and transformation, flutter between sea and sky.

The questions:

How can you bring beauty into your environment? Into your life? How can you create beauty for others?

GRAB THE UNTAROT APP:!

EMBARK ON A JOURNEY that intertwines fiction and reality as you dive into the captivating world of Kirsten Weiss's Mystery School series. With the UnTarot app, you can wield the very cards the characters from the books receive, tapping into a wellspring of ancient wisdom and boundless magic.

Imagine harnessing the power of the UnTarot cards to unlock hidden insights and unravel the threads of fate. With the UnTarot app, you gain access to a treasure trove of captivating readings and interpretations. As you explore this mystical experience, you'll be drawn into a world where the boundaries between fiction and reality blur.

- **Authentic Connection:** Immerse yourself in the enchanting ambiance of the Mystery School series. The UnTarot app faithfully captures the essence of the books, allowing you to connect with the characters and their adventures on a whole new level.

- **Ancient Wisdom, Modern Convenience:** The UnTarot app marries centuries-old divination techniques with cutting-edge technology, creating an accessible experience for both seasoned practitioners and curious novices.

- **Free Exploration**: Yes, you read that right! The UnTarot app is entirely FREE, ensuring that everyone can join in the magical journey of self-discovery, insight, and revelation.

Ready to embark on a journey that defies the boundaries of time and space? The UnTarot app beckons you to step into the wondrous world of Kirsten Weiss's Mystery School series. Download the UnTarot app and let the magic unfold before your very eyes!

Download the UnTarot app for FREE today and embrace the enchantment that awaits!

BOOK CLUB QUESTIONS

- For the person who selected the book: What made you want to read *Legacy of the Witch*?

- What did you like about *Legacy of the Witch*?

- What didn't you like about the book?

- Are April's "personal" ghosts real? Or are they all in her head? Is there a difference?

- What do you think the role is (or should be) of beauty in today's society? Has modern life made things more or less beautiful?

- How conscious are you in your daily life? How does that affect you?

- What spells have you cast upon yourself? Upon others?

- What is the role of truth in meaning making?

- How do you feel meaning is created in our lives?

- Why is faith important for April?

- Does April deal with the changes in her life in a healthy way?

- How was the mystery school used to advance the themes in the book?

- Did the worksheets and images in the book add or detract from your enjoyment of the story?

- How did you feel about how the story was told? E.g., was it too fast? Too slow?

- Was there any line or passage that stood out to you?

- Have you read other books by Kirsten? How did they compare to this book?

- Which recurring themes did you notice throughout the book?

- How would this story change if it were told from Mitch's perspective?

- What did you think about the ending?

- How does this book compare to other mystery novels you've read?

- After reading *Legacy of the Witch*, would you read other books by Kirsten Weiss?

About the Author

I BELIEVE IN FREE-WILL, and that we all can make a difference. I believe that beauty blossoms in the conscious life, particularly with friends, family, and strangers. I believe that genre fiction has become generic, and it doesn't have to be.

My current focus is my new Mystery School series, starting with *Legacy of the Witch*. Traditionally, women's fiction refers to fiction where a woman—usually in her midlife—is going through some sort of dramatic change. A lot of us do go through big transitions in midlife. We get divorced or remarried. The kids leave the nest. Our bodies change. The midlife crisis is real—though it manifests in different ways—as we look back on where we've been, where we're going, and the time we have left.

Now in my mid-fifties, I've spent more time thinking about the big "meaning of life" issues. It seemed like approaching those issues through witch fiction, and through a fictional mystery school, would be a fun and a useful way for me to work out some of these ideas in my own head—about change and letting go, faith and fear, and love and longing.

After growing up on a diet of Nancy Drew, Sherlock Holmes, and Agatha Christie, I've published over 60 mysteries—from cozies to supernatural suspense, as well as an experimental fiction book on Tarot. Spending over 20 years working overseas in international development, I learned that perception is not reality, and things are often not what they seem—for better or worse.

There isn't a winter holiday or a type of chocolate I don't love, and some of my best friends are fictional.

OTHER MISTERIO PRESS BOOKS

Please check out these other great *misterio press* series:
Karma's A Bitch: Pet Psychic Mysteries
by Shannon Esposito
Multiple Motives: Kate Huntington Mysteries
by Kassandra Lamb
The Metaphysical Detective: Riga Hayworth Paranormal Mysteries
by Kirsten Weiss
Dangerous and Unseemly: Concordia Wells Historical Mysteries
by K.B. Owen
Murder, Honey: Carol Sabala Mysteries
by Vinnie Hansen
Payback: Unintended Consequences Romantic Suspense
by Jessica Dale
Buried in the Dark: Frankie O'Farrell Mysteries
by Shannon Esposito
To Kill A Labrador: Marcia Banks and Buddy Cozy Mysteries
by Kassandra Lamb
Lethal Assumptions: C.o.P. on the Scene Mysteries
by Kassandra Lamb
Never Sleep: Chronicles of a Lady Detective Historical Mysteries
by K.B. Owen
Bound: Witches of Doyle Cozy Mysteries
by Kirsten Weiss

At Wits' End Doyle Cozy Mysteries
by Kirsten Weiss

Steeped In Murder: Tea and Tarot Mysteries
by Kirsten Weiss

The Perfectly Proper Paranormal Museum Mysteries
by Kirsten Weiss

Big Shot: The Big Murder Mysteries
by Kirsten Weiss

Steam and Sensibility: Sensibility Grey Steampunk Mysteries
by Kirsten Weiss

Full Mortality: Nikki Latrelle Mysteries
by Sasscer Hill

ChainLinked: Moccasin Cove Mysteries
by Liz Boeger

Maui Widow Waltz: Islands of Aloha Mysteries
by JoAnn Bassett

Plus even more great mysteries/thrillers in the *misterio press* bookstore

More Kirsten Weiss

The Doyle Witch Mysteries

In a mountain town where magic lies hidden in its foundations and forests, three witchy sisters must master their powers and shatter a curse before it destroys them and the home they love.

This thrilling witch mystery series is perfect for fans of Annabel Chase, Adele Abbot, and Amanda Lee. If you love stories rich with packed with magic, mystery, and murder, you'll love the Witches of Doyle. Follow the magic with the Doyle Witch trilogy, starting with book 1, *Bound*.

The Mystery School Series

The Doyle Witches have created a mystery school, and a woman starting over becomes a student of magic and murder...

This metaphysical mystery series is perfect for readers who love a good page-turner as well as the deeper questions that accompany life's transitions. These empowering books come with their own oracle app, the UnTarot, plus downloadable mystery school worksheets. The Doyle Witch magic continues, starting with book 1, *Legacy of the Witch*.

The Perfectly Proper Paranormal Museum Mysteries

When highflying Maddie Kosloski is railroaded into managing her small-town's paranormal museum, she tells herself it's only temporary... until a corpse in the museum embroils her in murders past and present.

If you love quirky characters and cats with attitude, you'll love this laugh-out-loud cozy mystery series with a light paranormal twist. It's perfect for fans of Jana DeLeon, Laura Childs, and Juliet Blackwell. Start with book 1, *The Perfectly Proper Paranormal Museum*, and experience these charming wine-country whodunits today.

The Tea & Tarot Cozy Mysteries

Welcome to Beanblossom's Tea and Tarot, where each and every cozy mystery brews up hilarious trouble.

Abigail Beanblossom's dream of owning a tearoom is about to come true. She's got the lease, the start-up funds, and the recipes. But Abigail's out of a tearoom and into hot water when her realtor turns out to be a conman... and then turns up dead.

Take a whimsical journey with Abigail and her partner Hyperion through the seaside town of San Borromeo (patron saint of heartburn sufferers). And be sure to check out the easy tearoom recipes in the back of each book! Start the adventure with book 1, *Steeped in Murder*.

The Wits' End Cozy Mysteries

Cozy mysteries that are out of this world...

Running the best little UFO-themed B&B in the Sierras takes organization, breakfasting chops, and a talent for turning up trouble.

The truth is out there... Way out there in these hilarious whodunits. Start the series and beam up book 1, *At Wits' End*, today!

Pie Town Cozy Mysteries

When Val followed her fiancé to coastal San Nicholas, she had ambitions of starting a new life and a pie shop. One broken engagement later, at least her dream of opening a pie shop has come true.... Until one of her regulars keels over at the counter.

Welcome to Pie Town, where Val and pie-crust specialist Charlene are baking up hilarious trouble. Start this laugh-out-loud cozy mystery series with book 1, *The Quiche and the Dead*.

A Big Murder Mystery Series

Small Town. Big Murder.

The number one secret to my success as a bodyguard? Staying under the radar. But when a wildly public disaster blew up my career and reputation, it turned my perfect, solitary life upside down.

I thought my tiny hometown of Nowhere would be the ideal out-of-the-way refuge to wait out the media storm.

It wasn't.

My little brother had moved into a treehouse. The obscure mountain town had decided to attract tourists with the world's largest collection of big things... Yes, Nowhere now has the world's largest pizza cutter. And lawn flamingo. And ball of yarn...

And then I stumbled over a dead body.

All the evidence points to my brother being the bad guy. I may have been out of his life for a while—okay, five years—but I know he's no killer. Can I clear my brother before he becomes Nowhere's next Big Fatality?

A fast-paced and funny cozy mystery series, start with Big Shot.

The Riga Hayworth Paranormal Mysteries

Her gargoyle's got an attitude.

Her magic's on the blink.

Alchemy might be the cure... if Riga can survive long enough to puzzle out its mysteries.

All Riga wants is to solve her own personal mystery—how to rebuild her magical life. But her new talent for unearthing murder keeps getting in the way...

If you're looking for a magical page-turner with a complicated, 40-something heroine, read the paranormal mystery series that fans of Patricia Briggs and Ilona Andrews call AMAZING! Start your next adventure with book 1, *The Alchemical Detective*.

Sensibility Grey Steampunk Suspense

California Territory, 1848.

Steam-powered technology is still in its infancy.

Gold has been discovered, emptying the village of San Francisco of its male population.

And newly arrived immigrant, Englishwoman Sensibility Grey, is alone.

The territory may hold more dangers than Sensibility can manage. Pursued by government agents and a secret society, Sensibility must decipher her father's clockwork secrets, before time runs out.

If you love over-the-top characters, twisty mysteries, and complicated heroines, you'll love the Sensibility Grey series of steampunk suspense. Start this steampunk adventure with book 1, *Steam and Sensibility*.

CONNECT WITH KIRSTEN

You can download my free app here:
https://kirstenweissbooks.beezer.com
Or sign up for my newsletter and get a special digital prize pack for joining, including an exclusive Tea & Tarot novella, *Fortune Favors the Grave*.
https://kirstenweiss.com
Or maybe you'd like to chat with other whimsical mystery fans? Come join Kirsten's reader page on Facebook:
https://www.facebook.com/kirsten.weiss
Or... sign up for my read and review team on Booksprout: https://booksprout.co/author/8142/kirsten-weiss

Made in the USA
Columbia, SC
29 May 2024